POINT OF CONTACT

BOOK 11

ALASKAN SECURITY-TEAM ROGUE

Jemma WESTBROOK

PLAYLIST

Could Have Been Me-The Struts
Raise Hell-Brandi Carlile
Demons-Hayley Kiyoko
Dirty Thoughts-All That Glitters
Daddy Issues-The Neighbourhood
Hard to Handle-The Black Crowes
Bad Habit-The Kooks
Delicate-Taylor Swift
Do You Feel It?-Chaos Chaos
Fire-Barns Courtney
San Andreas' Fault-Kathleen
Praise You-Fatboy Slim
Rude Boy-Rhianna
All out of Tears-Z Berg

CHAPTER ONE

COURTNEY

SHE TOLD THEM this was going to happen.

Tried to explain the severity of the situation she was facing, but no. No one was willing to consider for one single second that maybe she'd learned.

That maybe she was better.

It shouldn't have been a surprise. She should be used to people turning their backs on her when the life she had no choice but to live bled into theirs.

It still stung, the burn lingering as she watched the masked men ransack her house from the chair they'd parked her in, foolishly restraining her with nothing but a set of handcuffs as they dumped out drawers, swiped across tabletops, and shredded pillows and blankets, leaving nothing but pointless chaos in their wake.

Honestly, it would be a pretty fitting way for her to go. Forced to watch as the only things she really had in this world were destroyed moments before being destroyed right alongside them.

Except she didn't particularly feel like dying today. Not

when salvation was so close she could almost taste it. And that knowledge ignited the determination she'd been working so hard to fuel over the past year, making it flare hot enough to combust.

But in order to make it out of this, she had to be patient and calm. Neither was her strong suit.

One of the intruders turned to her, his cold eyes slowly dragging over her from behind the knit mask that was as pointless as the mess they were making. His gaze paused on where her tits stretched the tank top she'd pulled on before jumping on the treadmill. Like he was contemplating something more sinister than property damage and murder.

What did it say about her that murder didn't rank as the worst possibility? Lots, probably.

But, like every other person who put their eyes on her, he found her lacking. And for the first time, she was grateful. Watching the only world she'd ever known being ripped apart in front of her before her life ended was one thing. Being raped on her way out was another.

Except she didn't plan on going out today.

Not tomorrow either.

One of the other men came up beside the man now watching her with a disinterested, almost disgusted gaze. Like she was the offensive one. "Time to go."

Time to go. Shit.

She was running out of opportunity, and it was happening fast. It was either make shit happen now or end up the way everyone wanted: The dead daughter of a drug lord no one had sympathy for.

Schooling her features, she wedged one thumb against the cold, hard, metal cuff, using her other to press hard until the joint gave. She blinked a few times to clear the watering brought on by the pain but didn't flinch.

Not that it would have mattered. The men milling around the home she moved to less than a year ago weren't watching her nearly as closely as they should have been. They were clearly new to this. Green enough that they hadn't heard the rumors about her. About how problematic she once was. How she was capable of anything that might get her a shred of the attention she'd been denied her whole life.

And while the quest for attention from her father might have ended, her capabilities remained. Her willingness to do any and everything to get what she wanted lingered.

And right now she wanted to live.

Now that her thumb was dislocated, it was easy to slip her hand free of the cuff. But it wasn't time to act. Not yet.

She took a slow breath in through her nose, barely parting her lips to set it free as she used her other hand to set the misplaced digit where it belonged. Pain shot up her arm, tingling in a jolt that forced her to swallow down the whimper trying to break free. Stars danced in front of her eyes as her vision narrowed, but she continued her slow breaths through all of it. The setting was always worse than the dislocation, but fighting with her thumb flopping around would put her at a marked disadvantage.

She slowly felt around behind her, careful not to shift her body in any noticeable way as the fingers of her right hand teased along the underside of the table they'd been stupid enough to bind her in front of.

She wouldn't hold it against them though. She'd been stupid for a very long time. Played games and threw fits and metaphorically shot herself in the foot at nearly every turn.

That all changed a year ago when she realized there was

only one person in this world who cared if she was alive or dead. The only person she had to rely on. The only person she could trust.

Herself.

And so she made sure she was trustworthy as hell.

"It's set." The newly arrived masked man grabbed his friend by the arm when he didn't move fast enough, dragging him toward the back of the house her father bought her to shut her up. A house that had become both a home and a prison.

And, if she didn't figure something out soon, maybe a tomb.

Her fingers moved faster, sweeping the smooth underside of the table for what she knew was there. She'd put it there herself. The same way she'd done in every other available spot, tucking away everything she could, knowing this day was coming.

And knowing she would likely face it alone.

Her fingers finally brushed against the cool metal she was seeking, but it was just far enough away she would have to shift her body to reach it. The move would give her away. Alert her captors to the fact that she might not be as restrained as they believed.

But it had to be done. All she could do was hope she was faster than they were.

And she'd worked hard to be fast. Both on her feet and on the draw.

Just as she leaned, both men turned away, putting their backs to her and offering the opportunity she needed. The handgun was in her palm in a split second, safety switched off, ready to offer her the assistance no one else would.

But the men didn't turn around. They didn't point their

own guns at her, intent on taking out Vasquez's 'pride and joy'. It was almost laughable. If only they knew how little her father actually cared what happened to her, they wouldn't be wasting their time here.

And it almost looked like they weren't. The men disappeared down the hall, footsteps fast as they raced through her kitchen, door slamming as they ran out the back. Leaving her alone.

And, like her earlier gratefulness for being found lacking, finally being alone was a relief for the first time.

Right up until she heard an odd sound.

Courtney twisted in her chair, bringing both hands to the front of her body so she could tenderly inspect her injured thumb as she tried to determine if the sound was coming from behind her or in front of her. It might have been both.

She stood up just as it stopped. What in the world had it been?

Unfortunately, that odd sound was replaced by a much louder, more identifiable sound.

The explosion was sudden and unexpected, making the floor under her feet vibrate.

Shit. They'd set something off in her basement.

The smell of smoke followed the blast almost immediately, sending her racing for the front door, flying through the large, two-story foyer to grab the handle. She flipped the locks free and yanked, but it wouldn't budge. Her eyes dipped to the cut glass window slicing through the solid panel. A set of linear shadows dimmed the outside light, banding across her path to safety.

Holy shit. That sound was a drill. They'd barricaded her in.

That's why they hadn't bothered shooting her. They

planned for her to die another way. One more painful and slow than a quick bullet to the brain.

Pricks.

She turned and ran through the house, cutting across the formal dining room and into the Butler's pantry that led to the kitchen, even though she knew what she would find there. The back door was secured exactly like the front. Screwed in place by heavy chunks of lumber she could easily see through the clear glass of the back entrance.

"Fuck." Another rumble rattled the entire structure, signaling a second explosion that sent smoke billowing up through the open basement door and creeping from the vents.

She had to get out of there and she had to do it fast. There was no telling what else was in the basement. And as her captors clearly didn't plan on her making it out alive, she had to believe there was more.

Backing across the room as far as she could, Courtney raised the gun in her hand and aimed it at the large bank of windows overlooking the inground pool that took up most of her suburban backyard. She emptied the clip, holding her breath with every squeeze of the trigger, expecting each one to send a bullet ricocheting back at her as the thickening smoke made her eyes water.

By some miracle, not a single one came back to take her out and her aim stayed true despite the tears streaming from her eyes. She dropped the gun, now empty and useless, and raced across the kitchen. Grabbing one of the heavy chairs from the table, she used every bit of strength she had to slam it into the hole her bullets started. She'd built this house to be as safe as possible. To protect her when no one else would. But right now that was coming back to bite her like so many other things had.

The impact of the chair sent more fractures spider webbing across the surface of the giant window, so she hit it again. And again.

And again.

By the time there was a hole large enough for her to escape through, she could barely see and had given up on trying to breathe. She shoved the table as close as she could get it before climbing onto the surface and jumping through the jagged edged opening. Her body slammed into the patio harder than she expected, knocking any remaining oxygen from her lungs.

Another explosion, this one substantial enough to shake even the ground beneath her, sent her rolling away, trying to put as much distance between herself and the house as possible. In the confusion and chaos, she forgot about her pool, and rolled right over the edge, dropping into the water.

And thank God she did.

Courtney watched the surface as another explosion, the sound of it buffered by the water around her body, sent debris, angry smoke, and a few flames across her backyard. Particles of the sad life she lived dropped against the surface of the water, quickly turning the salty liquid from clear blue to a cloudy gray that burned her eyes almost as much as the smoke.

Closing her eyes against the sight, she rolled to her belly, kicking off the wall and swimming as far as she could away from the house before grabbing the opposite side and hoisting her waterlogged body free. She scrubbed at her face, trying to clear the water and ash from her eyes and her nose as she crawled across the grass. Once she reached the thick hedges lining the back of her property, she tucked her body behind them.

The air was blessedly free of smoke, but she continued struggling to breathe. A few coughs had her rolling to her stomach, heaving out water and what remained of her morning coffee into the freshly spread mulch. It tasted terrible, and burned like fire coming up, but she could finally breathe and gulped in a lungful of air, hoping the extra oxygen would clear the blurring in her brain.

They'd tried to kill her. Not just kill her, but burn away any evidence of her existence.

Her eyes drifted back toward the smoking remnants of her once beautiful house. The house that once held nothing but useless possessions and bitter memories. A laugh bubbled from her lips, high-pitched and slightly unhinged, speaking to the current state she was in.

Everyone would believe she was dead. That she'd finally fallen victim to any selection of the men always attempting to pry power from her father's greedy fingers. And maybe she should let them. Maybe this was her chance to finally be free.

It sounded great in theory, but there was one major flaw with the plan. She had nowhere to go. No clue how to genuinely disappear off the face of the earth.

If she was going to be dead, she had to act dead. That meant no using credit cards. No showing her face where someone might recognize her. No plane tickets and no passports.

She could probably get her hands on some cash, but outside of that she had nothing. No clothes. No identification. No way to get the fuck out of Miami.

The urge to vomit clenched her stomach again, but it had nothing to do with smoke inhalation or ingested pool water. She was fucked.

Courtney rolled to her back, allowing one single tear of

self-pity to leak free. Crying was a luxury she'd indulged in far too many times over the past year, and not a single one of them did her any good.

They didn't bring back her so-called friends. They didn't make her father give a shit. And they certainly wouldn't help keep her alive now.

She swiped at the wayward drop, rubbing it off her skin as she sucked in another deep breath, coughing out a little more of the smothering smoke still coating her throat before spitting it onto the ground. Courtney worked her body into a sitting position, collapsing back against the privacy fence as the sound of sirens rang in the distance.

She had to make a decision. Stay here and continue facing the perils of a life she didn't ask to be born into, or let it end right now. Leave it all behind and go somewhere none of these mother fuckers would ever find her.

She'd been somewhere like that before.

Courtney sat up a little straighter as realization hit. She could go back to Alaska. Convince Alaskan Security to help her again. She'd paid them plenty over the years. Certainly enough to cover one final disappearance.

And, conveniently enough, someone from Alaskan Security was already in Florida. Scheduled to be on her doorstep tomorrow morning even though she'd begged them to send him earlier. Explained until she was hoarse that this time she wasn't lying. This time she really was in danger.

And they'd blown her off. Left her alone, just like everyone else, to face the destruction of her life.

Helping her now was the least they could fucking do.

A slow smile worked on her lips as she settled into her escape plan. She'd find whoever was there and convince him to take her back. Say and do whatever it took to make that happen.

Because while she might technically have died today, there was no way she was giving up the chance to finally be able to live.

Courtney worked onto her hands and knees, keeping her body tight to the fence as she crawled away. Mulch dug into her palms and bushes scraped at her face and hair, but she didn't feel any of it. All she felt was the freedom now within her reach. The opportunity those pricks would never recognize they'd provided her.

She reached the corner of the lot where her back privacy fence met with the HOA required decorative panels lining the sides of her yard. Luckily the hedges planted along it were nearly eight feet high. More than tall enough to obscure her from view as she raised up, peeking through the branches to ensure no one was close enough to catch her movements before climbing the crossbars and maneuvering herself over the pointed spindles. Her feet hit the neighbor's yard, toes squishing against the saturated insoles of her sneakers as she dropped back down to a crouch. The sirens were loud now, so the police and firefighters would be descending on her house any second.

She picked up the pace, continuing to cut along the privacy fence blocking the back of each home's lot. Most had hedges that provided cover, but some didn't. That meant there was a chance she'd be caught on someone's security cameras, but there was no way around it. So she moved fast, keeping her head turned toward the fence and her arms around her body, doing her best to conceal as much of her identity as possible as she moved farther and farther from the wailing sirens.

She didn't let out a full breath until the edge of her neighborhood came into view. She ducked around the large water retention area camouflaged as a decorative pond, using the trees and foliage of the landscaping to stay as hidden as possible.

The tightness in her shoulders eased a little as she stepped onto the sidewalk. It was time to figure out where her mark was and sweet talk her way back to Alaska.

She glanced down at her athletic leggings and tank top. They weren't obviously wet, but they were clearly covered in smoke, and a little blood from where she must have scratched herself jumping through the window. Or rolling across the concrete. Or crawling through the bushes.

Or hopping a fence.

As much as she was ready to get this show on the road, she needed new clothes. Something that would make her less conspicuous. Her eyes lifted to the line of apartments across the street from her gated neighborhood. That's where she was going to find everything she needed.

Courtney straightened her shoulders, smoothed back what remained of her high messy bun, lifted her chin and strode across the street. Confidence was a great costume. One she'd worn more times than she could count.

Hopefully it would work as well today as it had in the past.

She skirted the property, angling her way along the edge of a familiar building. Avoiding the areas she knew had cameras, she ducked into the stairwell and took them two at a time until she reached the third floor.

She grabbed at her bun, pulling a hairpin free before looking side to side and sliding it into the deadbolt. Thank God she'd been too lazy to wash her hair this morning. She added a second hairpin, using it to provide enough strength to twist the lock. After a little maneuvering, it clicked open. She glanced around again before slipping into the apartment of someone she once believed was her friend.

But she wasn't. She was simply one more person who enjoyed the benefits of being around the wealthy daughter of a powerful man. The free drinks. The spa days. The shopping sprees and the fancy dinners. Her 'friends' were always happy to partake.

But when she really needed them, their true colors showed.

And now was time to pay up.

CHAPTER TWO

REED

REED STARED AT the smoking mess in front of him, still struggling to come to terms with what happened. Courtney's upscale suburban house was all but gone, reduced to nothing more than a pile of scorched debris.

The possibility of what it might contain sat heavy in his gut. Courtney wasn't his favorite person, but he didn't want her to end up like this.

Hopefully she hadn't.

His cell phone rang and he pulled it from his pocket, connecting the call as he turned away from the mess, unable to look at it anymore. "I'm here."

Heidi, one of Alaskan Security's primary hackers, hesitated a second. "Is it bad?"

He couldn't stop himself from turning back. Like he thought maybe another look would make the scene less terrible. It didn't. "They weren't exaggerating, that's for fucking sure."

If anything, the security company who monitored the system installed in Courtney's house had downplayed the severity of the situation. Losing contact when the power to her place dropped, they'd physically sent someone to verify her safety. They sure as hell could have been a little more specific with their description. Prepared him a little better for what he was going to find.

"So it really did catch on fire, then?" Heidi's skepticism mirrored his own when he first got the call that Courtney's house was on fire. He showed up expecting to find some small, primarily smoke-based issue. One he fully believed Courtney was to blame for, thinking she'd be able to play them into her hand one more time.

And he still half believed she was the cause of what he saw in front of him. Hoped she was the cause. That would mean she'd had a chance to get out.

"Calling this a fire would be a gross understatement." Reed stood along the sidewalk in front of the property, shoulder to shoulder with a handful of nosy neighbors who must not have anything better to do than gape at a disaster. He toed a chunk of singed pink insulation with his sneaker. "The whole structure collapsed. But somehow there's pieces of it twenty yards away."

Heidi was quiet for a second. "So it wasn't a fire. It was an explosion."

"Sure seems like it." He eyed one of the cops at the scene. "Let me go see what I can find out."

He had to tread lightly. Needed to remember this wasn't Alaska. His employment status carried no weight here, so chances were good the information he'd be able to obtain would be slim to none.

He was still going to try.

The cop taking statements from the neighbors loitering around was about his own age and appeared to be fairly proficient at his job, which didn't bode well for his chances of getting information. Older cops were cut from a different cloth and tended to be a little looser with their lips. The younger generation knew just how quickly information could travel, and the damage a simple screenshot could do, so they held their cards close to their chest.

Reed tipped his head at the officer in greeting. "Everybody make it out okay?"

The cop looked him over, taking in his shorts and T-shirt in a way that made him wish he'd stopped on his way to put on something a little more official looking. Something that might mark him as law enforcement adjacent.

Not that he was. Unfortunately.

The cop eyed him warily. "Are you a neighbor?"

Reed considered making that his claim, but decided to lean fully into his best option. "No." He let his eyes drift back to the smoldering pile before clenching and unclenching his fists. "My friend Courtney lives here."

It was a bold claim, but one he might be able to back up. To a point.

He did know Courtney. Had spent more hours in her presence than he could count.

All of them fucking miserable.

The woman was a spoiled brat. Used to getting her way in all things. Ready and willing to throw money around to make it happen. She'd tried to bribe him on more than one occasion, offering any amount he wanted for something as ridiculous as French fries from McDonald's.

But, while he normally struggled to turn down extra money, he took great joy in telling her no. Every fucking time.

The cop paused, his gaze narrowing. "You know the homeowner?"

"Yup." He glanced at the house again, shifting on his feet in a way that nervous people often did. "She's not usually home this time of day though. She's usually out shopping." He thumbed over one shoulder in the direction of the main road running alongside the private neighborhood. "I was driving past and saw the smoke." He met the cop's eyes, adding on information that would give his claim validity. "I have the code to the gate, so I came to make sure she was okay. She wasn't inside, was she?"

The cop clicked the end of his pen, pushing the tip back out before positioning it over his notepad. "Do you know what kind of car she drove?"

Fuck. He knew all kinds of shit about Courtney. What time she got up in the morning. What music she listened to. How long it took her to put her makeup on and how fucking used to getting her own way she was. But he didn't know what kind of car she drove. And calling Heidi to find out wasn't an option.

He shook his head. "Not off the top of my head."

The cop continued to watch him. "You said she's normally gone this time of day?"

Reed nodded even though he had no fucking idea what Courtney's schedule was like now. She disappeared from Alaska over a year ago, forcing them to track her down to make sure she hadn't been taken against her will. When they found her, she was back in Miami. Strutting around town like she didn't have a care in the world.

Which went directly against the story she'd told his boss when he'd agreed to hide her away.

The cop flipped his notebook closed, clicking his pen once more before straightening. "Thank you for your information. If you think of anything else that might be helpful, let me know." He pulled a card free, passing it off.

Reed stared down at the name printed across the plain white stock. The sight of it stung. Reminded him of what might have been. "Does that mean she's not in there?"

The cop hesitated, tongue sliding across his upper teeth before clicking back into place. "At this point, we aren't sure if the house was occupied at the time of the explosions."

Explosions. Plural.

"Shit." Reed raked one hand through his hair, his reaction completely genuine. "When do you think they'll be able to enter the premises?"

The police officer's expression carried a hint of surprise at the way he worded his question.

It was done with intent. Designed to hint at what he was in the hope it would get him what he wanted.

"The fire marshal is on his way over, along with a structural engineer. If they deem the location safe to enter, firefighters will attempt to canvas for," he hesitated just a second, "your friend."

The set of the cop's mouth was grim, conveying information he wouldn't disclose.

Reed focused on the driveway, looking closer at the portion of the house in front of him. "Was there a car in the garage?"

His stomach clenched as he waited for an answer. He was never Courtney's biggest fan, but that certainly didn't mean he wanted her to die. Especially not like this.

The cop worked his jaw from side to side, but finally offered a nod.

Fuck.

Reed backed away as the officer moved on to a neighbor, asking them questions about what they heard and what they saw. Guilt tugged the clench in his stomach tighter. Maybe if he'd come straight here after they landed—

There were many things he tried not to think about when it came to his job. Many parts of it he compartmentalized in order to continue doing what he was paid to do.

This wouldn't be as easy to shut away.

He crossed the road, walking the half block to his rental car without looking back, and slid behind the wheel. He started the engine and switched the air conditioning to full blast, angling every vent at his face as he took slow, deep breaths.

He knew what he was getting into when he came to work for Pierce. Knew employment at Alaskan Security was about as far from his initial career path as it got. The trade-off had been worth it.

But right now he was caught between who he'd wanted to be and the reality of the life he was forced to choose.

His phone started to ring over the speakers and Heidi's name flashed across the touchscreen at the center of the dash. He connected her call and let his head fall back against the rest, closing his eyes against the reality settling around him. "I think she was in there."

Heidi let out a long breath. "Shit."

Reed nodded even though she couldn't see it. "Yeah."

"When will you know for sure?" He could hear Heidi typing on her keyboard, no doubt attempting to glean any information she could from where she was. Unfortunately, none of it would tell them whether or not Courtney was inside that house.

"Don't know. They gotta make sure the structure is safe to enter before anyone goes in to do a search." He braced one elbow against the door, leaning his head into his hand.

"I'll stick around until there's an official determination made."

He'd anticipated this trip would be a short one. Fly down, spend a day at the parks with Nate and his family, head to the Miami suburbs to tell Courtney she was on her own, fly back.

Unfortunately, he hadn't understood how on her own Courtney actually was. She'd made so many claims over the years. Used them as errand boys and personal assistants while claiming to be in a danger that didn't actually exist. So when she really was at risk, none of them believed it.

And now the sky had fallen.

"I think that's a good idea." Heidi's typing continued. "I'm booking you a room at the Hilton around the corner. Looks like you'll be in room 453."

"Thanks. I'll talk to you soon." He ended the call, gave Courtney's obliterated house one final look, and slowly pulled away, turning around in the middle of the street. He paused as a nosey neighbor ducked behind their bushes so no one caught their morbid curiosity.

Hopefully it wasn't as morbid as he was afraid it was.

The address for the hotel flashed into his phone's GPS and he went straight there, making it into his room just as the sun started to set.

He dropped his shit on the pull-out sofa and started peeling his clothes off, ready to put this day behind him. He was fucking exhausted, and not just because of the time difference.

Years of walking an imaginary line were starting to wear on him. Beginning to break him down in ways he hadn't expected. And it would continue happening because it had to. Alaskan Security needed him and, like it or not, he needed them. More and more with each passing day.

He took a quick shower, scrubbing hard like he might be able to rid himself of the shame and guilt continuously crawling over his skin. It never worked, and tonight was no exception.

He brushed his teeth, tossed his towel over the hook and climbed into the king-size bed, flipping on the television before promptly passing out.

Only to be awakened what felt like seconds later, but had actually been more than an hour. The timer on the television had shut it off and the room was dark, any light from the parking lot outside blotted out by the heavy curtains layered over the window.

He scrubbed one hand over his face, rubbing at his tired eyes. The sudden silence from the television turning off must have woken him up. He snagged his cell phone from the bedside table and checked the time. Twelve thirty. He'd been asleep for a few hours, but it felt like minutes. Probably because his day had been such a fucking mess.

He set the phone down and rolled to his side, adjusting the covers before drifting back toward sleep.

He was almost out when the soft sound of rustling fabric sent his eyes flying open. It wasn't the television that woke him up. Someone was in his room.

His job had always been dangerous. Always put him one wrong move away from an early grave. He'd cheated death more than a few times and he'd do it again. Because dying wasn't something he could afford to do right now.

Reed continued breathing slow and deep, hoping to fool the intruder into believing he was still asleep. Unaware and defenseless, even though he was never either of those things.

He quickly scanned the space, but the darkness of the room was nearly complete, making it difficult for him to see exactly where he'd set his weapon. He'd been exhausted and distracted when he came in. Careless enough that his pistol wasn't beside his bed and he clearly hadn't flipped the safety latch on the door.

The soft sound of an inhale had the hair on the back of his neck standing up and every muscle in his body primed and ready to act. Without his weapon, he would have to rely on nothing more than his hand-to-hand combat skills. Skills he admittedly should have invested more time into maintaining.

Yet another way he was falling short.

When the mattress barely shifted behind him, he rolled, reaching out to grab whoever made the mistake of trying to sneak up on him. Yanking them into the center of the mattress, he straddled their hips, pinning their legs with his feet as one hand found their throat, squeezing just hard enough to cut off the oxygen without doing damage. "How the fuck did you get in here?"

He fought to keep his adrenaline from spiking out of control. He wasn't afraid. He was more angry than anything. Pissed that yet another thing was going fucking wrong here.

The person under him didn't move. Didn't fight his hold. Didn't grab at his hand or try to yank it away.

He eased his grip and they immediately sucked in a breath.

"I want a fucking answer. How did you get in here?"

Something hit him in the center of his chest before bouncing to the mattress beside him. He grabbed it with his free hand, thumb sliding over the smooth plastic of a key card.

What the fuck?

He shifted, keeping his knees tight and his feet locked, the hand at the intruder's throat barely tightening as he leaned to flip on the light. He blinked against the sudden brightness.

Then he blinked again.

And once more.

Courtney stared up at him, her dark eyes wide but unafraid. A slow smile curved her lips. "If you wanted me in your bed, all you had to do was ask."

Reed lunged back, sliding off the mattress and stumbling toward the wall, never taking his eyes off the ghost stretched across his sheets.

Courtney watched him, her eyes moving over his body. "I don't remember you sleeping in the nude, Reed."

One hand reflexively shifted to cover his dick. "Everyone thinks you're dead." He shook his head, still not quite believing what he was seeing. "*I* thought you were fucking dead."

Courtney's chin barely lifted, jaw setting in a defiant display. "I'm sure everyone is crying. Devastated at the loss."

Her eyes dragged over his body once again, lingering at his pecs and abs. "I'm surprised you're the one who came here." Her gaze came back to his. "Considering how much you hate my guts."

Hate was a strong word, but he'd let her keep it. "Pierce offered ten thousand dollars to whoever was willing to come deal with you."

Courtney's lips thinned, her head tilting to one side. "That sounds about right."

He stared at her a few seconds longer, still trying to wrap his mind around the fact that Courtney was not dead, but very much alive. And very much in his hotel room. "How did you get in here?"

She angled her body up to a sitting position, lifting one shoulder and letting it drop.

He waited for her to say more. Courtney always said more.

But she stayed silent. And her silence was unnerving.

"Fine. If you won't tell me how you got in here, then maybe you can tell me *why* you got in here."

Courtney had always been a pain in the ass, but this went above and beyond. Even for her.

She slowly worked her way to the foot of the bed before standing and coming his way. Now that she was standing, he noticed the difference in her appearance. She had on one of the most basic outfits he'd ever seen her in—a pair of jeans and a plain white T-shirt—and her dark hair was pulled back in a sleek ponytail, brushed back from her makeup-free face. It was a stark contract to the made-up woman who only wore the nicest clothes he dealt with in Alaska.

But the smug expression on her face as she closed in, claiming his space as her own, was familiar. "I'm here because, like you said, everyone thinks I'm dead. And you're going to help me keep it that way."

CHAPTER THREE

COURTNEY

REED STARED AT her like she'd lost her mind.

And maybe she had. She'd lost everything else, so why not that too?

He shook his head. "That's not going to happen."

Courtney moved closer, tilting her chin up as she stared him down. "Yes. It. Is."

She'd dealt with Reed before. Many times. In addition to being a stickler for the rules, the guy was generally an asshole to her. He was uptight and had zero sense of humor.

And was hot on an unfortunate level, all dark eyes, dark hair, and full lips. He stood nearly a full head taller than her five-foot-one frame and had broad shoulders and muscular thighs, which were kind of her catnip. She could almost imagine digging her nails into them as he lost control.

Not that she imagined a man like Reed lost control. He kept an iron grip on that shit.

Her eyes 'accidentally' skimmed down his naked body and she almost let out a groan of frustration. Of all the men they could have sent here, why did it have to be this one? There was something about him that always made her feel a little warm and tingly inside, in spite of his bad attitude.

Or maybe it was because of it. Maybe it was the constant frown he wore in her presence. The disapproving stares he shot her way. The constantly aggravated expression on his too-handsome face.

Whatever it was, she could never seem to stop herself from pushing his buttons. Shoving him closer to an edge that had to exist. Because she was unexplainably interested in discovering what happened when he reached it.

"I don't know what game you're playing right now, but I'm not gonna be a part of it." Reed tried to step around her, like he thought he'd be able to get away.

Silly boy.

Courtney stepped with him, blocking his path. She moved closer, enjoying the way he backed up as she closed in. How flustered he got as her body nearly touched his. "If you think this is a game, then you haven't been paying attention."

She couldn't really blame him for thinking that's what this was. And maybe a year ago it might have been.

Not now.

She held his gaze as she laid out the offer she'd worked hard to be able to make, just in case she ran into a situation just like this. "I have ten thousand dollars with your name on it if you help me get to Alaska."

After stealing a few bucks from her ex fake friend's cash stash, along with jeans and a T-shirt from her basic bitch wardrobe—and maybe hiding a can of tuna in the heating vent —she hadn't been able to resist the temptation of sneaking back to see who showed up at the sight of her untimely demise. And thank God she did. Because, from where she hid in the bushes, she'd been able to clearly hear Heidi disclose the location of Reed's hotel through the speakers of his rental car.

After he drove away, she'd picked up a few items at the local Walmart, hoping to disguise her identity before stopping at one of her storage units and snagging the cash she'd stashed there just in case.

Just in case ended up saving her ass more than once today.

Reed's eyes flicked to the bag she brought where it sat next to the bathroom. They lingered just long enough to make it clear the possibility of a little tax-free income appealed to him. But when his eyes came back to hers, they were angry and narrowed. "You can't buy me off, Courtney."

But it seemed like she could.

She inched in a little closer. "What if it was twenty thousand dollars?" She'd been raised by a father who taught her very little about life. But what he had passed on was to always look over your shoulder. Always expect the unexpected. Or, in this case, the expected.

Her father had more enemies than she could count, and over the past year it became more and more obvious they were outnumbering his friends. So she'd stashed weapons in her house and cash in storage units she rented under fake names. She wasn't excited about visiting another one, but if that's what it took to get Reed on board, she would.

His nostrils barely flared as he hesitated, thinking it over. When his jaw set, she knew what he was going to say before he said it.

"Not fucking happening."

Damn. He always did enjoy telling her no.

Courtney pushed her lower lip out, batting her eyes at him. "Please?"

She didn't imagine this angle would work with him either,

but it was worth a shot. She was willing to do whatever it took to get the fuck out of Miami. And to do it fast. She'd been able to obscure her identity on most things, but there was a chance someone would figure out she had storage units and go sniffing around, asking questions and looking at camera feeds.

If that happened, they would know she didn't die. And her days would be as numbered as her father's now were.

Reed leaned closer, the tip of his nose almost touching hers. "No."

Oh yeah. He definitely loved getting to tell her no.

But she wasn't giving up yet. She'd thought up more ideas than she could count when putting this plan together. Some more appealing than they should have been.

"Are you sure?" She reached out to trail one finger down the center of his bare chest. "I'll suck your dick every day until we get there." Her mouth watered a little at the possibility.

Being the daughter of a Colombian drug lord made it surprisingly difficult to get laid. No one wanted to end up on her father's bad side, so her opportunities for any sort of physical connection had always been limited.

Reed's dark eyes snapped to her mouth, lingering a second before coming back to meet hers. "That offer makes me even less likely to say yes."

This time she didn't have to force her pout. "Ouch. Careful. You might hurt my feelings."

"I don't give a shit if I hurt your feelings." He worked his jaw from side to side, gaze carrying no small amount of disdain as it moved over her, and he let out a snort of a laugh. "Let me guess. You're the one who set that fucking fire."

It wasn't a terrible guess, honestly. She'd done all sorts of things over the years in a bid to get attention from someone. Anyone. But this wasn't one of those instances.

"No." She lifted her wrist, showing him the red marks dug into her skin and the bruise blooming around her thumb. "Unfortunately it wasn't me being a pain in your ass this time."

Reed's focus zeroed in on the damage she'd done escaping what was intended to be an assassination. "If it wasn't you, then who was it?"

She dropped her hands, brushing them against the one still cupping his dick. "That's the twenty-thousand-dollar question, isn't it?" She smirked. "Unless you'd rather I get on my knees."

She was almost hoping he might pick the latter.

But Reed once again seemed unimpressed by her offer. "Who do *you* think it was?"

Apparently he was so unimpressed by her offer of a blow job that he was just going to ignore it completely. Fine.

"I would assume it was someone who mistakenly believed my father would be devastated at the loss of his only child." She couldn't keep the bitterness out of her voice even after years of seeing her father for what he was and what he would never be. She shouldn't still be disappointed, but she was.

Reed stepped away from her, and this time she let him go. "Who has your father pissed off now?"

Courtney watched him walk away, enjoying the flex of his well-defined ass as he went to grab his clothes. "Who hasn't he pissed off?"

Her father wasn't known for his even temperament or his fairness. He had a tendency to go around acting like he could do whatever he wanted, and usually he could. But things were changing in Miami, and her father didn't seem to be keeping up.

"I take it he hasn't slowed down any." Reed stepped into a pair of pants, not even bothering with underwear. Interesting.

"The only way my father will slow down is if he's dead. And based on the amount of force they used to get into my house, that might happen sooner rather than later." She'd been on her treadmill, exercising away her emotions, when the belt stopped moving and the screen went black. She thought it came unplugged and went to investigate as they started ramming her back door. It was barely noticeable above the bass coming through her headphones, so it wasn't until the fourth or fifth hit that she noticed the sound wasn't following the beat. By the time she got downstairs, they were already in. Already past the point of no return.

"So your plan is to just disappear?" Reed grabbed his shirt, yanking it over his head to hide the rest of his remarkably fit body from her roving gaze.

"Everyone already thinks I'm dead, right?" She lifted her shoulders in a shrug. "Might as well go along with them."

He studied her with a sharp gaze. "And you think living in Alaska will be better than staying in Miami?"

She couldn't stop the laugh that broke free. "Anywhere is better than Miami." She'd lived here her whole life, but it was never her home. Home was somewhere you felt comfortable. Safe. Protected. It was where the people who loved you lived.

There was none of that here, or anywhere for that matter, so she might as well get as far away from the people who tried to kill her as possible.

Reed's gaze turned skeptical. "I don't think Alaska is going to be what you think it's going to be, Princess."

He definitely meant that as an insult, but it actually didn't bother her. It made her think of fairytales and princes and knights in shining armor.

Granted, she didn't know of any fairy tales that took place in a frozen tundra like Alaska, but she hadn't come across any in the sun and heat of Florida either, so—

"Don't forget, I've already lived in Alaska." She moved toward Reed again. Her closeness seemed to make him uncomfortable and throw him off. Both would be helpful, and both amused her. "I'm sure Alaska will be exactly what I expect it to be." She stopped in front of him, looping both arms around his neck. "And I'm glad we've already gotten to the point where we have nicknames for each other."

Reed reached up, grabbing her forearms and unlinking them from his neck. "I've always had that nickname for you. I just never said it to your face."

She was unbothered by his chilly demeanor. Reed had always been all work and no play, so his reaction wasn't a surprise. Some of the other guys would humor her from time to time, but never him. He tolerated not a bit of her bullshit.

That meant she had to be absolutely on her game if she wanted to score a trip to Alaska. Luckily she was happy to pull out all the stops.

Courtney held his gaze, undaunted and undeterred. "Do you want to know what I called you behind your back?"

"No." His mouth flattened into an unamused line.

"Too bad. I'm going to tell you anyway." She reached out to tap one finger in the center of his chest. "I called you Captain Sour Pants." She walked her fingers up the center of his chest to press one against his lips. "Because you always greeted me with that sour look on your face."

"Because you were always a pain in my ass." He said it like she didn't already know.

"It seems like you're trying to hurt my feelings." She

pushed her lip out in another pout, tipping her head. "Maybe I should start calling you Mister Meany Pants instead."

"You don't need to call me anything." Reed grabbed her arm, once again avoiding her injured wrist as he pulled her finger from his lips. "Because I'm not taking you to Alaska."

"Yes, you are." He could argue with her all night. That was fine. But there was no way he was leaving Florida without her.

Reed laughed, shaking his head. "Typical. You think you can show up and make demands and that everyone will do exactly what you ask."

"You're wrong." That *would* be how he saw things. It was how most people saw things. But it wasn't the truth. It wasn't the reality she'd lived with her whole life. "I don't make demands. I make bargains." She held her ground as he glowered down at her. "I paid Alaskan Security for every request I've ever made of them." She let her eyes move down his front, lingering pointedly on the cock she'd gotten more than a good look at before he noticed it was on display. "Just like I'm willing to bargain with you now."

He crossed his arms over his broad chest, accentuating the corded muscle of his forearms. "Say I agree to take you to Alaska. How will you support yourself once you're there?"

Her heart skipped a beat. He was considering this. "That's not your problem, is it?"

"Somehow I feel like it will be." His scowl was on full display, and it said all kinds of things about her that it actually made him more appealing.

She'd paid for every person who'd ever been a part of her life. One way or another, they were compensated to be her friend. Her confidant. To be her lover. And they ate it up. They were happy to provide fake smiles and false laughter as they followed her around, reaping the rewards she offered.

But not Reed. Even when she was paying him to protect her, he never offered up anything but what he really thought. Not a single fake smile or bought behavior. And that made her respect him a little.

Even if the feeling wasn't mutual.

"I promise you won't ever see me again once we get back." She traced an X between her tits. "Cross my heart and pretending to die."

Reed stared at her, expression stony.

"Come on." She propped both hands on her hips, voice a little whiny. "That was funny and you know it."

He stared at her a second longer before turning away, refusing to admit she was as hilarious as she knew she was. "If I agree to take you back to Alaska—"

Courtney couldn't stop herself from making a squeak of excitement.

It sent Reed spinning back her way. He pointed a finger at her. "I said *if*, Princess. I still haven't decided what I'm gonna do with you."

She wiggled her brows at him. "I have a few suggestions if you're open to options."

She'd joked with the other men from Alaskan Security, but Reed was the only one she'd ever flirted with. Mostly because he was so clearly irritated by it. Jabbing at him gave her something to do all those months she was holed up in one of their off-grid cabins.

Even if it was always one-sided.

"You're not helping your cause any right now." His pointing finger dropped but he continued to glare. "If I agree to take you back to Alaska, you have to be on your best behavior." His voice was stern. "No making demands, no whining, and no fucking temper tantrums."

She gave him a bright smile, feeling hopeful for the first time in forever. "I promise I'll behave."

"I'm serious." He stepped closer, bringing the width of his sculpted chest almost to hers. "I'm not putting up with your bullshit."

Her thighs clenched around a feeling she hadn't had in months. Why did his grumpy demeanor turn her on so much?

"I'm serious too. I really will be good." She tried to look honest and innocent, which was a challenge. "And if I'm bad, you can spank me."

Reed shook his head, lips pressing tight. "See? That's the kind of shit I'm talking about."

She rolled her eyes. He really was no fun at all. "Fine. You don't have to spank me if I'm bad." She should leave it at that, but she couldn't stop herself from adding on, "You can spank me if I'm good too."

CHAPTER FOUR

REED

"HOLY SHIT. THAT'S great news." Heidi sounded relieved but exhausted, which made sense considering he was waking her up in the middle of the night. "I was feeling so guilty."

"There's no reason for you to feel guilty. Courtney worked hard to put herself in a position where we can't believe a thing that comes out of her mouth." Reed paced along the sidewalk, trying to wrap his head around the current situation he was facing.

This was not the trip he expected. He was supposed to come down here, tell Courtney they were done with her, and rid himself of one more of the ties binding him to the less than upstanding side of Alaskan Security's business. They would never be completely free of questionable jobs, but at least they would no longer be protecting criminals.

"I get that, but still." Heidi yawned, the sound long and loud. "What do you need me to do?"

Reed stopped his pacing and glanced up at the hotel. "I don't know yet. I haven't decided if I'm going to bring her back or not."

"You're kidding, right?" Heidi snorted. "You know as well as I do there's no way Pierce will let you leave her there. Not if she's actually in danger, which it sounds like she might be."

"Yeah, but it sounded like that before."

Courtney didn't hesitate to claim to be in fear of her life. She'd done it more times than he could remember at this point. And not in a single one of them did she actually end up being in any sort of real danger. She was just fucking with them. Amusing herself by seeing how many times she could make them jump through hoops.

They didn't have time for her bullshit. Not then. And sure as hell not while they were facing another threat they hadn't yet been able to identify.

Someone was focused on taking down Alaskan Security, but their motives were still unclear. He should be back there. Doing what Pierce had hired him to do—tracking down whoever was behind it.

Not here dealing with a spoiled brat.

Reed rocked his jaw from side to side, trying to ease the tension making it ache. "If Pierce is so worried about her, he can come here and handle her."

Courtney had always known how to push his buttons. Always did everything in her power to aggravate the absolute shit out of him any time they were in the same room. And while she might actually be telling the truth about her current situation, she still clearly intended to be a complete pain in his ass.

"You and I both know that's not going to happen. Pierce won't leave Alaska until this whole shit show is resolved. He can't stand to have Mona and the baby out of his sight right now." Heidi yawned again, but the faint sound of her keyboard carried through the line. "It looks like I can get Rico out there tomorrow afternoon." She paused. "Or maybe it's today afternoon. What the fuck time is it there?"

"After midnight." He'd gotten a couple hours of sleep before Courtney somehow managed to worm her way into getting a key to his room. "Afternoon is the earliest you can get him here?" He wanted to be rid of her. Done with Courtney once and for all so he could get back to real work. Maybe not the kind of work he'd hoped to be doing at this point of his life, but at least it wasn't as bad as it used to be.

Especially with her gone.

"Right now that's the soonest, but I'll look into it a little more and let you know if I can bump it up." Heidi continued typing. "And don't be a complete dick to her. If someone really did just try to kill her, she's probably terrified."

Reed glanced up toward the window of his hotel room. "I can promise you she's not terrified."

Determined, maybe. Terrified, absolutely not.

Which was a little surprising considering every other time she'd called for help, Courtney had claimed to be absolutely beside herself with fear.

Heidi groaned. "Whatever, just be nice anyway. I don't want to feel even worse knowing you're being a prick to her."

"Not putting up with her bullshit doesn't make me a prick." Everyone else could humor her as much as they wanted, but that was something he would never do. "And somebody needs to tell her she can't just do and say whatever she wants."

Heidi groaned again. "You sound just like my father." She snorted. "Better be careful with that, or she'll be calling you daddy."

He cringed at the possibility. "She better fucking not."

She would though. If the thought occurred to her, Courtney would absolutely do it. Especially if she knew how much he fucking hated it. The same way she kept pushing her offer of a blow job.

Although the thought of that wasn't as repulsive as it should be. He liked the image of the woman who'd tormented him unrelentingly dropping to her knees, submitting and swallowing him down, a little more than he should. Almost as much as he liked the thought of bending her over his knee and smacking her bare ass, giving her the spanking she asked for.

"Hello?" Heidi's voice was loud in his ear, dragging his focus back where it belonged.

Reed rubbed one hand over his face, trying to scrub away the images that came to mind way too easily. He was just tired. Exhausted enough that his mind was wandering all on its own. "Yeah. I'm here."

"I'm gonna get in touch with Rico and we'll figure out how soon we can get him to you. I'll send you the information as soon as I have it."

He gripped the tension building at the back of his neck, trying to get his mind back on track. "Just get me the hell out of here as soon as you can."

He ended the call, sliding his cell into his pocket before turning around and heading back into the hotel. He was half tempted to get them a second room while they waited this out, but he wasn't convinced Courtney wouldn't just find her way back into his anyway. The woman was fucking annoying and seemed to take great joy in it.

Standing in front of the door to his room, he took a deep breath before passing the key card over the sensor and letting himself in. Courtney was in the center of his bed wearing one of his T-shirts. Her bare legs were stretched out in front of her, crossed at the ankles, as she watched television and popped back an almond from the bag he had stashed in his backpack.

"Do you not understand personal boundaries?" He gritted his teeth as he plugged his cell into the charger on the nightstand.

Courtney's eyes swung his way, dragging up and down his frame before leveling on his. "Listen, grumpy pants, I almost fucking died today. All my clothes, all my jewelry, my fucking car, it's all gone. So you're going to have to deal with me wearing one of your shirts to bed." One of her brows barely angled as the corner of her mouth lifted. "Unless you want me to sleep naked too."

"No thanks. I'm not interested in whatever it is you have going on." He said it hoping to make it true, but tonight his mind was unusually weak. After Courtney planted that fucking vision of being on her knees or across his, there was a little part of him that was curious about what a fully nude Courtney might look like. And the fact that she was making him think inappropriate thoughts only pissed him off more.

"Are you sure?" Courtney seemed unbothered by his feigned disgust. "I've got really nice tits." She pulled her knees up before letting them fall open, the drape of his T-shirt barely covering what he was claiming to have no interest in. "And I just got a Brazilian."

Reed closed his eyes, taking a steeling breath. "Stop or I will leave your ass here."

"Ugh." Courtney rolled her eyes as she popped in another almond. "I almost forgot how unfun you are."

"I'm not here for fun, Princess." The word slipped out

before he could catch it, adding yet another layer of irritation to the piles stacking up around him. "I actually came down here to tell you that we were done with you. That you were on your own."

Courtney lifted her brows but looked relatively unbothered. "Oh yeah?" She tipped her head. "How'd that work out for you?"

"Considering you're in my bed, eating my food and wearing my clothes," he shook his head, "not well."

Courtney's eyes narrowed, like he was finally starting to get to her the way she got at him. "You know, there are lots of men who would love to have me in their bed." She tossed his bag of almonds to one side, leaning forward. "Or on my knees."

"Oh yeah? Where are they? I'd be happy to take you to them." One way or another, he needed to get rid of her. Unload this terror of a woman so he could get back to his life. Back to doing what needed to be done.

Courtney's lips pursed, pinching together as her nostrils barely flared. He'd hit a nerve. And he couldn't stop himself from hitting it again.

"What's the matter, Princess? Were you bluffing?" He moved closer, stalking toward her. "Does that mean there are no men who want you in their bed?" He leaned forward, resting his fists against the mattress as he leveled his eyes on hers. "That's probably because they want to fuck someone who's not a complete pain in their ass."

For a second, he felt like he finally had the upper hand. Like he was finally taking control of the situation and the woman within it.

But then Courtney's full lips slowly tipped up at the edges. "I didn't see anyone sleeping in your bed tonight." She held his gaze, completely undaunted as she fired back. "I bet you haven't had a girlfriend in years." Her eyes moved down his body. "That's probably why you're so grumpy." She tipped her head pushing her lower lip out in a pout. "Poor Reed hasn't been laid in so long he probably forgot how to do it."

Her assessment hit a little closer to home than he'd ever admit. "Careful, Princess. I'd love to leave you here to clean up whatever mess you made all by yourself."

Courtney, like usual, was unaffected by his threat. "But you can't. Because Pierce won't let you."

Once again, her assessment was more accurate than he'd like. That was one of the problems they'd faced in their dealings with this woman. She was much smarter than she let on.

"That's what I thought." She dropped back against the headboard, eyes going back to whatever bullshit television show she was watching. "When are we leaving?"

He didn't want to admit she was, in fact, leaving, but he was tired of sparring with her. "The plane will be here sometime after noon."

Courtney's spine went stiff, her skin paling the tiniest bit. "Why not first thing in the morning?"

"Because, contrary to what you think, we aren't at your fucking beck and call." Reed moved to the small pullout sofa lined against the wall. "You should be glad we're getting you out of here at all."

"I'm sorry." She turned his direction, the snideness in her voice making it clear this was not going to be an apology. "I was under the impression that was what Alaskan Security did. They protect people for money."

"Not everyone deserves to be protected, Princess." He regretted the words the second they were out of his mouth.

Mostly.

Courtney had wasted countless man hours during her last temper tantrum. She'd also occupied one of their off-grid cabins, taking up space someone else could have used.

Someone who sat on a more comfortable side of the law.

Courtney's head bobbed back like he'd slapped her, mouth gaping as she stared at him. After a few seconds, her lips clamped shut, jaw clenching as she swung her legs over the side of the mattress. "Whatever."

She stood up and strode toward the bathroom. But she didn't stop there. Courtney kept walking, flinging open the door to the room and walking right out into the hallway in nothing but one of his T-shirts.

"Fucking great." He rubbed both hands over his face, trying to scrub away the exhaustion making his eyes burn.

He shouldn't have antagonized her. He should have done what everyone else did when they had to deal with the spoiled daughter of one of Miami's most notorious drug lords. Played along.

But he couldn't do it.

She represented everything he shouldn't be a part of. Reminded him of just how much he sold out in the name of financial security. How far from his own ethics he'd been willing to drift when push came to shove.

And if he didn't go find her now, he'd be stuck with her for even longer.

He grabbed the keycard for the room and stalked out into the hall. It was empty, but there were only so many places she could go. The elevator wasn't moving and it was unlikely she had enough time to not only wait for its arrival, but also take it wherever she was planning to go. He turned toward the stairs, passing the well when he heard a soft sound from a few doors down.

He found Courtney in the vending room, tucked against the wall next to the ice machine. She sucked in a sharp breath when he walked in, turning away as one hand came to wipe at her wet cheeks.

He didn't like this woman. Never had. She rubbed him every wrong way there was.

But he still didn't mean to make her fucking cry.

It was one of the few emotions he'd never seen from her. And it was one of the few things he appreciated about her. At least she didn't manipulate with tears.

So seeing them now stopped him short. Made him force in a deep breath in the hopes it might calm some of the aggravation he connected with her. Not all of it was her fault and he should be better at remembering that. Better about not punishing her for his own choices.

"Courtney, I—" His attempt at an apology was cut off by a familiar noise.

One that sent a chill racing down his spine.

Someone was coming down the hall, the pattern of their steps making it clear they were trying to mask the sound. Anyone else wouldn't have noticed it, but after years of needing to know where everyone around him was in almost every situation, he picked up on it almost immediately.

Courtney, however, did not.

She spun to face him, her earlier sadness replaced by a more familiar expression. Anger. And he knew well how she handled that particular emotion.

Loudly.

Before she could open her mouth, he grabbed her, shoving her back into her original hiding spot as one hand clamped over her mouth. He held her wide gaze, praying that for once she wouldn't fight him.

Her hands came to his shirt, gripping tightly. But not to shove him away.

Instead, she held on. Going still except for a tiny nod of her head.

CHAPTER FIVE

COURTNEY

REED'S EXPRESSION WAS deadly serious as he slowly lifted one finger to his lips, like he didn't think she'd already figured out it was time to shut up.

She was a lot of things, but stupid wasn't one of them. The minute his body tensed up, it was obvious something was wrong. So right now, there was no way she'd open her mouth.

Not even if he asked her nicely.

Courtney pressed herself tighter to the wall, like it might make her invisible. Reed obviously thought whatever, or whoever, was out in that hall was a threat. She'd been careful, but there were cameras everywhere. The chances that she was able to make it here without being seen by anyone or recorded in any way, was slim to none. And the possibility she'd led them right to her had her stomach clenching around the almonds she'd scarfed down when she thought life was about to get better.

Wrong.

Reed started to step away and she gripped his shirt tighter, shaking her head. He couldn't leave her here alone.

His hands came to hers, warm and strong as they gently unwound her fingers from the fabric, his eyes holding hers the whole time. She knew what he was trying to tell her, but that didn't mean she had to like it.

He needed to go see what was up and couldn't do that with her tagging along.

She pressed her lips together and nodded, wrapping her arms around her middle as she tucked as tightly as she could into the corner where the machine met the wall.

Reed watched her a second longer before silently turning and creeping to the door. His steps were careful and quiet, graceful in a way she could never move. Proving he was right to leave her behind. She watched him until he was out of sight, disappearing around the edge of the icemaker that would only hide her for so long.

They must have discovered she wasn't dead. Must have discovered she escaped somehow and were coming to finish the job. It was an eventuality she always knew might happen. Her place in the world had many perks, like unlimited funds and the freedom that came with them, but being a pawn in a deadly game was definitely enough to tip the scales in the opposite direction.

She held her breath, listening for any sign of what was going on. Straining in the hope that she could catch a stray sound that might indicate who was out there. Where Reed was.

If he was okay.

The man definitely wasn't her favorite person, but she didn't want anything bad to happen to him. Maybe something minorly bad, like a paper cut or a stubbed toe, but definitely not death.

She was trying so hard to hear anything she could that

when he appeared around the corner of the ice machine she nearly yelped in surprise. Luckily, he was on her again, wide palm clamped over her mouth to stop the sound before it gave them away.

Like before, he held her eyes, expression serious and stern as he tipped his head toward the door.

Courtney shook her head almost violently. She did not want to go out into that hall. Especially since it was obvious something was going on. If there was no threat, he would have simply told her things were fine and dragged her back to the room. But his silence meant they were still in danger.

Or more accurately, she was still in danger.

Reed stepped closer, leaning down until their eyes were level as he pointed one finger at the center of her chest before turning it to his own and then stabbing it toward the hall. This time he didn't give her the chance to argue. He grabbed her hand in his and pulled her along, stealing any opportunity she might have taken to hesitate. To think of a better option.

Instead, she was stuck going with his plan. Forced to follow behind in bare feet, doing her best to be as silent as Reed was.

He paused at the door, leaning the tiniest bit around the corner to peer out into the hallway.

Then they were moving again. This time even faster. His grip was tight on her hand as he dragged her down the hallway and into the stairwell. He only let go of her long enough to grip the handle as he quietly let the door slide shut behind them, silently releasing it before grabbing her again and racing down the stairs.

It took everything she had to keep up with him. To keep from tripping over her own feet and falling down the metal treads of the cement stairs. They quickly reached the main floor and Reed paused, peeking out the narrow window into the hall before once again quietly opening the door and leading her out. She was barely over the threshold before the sound of a door opening in the stairwell above them sent her stomach dropping.

Heavy bootsteps banged against the stairs, keeping time with the racing of her heart as she rushed into the hall. Reed was less careful closing the door this time. Probably because there was no time to waste. He looked both ways, jaw clenching tight before he turned away from the lobby and headed down the line of doors leading to the first-floor rooms. She did her best to keep up with him, but he still had to pull her along. She worked out, but it turned out running on the treadmill and running for your life were two completely different things.

He hit the exit door full force and they hurtled through it, the exterior door slamming shut behind them. She immediately shivered, regretting her decision to torment Reed by stealing one of his shirts. Even in the winter, Miami days were decently warm, but damn could it get chilly at night. Especially when all you were wearing was a borrowed T-shirt and a stolen thong.

Reed yanked her closer to his side, bringing them tight to the building as he moved behind the large line of hedges flanking the perimeter.

She winced a little as the mulch dug into the soles of her bare feet, adding another layer of pain to her aching body. It probably wouldn't have been so bad if she hadn't already dragged herself through bushes and over fences once today, but her earlier escape left her sore and tired and not so much in the mood for a repeat performance.

But living was fun, so she sucked it up and kept moving,

doing her best to ignore the sting as little splinters worked their way into her skin.

Reed's eyes came to her, narrowing slightly as they swept her from head to toe, stopping when they reached her suffering feet. He quickly shifted, putting his weight on one foot as he yanked off a boot and shoved it her way. Normally, she would have resisted. Convinced him and herself that she didn't need it. That she would be fine. But this fucking day wouldn't quit, and who knew how long it was going to keep going.

She grabbed the boot and shoved her foot in, tightening the laces as much as she could before repeating the process with the second one. They were way too big, but she was able to secure them at her ankles, so hopefully she could still run.

Because it looked like they were getting ready to run.

Reed pulled her along, peeking through the branches as he moved them toward the back of the hotel.

She leaned into his ear, keeping her voice low. "Where are we going?"

She half expected him to chastise her for daring to open her mouth, but Reed only continued leading her through the bushes. "We need to get to my car."

Hope ballooned in her chest. Maybe she wouldn't die today. Maybe they could get out of this. "You brought the keys?"

His eyes came her way and his expression turned cocky. "I don't need keys to start a car, Princess."

She shouldn't like that he kept calling her princess. Especially since he meant it as an insult. But everyone wanted to protect the princess. They looked out for her and kept her safe. And Reed was a lot of things, many of them irritating as hell, but he had a sense of duty like no one she'd ever seen before. He might be pissed about it. He might hate every fucking second of it. But he would keep her safe. And hearing him call her princess reminded her of that fact.

They reached the end of the building, stopping at the corner. Reed turned to face her, his voice so low she had to lean close to hear it. "Stay here. I'm going to go get the car. When I pull up, run out and get in as fast as you can, okay?"

She nodded. "Okay."

Reed seemed satisfied with her answer, giving her a single nod before turning away.

It took everything she had not to grab him. She didn't want him to leave her. Didn't want to be on her own for a single second right now. She understood it was safer if he went to get the car on his own, but what if something happened to him? What if he got hurt or captured and she was left—

But before Reed could step away, the whole world shook. The sky lit up as the ground seemed to rock under her feet. She stumbled, latching onto Reed, trying to keep her balance as the shrubbery barricading them in shuddered in a sudden stiff and unrelenting breeze. Her ears were ringing. Her heart was racing. Bits of hot metal rained down, sticking in her hair and to her skin.

Reed's lips moved as he tried to shove her in the opposite direction, but she couldn't hear a word he was saying. He pushed harder, but for some reason her body wouldn't move. Nothing seemed to be working right.

She pressed both hands to the sides of her head, trying to block out everything that was happening. It was too much.

And then the world shifted again, flipping upside down as it once more began to shake, making her dizzy and nauseous and terrified.

She squeezed her eyes shut, covering her face as she tried

to ride out the disorientating sensations. After a few seconds, the scrape of branches was gone, replaced by a sense of freefalling that was almost worse. The ringing in her ears started to quiet, but was replaced by equally horrifying sounds. People were screaming. Alarms were going off. There was chaos all around as guests poured from the hotel, spilling out into the debris covered parking lot that sat at an odd angle.

Odd, because she was currently upside down. Reed had thrown her over his shoulder, hands gripping her thighs as he raced away from the hotel and whatever the fuck just happened there.

He moved so quickly, making it across the parking lot and behind the privacy fence separating it from the swampy area just beside it. But he still didn't slow down. He kept moving, feet splashing through knee-high water as he crossed an area that was most definitely inhabited by alligators.

She wanted to warn him, but her voice didn't work when she opened her mouth. No sound came out.

So she just held on for dear life, praying that she didn't escape two attempts on her life just to be eaten by a giant lizard.

Her stomach rolled as Reed changed directions, switching up his trajectory, socked feet continuing to move through the stinky, murky water as he headed for an area of higher grass and trees. He carried her straight into it, continuing on a few more yards before finally moving up onto the bank and setting her on her feet.

She gripped his shoulders as the world spun again and spots danced in front of her eyes. "I feel sick."

Reed grabbed the back of her neck, bending her forward. "Deep breaths. In through your nose, out your mouth." He was practically holding her up at this point as she tried to reorient herself to the world around them.

A world that was dark and scary and smelled like shit.

She braced both hands against her knees, pulling in gulps of the shit-stinking air even though it was the last thing she wanted in her body. "What the fuck happened?"

Reed slowly angled her upright. "It doesn't seem like anyone wanted us taking my car anywhere."

She squeezed her eyes closed as everything started to blur, fighting nausea and dizziness as her brain picked its way through the past few minutes. The intense brightness. The sudden ringing in her ears. The way everything seemed to move and shake just like it had earlier in the day. "Was there an explosion?"

"Don't worry about it. Just keep breathing." Reed's hand rested on her back, steady and solid. "We aren't going to get anywhere if you can't stand upright."

They couldn't get anywhere? It was almost laughable. "Where are we going to go?"

They couldn't go to her house. It was gone. They couldn't go back to the hotel. Whoever blew up Reed's car was most likely crawling all around the place, hoping to find her.

Hoping to finish what they started.

She pulled in another slow, stinky breath before opening her eyes to find Reed watching her closely, his expression pinched in something that almost seemed like concern. But that couldn't be it. She probably just didn't recognize what that emotion actually looked like since it was never directed at her.

"Seems like they really want to kill me."

Reed's jaw worked from side to side before he finally admitted, "It does seem like that."

The urge to cry again was strong, but she fought it. She wasn't going to give them the satisfaction of making her break her no crying rule twice in one day. "I don't have anything now." Courtney wiped both hands over her face, sinking down into the despair that had been hot on her heels all day. "All the money I could get my hands on is in that hotel room."

There was no way she could go to her storage units now. If they found her at the hotel they could find her anywhere. The realization dug hopelessness deep into her chest.

She'd lost nearly everything in the explosion at her own house, but somehow it made her feel better to know she was capable of continuing on anyway. Able to do whatever it took to survive.

But maybe she wasn't. Maybe there was no escaping this. Maybe she really would end up being taken down for someone else's bad behavior. Someone who was supposed to put her above everything else. Someone who was supposed to put her life above his own.

Someone who was supposed to protect her.

"Perk up, Princess." Reed's no-nonsense tone almost snapped her out of the cycle of self-pity. "We've got a long day ahead of us."

She sucked in a breath, this one not smelling nearly as bad as the ones before it. "Fine." She smoothed her hair back from her face and readjusted the messy ponytail hanging on by a thread. "What do we do now?"

A slow smile spread across Reed's lips, making it impossible to ignore how handsome he was in spite of his asshole-ish nature. "Now we get back in that water."

CHAPTER SIX

REED

HE EXPECTED HER to argue. To throw a fit just like she had every other time he asked her to do something she didn't want to do. And, based on the look on her face, it was clear Courtney did not want to get in that water.

Her eyes drifted back the way they came, lingering over the shadowy swamp. "Is it because if we go through the water they can't track our footsteps?"

He might have been impressed with her conclusion if the woman hadn't done everything in her power to drive him absolutely insane for as long as he'd known her. "Bingo."

Courtney pressed her lower lip between her teeth, dark brows pinching together in the moonlight. "You know there are alligators in every body of water in Florida, right?"

The thought actually hadn't occurred to him. He knew Alaska inside out and upside down, but Florida was a different beast entirely. One he wasn't quite as equipped to wrestle.

But he wasn't going to tell her that.

"We've got two options, Princess." He pointed down the muddy shoreline. "We can stay out of the water and leave them a trail to follow us," his eyes swung pointedly to the murky depths, "or, we can take our chances with the alligators."

Courtney sucked in a breath, digging the heels of her hands against closed eyes. "Okay. Fine." She turned and took a tentative step into the soggy wetland, visibly cringing as her foot sunk into the muck. "I hope you don't want these boots back."

He hid his surprise at her willingness to slosh their way through an escape. "Let's just call them yours."

Reed followed Courtney into the water, his own socked feet splashing through the mess as she carefully picked her way along. She barely made it ten feet before wobbling, forcing him to grab her by the hand to keep her steady.

Her eyes came his way before dropping back to the water. "Thank you."

"Don't thank me. I just don't feel like arm wrestling an alligator over you." He put himself on the deeper end, giving her the shallower water since she seemed to be struggling. It actually wasn't that much different from trudging through the snow. Snow might be a little more forgiving, and not infested with anything that might murder you, but at least this was warm. Especially since he'd offered up his boots in the hopes it would keep her moving.

And it had.

Courtney continued making faces as they walked. She cringed at every sucking sound made as her feet pulled free from the bottom of the mucky mass, but she didn't stop. And she didn't slow down or complain.

They continued along what might have been considered a river by some people's standards, sticking to the shallower water as they put more and more distance between themselves, the hotel, and the men who forced their way into his room. He hadn't decided if or when he would tell Courtney about that part. He'd seen how she acted when she was pretending her life was in danger, so he could only imagine the fuckery she would unleash when she was actually in danger.

Which he still hadn't been entirely convinced she was, right up until he saw the masked men standing outside of his room.

They clearly weren't trained the way he, or anyone else at Alaskan Security, was. Which led him to believe they were likely tied to Courtney's father's dealings. Dealings which seemed to have placed a target right on her back.

A back that was now slightly more slumped than normal.

She was getting tired. Her breathing was a little heavy and bits of hair had fallen from her ponytail and now clung to her sweaty skin. Each step seemed to take more effort than the last, even if the pace was the same. Courtney wasn't cut out for this.

Not like he was.

He slowed, directing her to the shoreline. Guilt wasn't something he was used to feeling when this woman was involved, but there was a first time for everything. "We can move up to dryer land now."

Courtney's shoulders lifted the tiniest bit. "Really?"

He nodded. "Really. I think we've come far enough." He sloshed up onto the bank, fighting the last of the muck before finally landing on something stable. They'd probably come half a mile. Far enough to hide the path they'd taken away from the hotel, but still not out of danger. The overgrowth of the shoreline had thinned to the point there was little keeping anyone driving down the road from seeing them, so they still needed to move carefully.

"Thank God." Courtney trudged up the bank, swiping one forearm across her brow as she let out a long breath. "I really didn't want to get eaten today." Her eyes slid his way and her lips twitched. "At least not by an alligator."

Normally, her comment would aggravate the piss out of him, but she'd just done something most men wouldn't do. She'd hiked through alligator infested waters, and hadn't complained at all. He could cut her some slack. "Funny."

The twitching of her lips bloomed into a small smile. "I told you I was funny." She looked around, the humor slipping from her face. "Now what?"

"Now we figure out how to get to the airport so Rico can come pick us up." It was really the only option they had. His phone, his wallet, his laptop—all of it was in the hotel room. Or more likely in the hands of whoever was after Courtney.

And they clearly didn't believe she was as dead as she hoped.

Courtney looked him over before glancing down at her mud splattered legs. "Should we get some clothes so we don't look quite so—"

Reed lifted his brows, waiting for her to explain exactly what she believed she currently looked like. Courtney was all about appearances, so he had a few good guesses of what was about to come out of her mouth.

Her lips quirked to one side as she tugged at the hem of his T-shirt. "Questionable."

"Questionable?" He huffed out a laugh. "That's how you think we look right now?"

Courtney propped both hands on her hips, looking a little offended. "I definitely wouldn't stop to help us. We look like we're more than capable of mugging someone and leaving them in a ditch."

She wasn't wrong, it was just surprising that this was the observation she made. The Courtney he knew would be completely disgusted at her current state. She was covered up to her knees in God knows what, wearing nothing but his borrowed T-shirt, her hair a sweaty mess. Definitely nothing like the always made-up prima donna he'd dealt with in Alaska.

"And where do you suggest we find these new clothes?" He watched her closely, mildly interested in what she would say next.

Courtney's eyes left his, roaming all around them as she lifted one shoulder in a halfhearted shrug. "I don't know. I'm sure we could find some somewhere."

She was acting strange. Almost like she had something to hide, but he didn't know what it might be. "I'm pretty sure there aren't fresh, clean piles of clothes stacked around here." He dug one hand into his pocket, hoping to find something besides the room card, but came up as empty as he expected. "I've got no cash. No credit cards. No way to get us anything new to wear." He pinned his gaze on her. "And I'm guessing you don't have a credit card hidden anywhere on you."

Courtney snorted. "I fucking wish." She shook her head. "After this, you can bet your asshole I'm gonna hide prepaid cards all over the place though." She turned to face the roadway. "I guess we better start walking. The farther we make it before the sun comes up, the better off we'll be since I'm pretty sure anyone who sees us coming is going to call the cops."

Reed paused, thinking over what she said. "Maybe that wouldn't be the worst thing that happened. Whoever's after you clearly suspects you're not actually dead, and has already tied you to me. So maybe involving the police is the smartest thing we can do."

If nothing else, it would give him an opportunity to contact his team, verify who he was, and get them to the airport. To keep her safe until she made it to Alaska and could go on her merry way.

But Courtney immediately rejected his idea, shaking her head vehemently. "No. No cops."

"They already believe you're alive, Princess." He pointed one hand in the general direction of the hotel. "And considering the clothes you came in wearing are still in that room, they're going to be even more sure now."

Courtney's eyes narrowed at him as she moved closer. "In case you didn't realize it, most cops don't look favorably on drug smugglers."

It was a fact he was quite aware of. Probably more than she'd expect.

"But you're not a drug smuggler." He almost didn't believe the concession came out of his mouth.

She huffed out a bitter laugh. "It doesn't matter what I am. It only matters what my father is."

There was no point in arguing with her. She was right. How many times had he put blame for her father's misdeeds right on Courtney's head?

Too many to count.

Not once had it bothered him. Not once had he felt bad about it. Not once had he considered he might be in the wrong.

"Fine." Reed crossed his arms, forcing his focus from the tug of guilt trying to make him feel sorry for her. "What would you suggest we do then?"

Courtney seemed to perk up a little. "I think we should break into a house and steal some clothes." She pursed her lips. "And maybe a car."

He almost laughed. For a second there he'd started to let himself look at Courtney as a victim instead of a criminal he was forced to protect. "You said that pretty easily, Princess. Like you go around breaking into houses all the time."

Courtney's eyes narrowed as she stood taller. "Are you seriously judging me right now? That's awful hypocritical of you, Sexy Pants." She stepped closer, the hint of frailty when they discussed her father all but gone. "Because I'm pretty sure more than a few lives have ended because of you." She smirked. "And I can say with complete certainty I've never killed anyone."

There were so many parts of her statement that rubbed him the wrong way, but only one he cared to comment on. "Did you just call me Sexy Pants?"

Courtney's eyes widened in fake innocence. "Would you prefer Sexy No-Pants?" Her eyes dropped down the front of his body. "I mean I have seen your—"

"I'd prefer you don't call me anything." He cut her off before she could remind him of their initial run-in.

Courtney tipped her head. "I guess that's too bad for you." She moved even closer and ran the tip of one finger down the center of his chest. "Sexy No-Pants."

He stared down at her, trying to dig up his normal level of irritation. "You're a real pain in the ass, you know that, Princess?"

"I do know that." She walked her fingers up his chest before booping him on the end of his nose. "But even though it's in pain, your ass is still pretty damn nice." She pressed her smiling lips together. "I got a pretty good look at that too."

She turned toward the road. "So are we gonna keep walking around like this, or are we gonna get ourselves some clothes?"

He didn't want to have to answer that. Didn't want to have to cross yet another line he would never be able to forget. But they were running short on options. "You sure you don't want to call the police?"

Courtney's eyes came his way, one dark brow cocking. "Do you have a boner for the cops or something?" She widened her eyes as they swung back to the roadway. "Because I wouldn't think someone who works in the line you do would be so interested in bringing them into this."

Any tolerance he'd accidentally developed for the woman beside him evaporated in an instant. "Watch it." He glared at her a second longer before shoving his way through the last bit of scrappy overgrowth, leaving her to follow behind him.

Or not. Hopefully, not.

Courtney groaned behind him. "God you're an asshole." She stomped through the tall grass. "Just when I was starting to think you might not be a complete dick, you go and remind me why you were my least favorite babysitter."

"Aren't you a little old to have a favorite babysitter?" That's what his time with her last year had been though. Nothing more than glorified babysitting. Taking care of a brat throwing a temper tantrum.

"You're awfully ungrateful for someone whose salary I probably paid." She continued behind him, ranting as they moved. "But I guess if it wasn't for me taking up all your time, you could've added a few more notches to your murder belt."

He stopped short as she stuck her finger right in a festering wound. When he spun to face her, she didn't even have the sense to look surprised. "You're pushing me, Princess."

Courtney rolled her eyes. "I'm so fucking scared." She stepped in, squaring up to him. "What are you gonna do? Leave me out here?" She snorted out a laugh. "I don't think so. Don't want to sully your pristine mercenary image. Gotta make people think you're the best at your job."

This was how things always ended up with her. She knew exactly what buttons to push, and she nailed each one with a sledgehammer.

"At least I have a fucking job." He inched in more until they were toe-to-toe and nose to nose. "All you do is sit at home on your ass, pretending like your life matters."

Courtney didn't even flinch. "That's where you're wrong." Her nostrils barely flared. "I know my life doesn't matter to anyone but me." She planted one hand in the center of his chest and shoved, pushing him out of her way before storming past him, going straight for the road as a set of headlights cut through the darkness.

The chances of someone finding them were slim, but not none. Instinct took over, sending him right into her, taking her down as the car slowed to coast past them.

Courtney grunted as they hit the dirt, all the air rushing from her lungs. She kicked back at him, fighting against his weight until she was free. Then she jumped up, looking down at her filthy front. "You prick. You did that on purpose." She tried to brush away the debris clinging to the shirt and embedded in her knees. "You're trying to punish me for making you do your job."

Was that what he was doing? Taking out his own pent-up frustrations about the twist of fate that had forced him to join Alaskan Security?

Courtney flailed around, knocking bits of whatever was under their feet from her hair. "You know what? It doesn't even matter." She held both arms out. "I relieve you of your duty. Go back to Alaska. I'll figure this out on my own." She turned away from him, marching along the narrow bit of cover.

She was about twenty feet in front of him when the car that passed earlier stopped, brake lights illuminating in the darkness.

Then it started to back up.

"Fuck." Reed shoved up from the ground and took off after her. Stepping as carefully as he could to keep his path as quiet as possible, he kept one eye on Courtney and one on the car as he went. He was almost to her when she seemed to notice the car was coming and ducked down.

But it wasn't the car she was avoiding. A second later his forehead connected with the metal crossbar of an abandoned footbridge, and everything went dark.

CHAPTER SEVEN

COURTNEY

NORMALLY SHE WOULDN'T mind sparring with Reed. Part of her loved giving him shit, even if he was all too eager to give it back.

Or maybe that was why she enjoyed it so much.

Reed wasn't fake. He didn't tell her what she wanted to hear in the hope she would make his life better. Buy him clothes. Buy him drinks. Connect him with someone who might invest in some ridiculous business idea.

Courtney shot a glare over her shoulder in Reed's general direction. "Stop following me."

It was a testament to how exhausted she was. Physically. Mentally. Emotionally. She'd been in survival mode for almost twenty-four hours and was wearing down. Desperate for help from Alaskan Security for weeks, she'd called every day, hoping they would finally whisk her away from the threat she knew hung over her head. Because, while there was no denying she benefited from her father's position, she most definitely suffered for it as well.

Especially since it seemed like his reign over Miami's more

questionable imports was about to be over as two groups fought for power. One led by an aging perv and the other led by a man she might have tried to get her hands on a time or two. Right up until he fell in love with some chick from out of town and became all obsessed with her.

Which was fine. She wasn't actually that interested in him anyway. Her attempt to catch his eye was more about self-preservation than anything. A way to save her own skin as her father's empire began to crumble.

She ducked under the remnants of a footbridge, frustration mounting as she tried to figure out what in the hell she was going to do next. She'd done everything she could think of to avoid this situation. She'd moved out of the city, hoping distance would make people forget she existed. She'd laid low, hidden in her house for nearly a year hoping to fade away without notice.

And now here she was. Hiking through the dark in nothing but a T-shirt and borrowed boots, telling the only man who could save her to stop following her.

She was a fucking idiot.

A heavy thud echoed behind her, coming right as a passing car hit its brakes, tires screeching at the sudden stop before it began backing up.

"Shit." She crouched down, glancing back to tell Reed to do the same, but he was already flat to the dirt. So, she did the same thing, pancaking her body against the same dirt and debris she'd just knocked out of her hair, crossing her fingers she had more time.

Time to apologize for being such a bitch. Time to find her way back onto Reed's sliver of a good side.

Time to figure out how to survive.

The car slowly coasted past, a beam of light dancing across

the space around them as whoever was on the roadway searched the overgrowth for whatever they were looking for. Hopefully it wasn't her.

After what felt like an eternity, the light disappeared and the car switched directions again, creeping forward through the darkness before finally disappearing from sight.

Courtney let out a breath, closing her eyes and letting her forehead drop to the stinking ground. That was close. Another lucky break. But luck was a finite resource. One she would no doubt run out of soon. At some point, luck would no longer be on her side. And she planned to get out of Florida before that happened. Whatever it took, she would do.

No matter how much it pissed Reed off.

It seemed like he had some sort of a hang up when it came to stealing, which was crazy considering his chosen profession, but whatever. She was happy to do the dirty work to save her skin.

"Listen." Courtney worked up into a sitting position, not even bothering to attempt to wipe away everything stuck to her skin and tangled in her hair this time. "I'm not trying to be a bitch. I'm just really stressed out."

Reed didn't budge. Didn't acknowledge her apology.

"Are you fucking kidding me?" She crawled toward him. "I'm trying to tell you I'm sorry. You don't have to be such a fucking dick all the time." She reached his side, stopping short at his unmoving form. "Reed?"

Nothing.

Oh fuck.

She grabbed his shoulder, shoving it hard, but he was surprisingly heavy, the dead weight of his body shockingly difficult to move. "No, no, no, no."

He couldn't be dead. If he was dead, then she was completely alone. Abandoned by literally everyone.

Courtney managed to get him on his back and ran her hands over his chest, looking for some sign of what happened. Why he was—

She swallowed hard, refusing to consider the worst.

Unconscious. Reed had to be just unconscious. She couldn't handle the alternative.

Courtney dropped her ear to his chest, pressing it against his sternum as she listened. All the air rushed from her lungs as his heart beat under her, steady and strong. It was a relief, but one more bit of the limited luck she would surely use up soon.

That meant she needed to start making her own luck.

She went back to investigating. His chest seemed fine, stomach intact, legs and arms perfectly perfect. As she felt around, even in this fucked-up situation, there was no denying the effort Reed put into maintaining his form. Every inch of him was solid and strong. Firm with hard-earned muscle that she would appreciate more if she wasn't so worried he was going to die on her.

Her fingers brushed over the skin of his neck, looking for something to explain what was wrong, but it was fine too. As was his jaw, nose, and mouth. But then she reached his forehead, and a patch of sticky warmth made her stomach turn.

A head injury. It didn't feel like a hole, so hopefully he hadn't been caught by a wayward shot she didn't hear coming.

She lifted her eyes, barely making out the footbridge she'd seen coming and ducked under. It seemed like maybe she was the only one.

"Godammit." She sucked in air, trying to come up with a plan as her frustration with Reed grew. "You're supposed to be the one who's doing this, jerk." Panic had her scanning the space around them as her mind raced. A slightly denser area of growth sat about twenty yards away. It would provide decent cover, even as the sun came up.

Courtney wobbled to her feet, crouching down at Reed's head as she hooked both arms under his, grunting a little as she lifted his upper body off the ground. "God, you're heavy. You need to go on a fucking diet."

She tried to take a step backward but stumbled, going down hard on her ass with Reed's head falling right into her lap. She let out an unhinged sounding groan of frustration before wrestling her way back to her feet, hooking her hands under his arms a second time and starting to move.

It was slow going, and the exertion of dragging his heavy body made her already sweaty skin wet and sticky, attracting every mosquito within a twelve-mile radius. But she wasn't fucking giving up. If there was one positive thing she'd learned about herself over the past year, it was that she didn't give up. No matter how many people gave up on her, she would never give up on herself.

And, apparently, Reed. Because as tempting as it was to leave his grumpy ass out there, she just couldn't do it. It would be a waste of such a nice body if it was to get eaten by an alligator.

After what felt like forever, she finally made it to the overgrown area. She set Reed down, making sure not to bang his already injured head against the ground, before kicking her way through the growth to check for snakes or anything else that might try to murder him while she was gone. Leaving wasn't ideal, but there was no way she could take him any significant distance. Hauling him with her would only slow her down, and morning was approaching rapidly, so she needed to be able to work fast.

Breaking the law was always so much easier in the dark, even when you wanted to get caught.

Which she did not.

Once Reed was as camouflaged as he could get, she patted his cheek, giving him one more opportunity to wake up before he was on his own. "Wakey, wakey. Eggs and bac-y."

He didn't react at all. She didn't expect him to laugh—he made it clear he did not find her amusing—but the least he could do was groan. Grunt. Moan. Something. Just so she knew he wasn't already half brain-dead. Because that would mean she'd have to make a stop at the hospital on her way out of town to leave him outside of the emergency room. And while she wasn't against breaking little laws, that seemed slightly more illegal than she wanted to be.

"Fine." Courtney stood up, propping her hands on her hips. "Be good while I'm gone, Sexy Pants."

It was harder than she expected to turn away. There was some sense of safety that came with Reed, regardless of his feelings for her. He seemed to have a moral compass that was unusually high, especially given his line of work. He might bitch and piss and moan, but he would never abandon her.

Hopefully he didn't wake up and think she'd abandoned him.

His water-logged boots were heavy on her feet as she raced through the last of the overgrowth, breaking through the other end to find herself on the backside of a subdivision. It wasn't nearly as nice as the one she lived in—used to live in— and that was probably a good thing. It likely meant fewer cameras and safety measures.

Courtney scanned the closest homes, looking for one that

jumped out. Unfortunately, they were all almost identical, with matching clay roofs and slightly untended yards. At least until she got to the corner lot.

A smile curved her lips as her eyes locked on something peeking out from behind the detached garage. "Bingo."

She took off at a run, covering the distance as fast as she could. The sky was already starting to lighten up, and daylight was her worst enemy, which was saying something.

She reached the corner house and slowed, looking for any sign of dogs or cameras. The place had an almost abandoned look to it, but she didn't want to assume no one was home and end up getting caught. So she crept quietly along the privacy fence enclosing a section of the back yard, ducking down as she peeked through the dilapidated panels. More than a few were knocked loose and hanging by a single nail, making it easy to get a good look at the back of the house. The yard was completely grown over and filled with all kinds of shit. Boxes, bags, sun-bleached toys and furniture, and clothing littered the space.

Holy shit. She'd found a hoarder.

That meant her earlier discovery might not be as exciting as it first seemed.

She paused for a second, considering abandoning this house and hunting for another, but she couldn't walk away. Not yet. Not until she knew the thing that brought her all the way over here was a no-go.

The birds were just beginning to chirp when she reached the back bumper of the biggest vehicle she'd ever considered driving. It wasn't new. It wasn't fancy. It definitely wasn't in great shape. But it was exactly what she needed.

Even better, no one inside the house would even notice it was gone unless they came out and looked for it. It was hidden at the very back of the property, parked behind an outbuilding that was probably also filled with piles of shit.

She hustled up the side, headed for the driver's side door, looking along the ground for anything that might help her break-in. Surely there had to be at least a few wire hangers hanging around the mess. But the area was surprisingly clean. Clean enough she paused to consider someone might actually be living in the camper she was planning to steal.

Courtney backtracked, pushing up on her tiptoes in an attempt to peek into the windows as she made her way around the rear and up the driver's side. The entry door to the back portion was incredibly close to the building, so it could only open less than a foot before being stopped. It hardly seemed like a convenient place to put it if someone was planning to live there, and she hadn't seen any wires hooking it up to an electric source. So she took a deep breath, grabbed the levered handle and pulled, cringing a little when it immediately opened.

On one hand, she was thrilled to be able to get inside. But on the other, there was a chance someone might be waiting for her on the other side.

It was a chance she was going to have to take. She was getting out of this alive. Her whole life had been lived in a shadow. One that drowned out any chance she had for friends or lovers or jobs. Yes, she had money, every bit of it dirty, but money couldn't buy people.

She knew. She'd tried.

After one more deep breath, Courtney carefully wedged her body into the small opening, wiggling a little to get through before quietly stepping into the musty smelling space.

It wasn't filled to capacity with random items, so that was good. Maybe.

She stepped up, making her way in, listening for any sign someone else was there with her.

But all that met her was silence.

"Hello?" she whispered quietly. Quiet enough no one outside would hear, but loud enough anyone inside would. If someone was, in fact, in here, she wanted to find out now. While there was still a chance to escape.

But there was no response. So unless whoever was in here was as unconscious as Reed was, she was in the clear.

She held her breath, doing a quick check of the back end and finding nothing but an empty bed and a bathroom you couldn't pay her to step inside. The front end had a small couch, a booth-style dinette, and a tiny kitchen area, along with some sort of a bunk thing over the swiveling driver's and passenger's seats.

It was old. It was stinky. But it was empty.

And hopefully it had gas.

She quickly pulled the side door closed, flipping the lock before hustling up to the front and dropping into the driver's seat. She'd hotwired more than a few vehicles in her years, but never one like this. And the dashboard looked a whole hell of a lot different than she was used to. She felt around, looking for a way to get at what she needed, but then paused, her eyes going to the visor. It wouldn't be that easy, would it?

But if a person lived in a house so packed with crap they could never find what they were looking for, maybe it would make sense to keep the keys somewhere safe. Somewhere they would never forget.

She straightened, taking a deep breath before grabbing the visor and flipping it down.

A set of keys and a dead moth dropped into her lap. She stared at them both for a second, a little in shock and a little terrified. It was more good luck. More bleeding from a limited well. And she hadn't even made it out of the state yet.

Of course, the thing could still be out of gas. Or the engine might not function at all. There could be a reason it was sitting here unlocked. Not because the owner didn't believe anyone would steal it, but because they knew they couldn't.

She picked up the keys, selected the one that looked like it went to the ignition, and shoved it in, saying a little prayer before twisting it away from her.

The fucking thing started right up. Sure, it sounded a little rough, but it was running. Even better, the gas gauge said the tank was full.

And as much as she hated all this good luck, she wasn't gonna look a gift horse in the mouth.

She switched it into drive and eased onto the gas, trying to keep her escape as quiet as she could. Just in case whoever was in that house decided to wake up and end her lucky streak. The camper bumped along the uneven ground, making terrifying rattling noises that she was pretty sure meant the whole fucking thing was falling apart. But once she hit black-top, those seemed to calm down a little, and she floored it, getting out of the neighborhood as fast as she could.

CHAPTER EIGHT

REED

HIS WHOLE BODY hurt. Every inch of skin felt like it had been raked over a cheese grater and his head was throbbing. The fact that the world wouldn't stop moving wasn't helping matters any.

Reed groaned as a particularly violent shift bounced his head, rocking his tender brain inside his skull. He pressed one palm to his temple, trying to stop the movement. But instead of finding the cropped line of his short hair, his palm rested against a thick band of webbing. He traced his fingers along the edge, following its path across his forehead and around his skull.

His head was bandaged. Why in the hell was his head bandaged?

It took every ounce of strength he had to push into a sitting position, and the change in elevation made the throb behind his eyes even worse, dragging another groan free. What the fuck happened to him? The last thing he remembered was—

He sat for a second, trying to piece together the events of the past twenty-four hours.

He was in Florida. Here to deal with Courtney. But, shocker, that wasn't going as planned. She came to his room, begging him to take her to Alaska. The explosion. Their escape.

They'd been in the overgrowth. Hidden between the road and the swampy waterway. She'd tried to storm off after he was an ass—again. He tried to chase her down, but...

That's when everything went black. Literally.

He rubbed at his burning eyes, rolling them around behind his lids as he tried to work up the gumption to open them. Discovering where he was wasn't necessarily something he was in a hurry to do. He worked his eyes open anyway, fighting against the confusion still making it difficult to focus.

Reed blinked a few times, then rubbed his eyes again, sure they were playing tricks on him. He didn't expect to still be outside, based on the softness of whatever he was lying on, but he certainly didn't expect this.

Was he in the back of a camper?

It would explain the constant movement. But how the fuck would it have happened?

He dropped his feet over the edge of the bed, cringing a little as his raw soles hit the floor. He'd been in socks as they ran through the river. It was better than nothing, but, based on the pain he was experiencing now, not by much. He glanced down, ready to assess the damage, but found his feet were wrapped in gauze and webbing and just as bandaged as his head.

He was also wearing fresh clothes. He wasn't in anything fancy, but the knit shorts and graphic T-shirt were new and clean.

And nothing he owned.

The camper bounced again, making his aching head bounce along with it. Getting to his feet was both an act of determination and focus. Between the pain in his feet, the pain in his head, and the blurriness still lingering at the edges of his vision, it took way too much effort to get upright. Even more to take slow steps through the dated vehicle. It had a musty smell and, from the paneling on the walls to the chipped yellow countertops, looked like something straight out of the seventies. A fact that made it impressive the thing was holding together as they flew down the highway.

And they were definitely flying.

He managed to make it to the front of the vehicle and fell into the passenger's seat, closing his eyes as his head dropped back against the rest. "You need to slow the fuck down before we get pulled over."

"Damn." Courtney glanced at him from the corner of her eye, both hands gripping the large steering wheel. "I was kind of hoping a concussion would make you a little less of a dick." She tossed back a long gulp of an energy drink in a black can. "Looks like that was a fail."

He peered back down at his clean clothes and the bandages on his feet before closing his eyes again and taking a deep breath. "Sorry."

Courtney shrugged one shoulder. "It's fine. It's your thing. I get it." There was an edge to her words that made it seem like even if she did get it, his attitude still hurt her feelings.

And it made him feel like an ass. An ungrateful one.

"Thank you."

Courtney glanced his way again, looking him over. "You're welcome."

They sat quietly for a second, but he had too many questions to keep his mouth shut. "Where did you get the camper?"

Courtney's eyes stayed glued to the road. "I don't think you want me to answer that.

"What about these clothes I'm wearing?"

Courtney pressed her lips together as she shook her head. "No comment."

Her non-answers told him enough. "Should I expect the police to be coming after us?"

Courtney snorted. "The police coming after us is the least of my concerns." She reached into a bag beside her seat and pulled out a bottle of water, holding it his direction. "Thirsty?"

His eyes fell to the drink. One that had most likely been lifted from a convenience store by the woman next to him. Normally, something like that would have him turning it down on principle alone. But right now principles didn't seem very useful.

He took the bottle and cracked the lid. "Thank you again."

Courtney's lips barely lifted in a smile. "You're welcome again." Her brows pinched together as she looked his way. "How are you feeling?"

He swallowed down half the bottle, hoping rehydrating would ease some of the throbbing in his skull. "Like I was dragged to hell and back."

Courtney chewed her lower lip, looking into both side mirrors before changing lanes. "I didn't drag you to hell, but I definitely dragged you at least a quarter of a mile." She settled into the new lane and gave him another glance. "You weigh a fuck ton, by the way."

He laughed as he downed the rest of the water, wiping his forearm across his wet lips before shooting her a grin. "You should just be glad you didn't have to carry my ass down a river in socked feet."

Courtney's brows jumped up, her mouth dropping open. "At least I was conscious while you carried me." She slapped at him, lightly hitting him in the shoulder. "You were dead weight."

He continued to smile, a little amused that the woman who tormented him endlessly had to suffer. And also because the woman who tormented him endlessly saved his ass even though he'd been a complete dick to her. He still might not be Courtney's biggest fan, but he had to give her props right now. Her means might not be something he agreed with, but she definitely made it to a relatively successful end.

Even if the path getting there was a little… colorful.

And while he didn't feel the need to jab at her like normal, he couldn't stop himself from teasing her. Just a little. "What about when you changed my clothes? Was I dead weight then too?"

"Did you want me to leave you in your disgusting clothes?" She took another swig of her energy drink. "They smelled like shit and were covered in blood. And I didn't want to have to smell you the whole way to Alaska." She peeked his way, her cheeks pinking up the tiniest bit. "And I didn't really even look at anything. I was very respectful." Her eyes moved back to the road. "I'm not the kind of girl who mauls unconscious men."

"Only conscious ones, then?" The snarky words slipped right out of his mouth, hanging in the air between them, unable to be taken back.

And, for the first time, he wanted to take them back.

Courtney gripped the wheel, her expression tight as she changed lanes again, quickly jumping onto the exit ramp in a move that had him sitting straighter in his seat.

"Why are we pulling off?"

Courtney worked her jaw from side to side, before letting out a long sigh. "Because I have to pee." She faced him, lifting her brows. "Is that okay with you, or would you like to talk more about what an awful person I am?"

Fuck. He shouldn't have said that last bit. She clearly worked hard to save their skins and he was being ungrateful as fuck because she broke the law to do it.

Like he hadn't broken the law a few times himself.

Courtney whipped the RV into a spot, parking it and jumping out, keys looped around one finger like she expected him to take off without her.

Because he probably made her think he would take off without her. Abandon her at any moment, leaving her to fend for herself. Even worse, he acted like she would deserve it. Like everything that happened would be her own fault.

And even after everything, she still didn't do that to him. Even though saving him was certainly a huge risk, and she would have been better off to get the hell out of Dodge and leave him where he laid, she didn't do it.

And she wasn't holding it over his head.

"Godammit." Reed shoved open the door, pausing before climbing out. His feet were still bandaged, and there probably wasn't much gauze to go around, so destroying it by running across the parking lot didn't seem like a great idea. He pulled the door shut and stood, wedging himself back into the narrow walkway between the dinette and the sofa that led to the back bedroom. He opened one of the tiny cabinets, and sure enough a few more clothing items and a set of slide-on sandals sat inside, the tags still on them. He grabbed the shoes, yanking them in different directions to pop the plastic binding them and dropped them onto the cracking floor before slipping his tender feet inside. Once both feet were appropriately protected, he opened the side door and stepped out into the parking lot, giving it a quick scan for any sign of trouble before hustling to the rest stop bathroom. The place was nearly deserted, so he didn't slow down as he marched into the women's bathroom.

"Courtney?" He strode down the line of stalls, looking for a set of familiar feet. He reached the only occupied stall and stopped, staring at Courtney's dirty toes. He looked at the dirt crusting her nails and skin before taking another scan of his own body. Every inch of him was clean. Free of all the disgusting shit they'd hiked through the night before.

"Did you come in here to listen to me pee?" Courtney's voice was sharp on the other side of the door. "Because I can make you a recording."

He relaxed a little as she gave him shit. At least she was talking to him. "Finish up and get your ass out here."

Courtney groaned. "Are you serious? You're really going to stand in here while I go?"

He leaned against the stall, gripping the top edge. "You wanted somebody to come protect you, Princess. You asked for this."

Courtney made an indignant sound on the other side of the door. "Can you at least go stand by the sinks? I can't go with you standing there listening to me."

He ran his tongue over his teeth, cringing a little at the stale taste of his mouth. "Fine."

He went to the sinks, ripping off a few paper towels and running them under the water before scrubbing at his scummy feeling teeth, getting them as clean as he could before rinsing out his mouth and chucking everything in the trash. It wasn't as great as a toothbrush and toothpaste would've been, but it went a long way.

It was another few minutes before Courtney finally came out, eyeing him warily as she went to the sink to wash her hands. She was still wearing his T-shirt, along with a fitted pair of stretchy shorts and sandals almost identical to his.

He propped against one of the wall-mounted sinks, crossing his arms as he watched her. "Did you clear out a Walmart?"

Her eyes rolled his way as she scrubbed at her hands, working the soap up her dirty forearms. "Have you ever been to a Walmart?" Courtney carefully rinsed away the suds. "It would take me a decade to clean one out."

Reed looked her over, trying to gauge what she was thinking. "They weren't suspicious when you walked in, covered in dirt wearing only a T-shirt and my boots?"

"Again, have you ever been in a Walmart?" She yanked off a few paper towels and went to work drying her skin. "I was the least unhinged looking person walking around the store at four thirty in the morning."

He couldn't help but be impressed by her ingenuity. "So while I was out, you stole clothes, bandages, beverages," he glanced in the direction of the parking lot, "*and* an RV?"

Courtney tossed her paper towels into the trash can. "Well I didn't see you doing anything to improve our situation." She bumped his shoulder as he walked past, still hell-bent on irritating him as much as possible. And it was working, but the irritation didn't chafe as much as it once did.

Reed snagged her by the hand, pulling her back before she could get away. "You did good, Princess."

Courtney wouldn't meet his gaze as she let out an almost

defeated sounding sigh. "I just don't necessarily want to die today."

"Understandable." He should let go of her hand. Let her move away and give them both some space. But he wasn't going to. He had a whole team of men who were required to have his back. Hired to do the same job he was and all their lives depended on each of them looking out for the other one. But this was different. Courtney didn't have to have his back. She didn't have to look out for him. Hell, she probably shouldn't have. He probably deserved to be left as alligator food. The fact that she didn't, had him looking at her a little differently.

"I don't want you to die today either." His thumb accidentally moved across her skin. "Tomorrow might be a different story though."

Courtney huffed out a laugh, rolling her eyes as she yanked her hand away. "I'll remember that when you want me to help you bandage your head again." Her eyes fixed on his forehead. "How's it feeling? You hit it pretty hard."

"It feels like I knocked the shit out of myself." He fisted the hand that just held hers. "But I'll survive."

"That's good, because I'm pretty sure Pierce would charge me extra if you died." Her shoulders slumped a little. "Not that I actually have any way of paying him at this point."

She looked a little lost. A little unsure, which was nothing like the brash, confident Courtney he'd come to know.

"Are you sure you really want to do this?" He thumbed over his shoulder, even though he had no clue which direction Miami was. "We can always find a way to get you back to your dad."

Courtney seemed to wilt even more. "For what? He doesn't even care that I'm dead." She reached up to swipe at her messy hair. "I hid in the neighbor's bushes, watching as people showed up, and he never came."

Her sadness was palpable, and it made him do something he would have never thought might happen. He snagged her hand again, using it to reel her in, pulling her close, tucking her against his chest. "He's a fucking idiot, Princess." He'd interacted with Courtney's father a couple of times over the years, and each one left a bad taste in his mouth. "He's an even bigger asshole than I am."

Courtney leaned back, her eyes coming to meet his. "You're not really an asshole. You just act like one."

He smiled, the expression still feeling odd on his lips. "I think that's the nicest thing you've ever said to me."

Courtney's lower lip pushed out on a pout that could almost be considered cute. "I can be nice."

He held her gaze, caught up in a moment that didn't entirely make sense. He shouldn't be comforting Courtney. He sure as shit shouldn't still be holding her so close. She annoyed the shit out of him. Drove him absolutely fucking crazy.

"You're a pain in my ass, you know that?" He needed the reminder. To refocus on the situation and the woman at hand.

Courtney slowly smiled. "I know." She tapped one finger in the center of his chest. "And you piss me all the way off." Her eyes held his as the seconds stretched out between them.

And then they collided.

It was impossible to tell who moved first. Whose bad idea what happened next was.

Odds were good it was his.

However it happened, the next thing he knew, Courtney was pulled against him, her soft mouth opening under his.

CHAPTER NINE

COURTNEY

THAT ESCALATED QUICKLY.

Somehow Reed had gone from hating her guts to acting like he wanted to rearrange them in the span of five minutes. And honestly, she was here for it.

It had been forever since someone touched her like this. And even then they'd done it with some sort of ulterior motive. Usually one involving money or power. Everything in her life always came with a price. But she had nothing to give anymore, and Reed knew it. So the second he leaned in, dark eyes focused on her lips, she was already meeting him halfway. Mouth hitting his so hard her teeth dug into her lips. It wasn't so much a kiss, but a clash. A new way to fight and attack each other.

It was fucking amazing and absolutely intoxicating.

She channeled every bit of her frustration and aggravation into the moment, tangling her fingers in his dark hair and pulling tight as their kiss intensified, his tongue slicking along hers without hesitation or caution. His hands gripped her hips, hefting her up before dropping her ass on the edge of the wall-mounted sink. She locked her legs around his waist, pulling his body flush against hers and letting out a little gasp when the hard line of his dick met her pussy, providing a blessed amount of friction.

Reed's hand worked into her drooping ponytail, gripping tight at the back of her skull as his mouth devoured hers. There was nothing hesitant or exploratory about his kiss. This was complete possession and ownership. Control and demand. Every breath was a struggle as his tongue flicked against hers, his large body crowding her closer to the chipped mirror mounted on the block wall.

She grabbed at the men's T-shirt she'd managed to sneak out of Walmart, yanking it up so she could get her hands on the hard plane of his abs. Her palm skimmed over warm skin and solid muscle. There wasn't an inch of fat on this man, and she wanted to explore every bit of him. With her hands.

Hopefully with her tongue.

But, just in case this turned out to be the only opportunity she had, she was going to make the most of it.

She slid her palms higher, finding the solid swell of his pecs before giving his nipples a hard pinch. Partly because she wanted to see his reaction, and partly because the man deserved a little bit of pain for all the bullshit he put her through. Sure, he thanked her for saving his ass and bandaging him up, but that didn't even scratch the surface of what she was owed.

Reed hissed against her mouth as his nipples tightened under her fingers, but the move only seemed to make him more focused. More intent.

"Is that how this is gonna be, Princess?" He palmed her ass with the hand not currently fisted in her hair. "I try to apologize and you keep making me pay?"

She smiled against his lips at the accurate assessment as one hand slid down to grip his rigid cock through the thin fabric of his jersey shorts. "You don't seem too bothered by it."

Reed groaned, the sound passing from his mouth to hers as he sucked on her bottom lip. "I'm fucking bothered by you."

"Good." She worked her hand into the waistband of his shorts, wrapping her fingers around him. "Because I'm fucking bothered by you too."

He was absolutely infuriatingly irritating, and apparently that directly translated into the uncontrollable urge to rip his clothes off and fuck him right here in the rest stop bathroom.

Because that's what she was about to do.

Right up until the earth fell out from under her.

Or, more specifically, the sink.

Courtney yelped as the porcelain under her ass suddenly gave way, dropping her straight toward the cement floor. Luckily, Reed's grip on her was tight enough to keep her from ending up even grosser than she already was. He pinned her to his chest as the sink went crashing down, breaking into two pieces on impact. The separation of the pipes sent water spewing out at them, soaking her back and Reed's bandaged feet.

She stared at the growing mess, legs still locked around his waist. "We should go."

"Agreed." Reed carefully set her down before grabbing her hand and leading her out of the bathroom, through the lobby of the small building housing the restrooms and a vending area, and into the parking lot. They were almost to the camper when he glanced her way. "You always go around breaking shit?"

She scoffed. "Me?" She shoved at his shoulder with her free hand. "You're the one who put me up there. That was definitely your fault."

"It wasn't my ass that broke it." He grabbed the passenger's door and yanked it open, motioning for her to get in.

Courtney shook her head. "That's your seat. I'm the driver."

Reed reached for her, snagging the front of her filthy shirt before she could get away and hauling her toward the seat. "You *were* the driver. I'm the driver now." He all but picked her up and dropped her into place before plucking the keys from her hand. buckling her in and closing the door.

She glared at him as he rounded the front and jumped in beside her. He started the engine and shifted into drive. "Don't look at me like that."

Courtney crossed her arms, continuing to glare. "Like what?"

He adjusted the side mirror as they moved toward the on-ramp. "Like I'm being unreasonable." He brought them up to speed and merged into the slow lane. "You're fucking exhausted. I can see it in your eyes. You need to rest." He jerked his chin toward the back end of the camper. "Why don't you go lay down and get some sleep."

She wrinkled her nose. "Ew. No. I'm not laying down on that gross bed."

His head snapped her way, brows pinched together. "But you laid me across it?"

"What was I supposed to do with you? Leave you on the floor?" Courtney slumped down in her seat, propping both feet up on the dash. "And for the record, I put fresh sheets on the mattress before I laid you on top of it."

Reed worked his jaw from side to side as they continued

down the highway. "So you managed to make it out of Walmart with clothes, shoes, beverages, and a set of sheets?"

Courtney wiggled one finger in his direction, aiming at his head. "Don't forget the bandages." She paused "And a couple towels and some soap."

Reed glanced down at himself before peeking her direction. "Why didn't you clean up too?"

She shrugged. "I didn't really have any injuries I needed to worry about getting infected. And it was getting late and I wanted to get the fuck out of Florida."

He was quiet for a few minutes, leaving her to wonder what he was thinking. It sure didn't seem like he was thinking about what happened back at the rest stop. Which was unfortunate, considering it was all she could think about.

That might have been the hottest, most intense three and half minutes of her life. And the memory of it left her with an ache between her thighs. "Maybe I am tired. I think I will go lay down." Courtney gripped the back of her seat and hefted to her feet before wobbling down the narrow path leading to the back bedroom. She dropped onto the mattress, settling into the same spot where Reed had been lying not so long ago, before slipping one hand into the waistband of her shorts.

She was ridiculously wet from just that little bit of contact in the bathroom and desperately needed a release after storing up so much fear and frustration over the past twenty-four hours. Too bad that damn sink broke before Reed could take care of it for her. The man ran so hot—burned with so much focus and drive—that she could only imagine what he was capable of accomplishing when it came to physical interactions. He probably ate a pussy like a fucking champ. Went at it like his life depended on the satisfaction he provided.

She could almost picture his half angry expression as he

wedged his broad shoulders between her thighs. Shoving them wide as his frowning mouth went to work on her clit, licking and sucking with unerring precision. Bringing her right to the edge before stopping. Punishing her for being so fucking difficult.

That's what he'd do. He'd edge her until she was ready to claw his eyes out before finally letting her come on his tongue. She worked herself with the tips of her fingers, rubbing faster as she imagined what would happen next.

Because what happened next almost aroused her more.

Getting on her knees for him. Swallowing his thick cock so deep she choked. Sucking hard as she worked his balls in her hands. Waiting until he was ready to come before working one finger into his ass, blowing his mind while he blew his load.

He'd be so fucking pissed at her he might make good on his earlier threat and bend her over his knee. Give her a few, well-placed slaps across her ass and the bit of her pussy that would peek out between her thighs. That was what had her coming, hard and fast. The thought of Reed's hand on her skin. The sting it would bring. The bit of reprimand that came with it.

No one had ever cared about her enough to give two shits when she fucked up. Thinking that Reed might, had her thighs jerking as her pussy clenched around nothing, fingers still working as she tried to drag the release out as long as she could.

No doubt Reed would be pissed about this too, and the possibility made her smile. Made her wish she'd been a little more obvious.

Maybe next time.

And next time could come as early as the next five

minutes, because she was two years into a dry spell and her body was already considering round two.

"Hey, Princess?" Reed's deep voice shot straight to her still-throbbing lady parts, reminding her of the way he growled against her mouth as she fisted his cock.

Five minutes might have been generous. Hearing him call her Princess knocked it down to a solid minute and a half. "Yes, Sexy Pants?"

"Did the check engine light come on while you were driving?" His voice carried a hint of concern.

Concern that had her sitting up straight, post orgasm glow snuffed out almost immediately. "No." Courtney jumped up, bumping into the tiny bank of cabinets as she wobbled her way toward the front. Reed never sounded concerned. Angry, yes. Frustrated, yes. Confident? Always. Serious? Definitely.

But never concerned.

She wove her way to the cab, dropping into a crouch behind his seat. Sure enough, the check engine light was glowing bright and threatening from the dashboard. "What do you think that means?"

"I think it means you stole the biggest piece of shit you could find, and now it's doing exactly what anyone else would've assumed it would do."

Courtney stared at the side of his head, shocked even though she shouldn't be. "Are you fucking kidding me?" Was he really gonna be like this? "I didn't see you doing anything to get us the fuck out of there."

The urge to retaliate was strong. Before she thought it through, the tip of one finger was in her mouth and then immediately shoved in his ear, wiggling her spit right into the canal.

Reed jerked away, the camper swerving as he swatted at her offending hand. "Did you just fucking wet willy me?"

"If you're going to be an ass, I'm going to treat you like an ass." She immediately licked her middle finger and went after him again, fighting against Reed's hold as he caught her by the wrist.

"I don't think that's the precedent you want to set, Princess." He held her tight, too strong to overcome. "Because if we're going to go there, then you're gonna start getting treated like the brat you are."

Did he think that would be a deterrent? Because it definitely wasn't.

"I'll stop being a brat when you stop being an ass." She quickly snaked her free hand around to pinch his closest nipple through the fabric of his shirt. Giving it a twist between her fingers as his eyes snapped her way.

"I don't think that's gonna have the effect you want it to."

Courtney yanked her hand from his grip and shoved it into his lap, sliding it over his rapidly thickening cock. "Seems like it did." She stroked him through the fabric a couple of times, rubbing at the head with her thumb before retreating. "Take that."

She wanted him to be as sexually frustrated as she still was. Rubbing one out had done nothing to help. If anything, it made everything worse. Because now she had all those imagined fantasies frolicking around her mind. Clogging it up when it should be focused on the fact that their only mode of transportation was having a moment.

"I think you underestimate me, Princess." Reed looked calm and cool and nowhere near as worked up as she still was. "I wouldn't be very good at my job if I got distracted every time I had a hard-on." His dark eyes slid to the side mirror before going back to the dash. "I think we might be coming to the end of our time in the RV."

Her lower lip pushed up to cover her top one in something that wasn't necessarily a pout.

But wasn't necessarily not a pout.

How could he act like everything was fine? Like he didn't need to finish what they'd started?

It was bullshit.

Reed scanned the exit sign coming up. "Looks like this is our next stop."

Courtney scowled at the sign. "We're still in Florida."

"For now." Reed eased onto the exit, his eyes continuing to flick to the dash on regular intervals as the engine started to make an odd sound. "Don't worry, Princess. I've got everything under control."

That was an understatement. She knew he was focused. She knew he was dedicated. She knew he was intense.

And she liked all of it. It made her feel like she could rely on him. That he was capable of handling all that came their way.

But right now his level of self-control was a little annoying.

Reed coasted into the closest parking lot right as a thin stream of smoke started to leak from the edge of the hood. He parked the camper at the farthest end of the lot before shutting down the engine and turning to her. "Start packing our shit. We've gotta come up with plan B."

CHAPTER TEN

REED

REED PULLED THE dipstick on the engine, tipping it to the side to confirm his suspicions. "Looks like this thing hasn't had its oil changed in a decade."

Courtney leaned closer, squinting at the strip of metal. "How can you tell?"

He tipped his head to look her way, a little surprised that she gave a shit about something like this. "See that black liquid at the bottom?"

She nodded, her eyes coming to his face before going back to the dipstick.

"That should be a lot higher than it is." He put it back in place, before reaching for the prop holding up the hood.

"So can we just add more oil to it?" Courtney sounded hopeful. Like she didn't mind cruising down the highway in a camper older than she was.

"Maybe?" Reed clipped the prop stand in place before dropping the lid. "It might help, it might not. The water we put in the radiator could fix our immediate issue, but it looks like it's not our only issue." He faced her. "And I don't happen to have any oil on me, so I'm not sure we should count on this thing getting us very far."

Courtney chewed her lower lip, her dark eyes drifting over his shoulder. He turned around to see what she was staring at. A Walmart Supercenter stood behind him. He shook his head. "No way. You're not trying to lift oil from Walmart."

Courtney gave him a grin. "Who said anything about trying?" She started across the parking lot, headed straight for the front doors, forcing him to chase after her.

He caught her by the hand, stopping her. "I know you got away with it once, but that's a huge risk, Princess. You said you don't want the cops involved, and if you get caught, I can promise you they will be involved."

Courtney's head tipped and she gave him a smile, reaching out to pat the side of his face with one hand. "That's so sweet that you think I've only done this once." She pinched his cheek, wiggling it around. "Don't worry, Sexy Pants. I've got this. I was a professional juvenile delinquent." She released his cheek and immediately gave his face a light slap. "And if I get caught, you can spank me."

He took a slow breath, trying to will away the sudden stiffening of his cock. "Someone who misbehaves as much as you do probably shouldn't go around offering up her ass for paddling. Someone might take you up on it."

Courtney smirked. "Do I look scared?" She pulled her hand from his, giving him a wink as she backed toward the store. "Because you sure as hell do."

He shook his head. "Definitely not scared, Princess." He jerked his chin toward the door behind her. "Let's see what you can do." He held up one hand before she managed to get away. "But, if I have to save your ass, it's definitely going to see the business side of my palm."

Courtney wiggled her brows. "Careful. You give me too much incentive, I'll get caught on purpose."

Reed was still shaking his head as she took off toward the store, an extra bit of swagger in her step. He'd been almost positive he knew exactly who Courtney was, but he might not have been giving her enough credit.

Or enough grace.

She was most definitely everything he thought she was, but there might be a little more to her. Something beyond being a complete pain in his ass.

Unfortunately, that something led to him making bad choices in the rest stop bathroom. That couldn't happen again. If for no other reason than because he needed to keep his head clear right now. They were in a bad situation. One that could get exponentially worse with little to no warning. He needed to be at the top of his game. Alert and prepared every minute.

And he'd been anything but alert or prepared with her legs wrapped around his waist.

He shifted on his feet, tugging at the hem of his T-shirt to hide the jut of his cock as it focused a little too easily on Courtney and that very bad decision. The woman burned hot in every sense of the word, and fire was fucking dangerous. He had to make sure neither of them got burned.

He turned back to the camper, deciding to be optimistic and popping the hood for a second time, propping it open and carefully working the oil cap free just in case they needed to move quickly when she came out.

He leaned against the side of the vehicle, crossing his arms over his chest as he waited. And waited.

And waited.

He was just about to go in after her when Courtney's dark head came sashaying through the sliding doors. He expected her to look awkward, considering she likely had a quart of Valvoline shoved into her shorts, but she might as well have been a runway model as she strode through the parking lot.

Carrying three full bags.

He held his hands out when she got close. "What the fuck are you doing?"

Courtney's brows pinched together. "What do you mean what am I doing?" She shoved one of the bags in his direction. "I got what we needed."

He took the bag, looking down inside it at the three bottles of motor oil. "Why is it bagged up?"

Courtney looked at him like he was the biggest fucking idiot she'd ever seen. "How did you think I was gonna get out of there? If you have it already bagged up, they assume you bought it in a different department."

He glanced back at the sliding doors, half expecting to see someone running across the lot in search of the woman who just raided the store.

And it had definitely been raided.

Reed pointed at the other bags she carried. "What else did you get?"

Courtney's chin tipped. "Stuff." She clutched the remaining bags tight to her chest before opening the side door. "Pour that shit in so we can go."

She slammed the door, leaving him with no choice but to make it seem like he was doing her bidding. Which he was not.

He quickly added the Valvoline—hoping she grabbed something semi-close to what the engine required—before capping it off, dropping the hood, and climbing into the driver's seat. Courtney was already seated in the passenger's side, chewing through an energy bar. She reached into the bag between them and tossed one into his lap. "It's the best I could do given the circumstances."

He picked up the package and tore into it as he started the engine, breathing a little easier when the check engine light didn't immediately flare to life. "It's better than what I made." He bit off a chunk. "But I'm more worried about how to fill the gas tank than how to get food." He knew calling Alaskan Security was what would get them out of this, but figuring out how to do that was easier said than done. Strangers didn't typically hand over their phone for use, and Walmart certainly wouldn't be interested in letting him use their system to make an out-of-state call.

"That's a good point." Courtney chewed on her lower lip. "Can we call Heidi or something?"

It was a little unsettling how quickly her train of thought aligned with his. "With what phone?"

Courtney shrugged. "Any phone. Do we need a special phone to call them?"

"No, but I don't have a phone and neither do you." He glanced into the back end of the camper. "I'm sure this thing didn't come with its own landline."

"So why don't we just go ask somebody to use theirs?" Courtney said it like it was a completely reasonable plan.

"Because people don't generally like to let strangers borrow their cell phones."

Courtney smirked at him again. "No. Strangers don't like to let *men* use their cell phones." She held out one hand, wiggling her fingers. "Give me the number."

Reed looked down at his shirt and shorts. "Do I look like I have a pen?"

Courtney rolled her eyes. "You're so fucking dramatic." She pushed up out of the chair, going back to the tiny kitchen area and yanking open the drawers. A few seconds later she came back with a pen that looked like it came from the eighties. It was emblazoned with the logo of an auto repair shop and the white plastic was stained yellow at the edges.

Reed lifted his brows. "You really think that thing's gonna work?"

Courtney held her hand out. "If nothing else, you can use it to carve the number into my skin."

He studied her for a second. "You're a strange woman, Princess."

"Not strange." Courtney pushed her palm closer. "Just ready to get the fuck out of here."

His eyes moved over her face, cataloging her determination for a second, before dropping to her smooth palm. The one that had been stroking his dick not so long ago. He gritted his teeth against the memory as he yanked the cap off the pen and rolled the tip across the dashboard, hoping to get the ink moving. It left a faint, but legible line after a few swipes.

"Whew." Courtney blew out a breath. "I was really hoping I wouldn't have to follow through on that skin carving suggestion."

Reed brought the pen to her palm and started writing out the numbers, being careful not to press too hard into her skin. "You in the habit of writing checks you don't want to cash, Princess?"

Courtney's dark brows pinched together. "I don't think anyone even writes checks anymore." She leaned closer. "How freaking old are you?"

"It's a saying." He finished with the pen just as it stopped working. "And how old do you think I am?"

She shrugged, turning her hand toward her face. "I don't know. Fifty?"

He scoffed. "Are you fu—"

She shot him a grin as she pushed open her door. "Was I wrong?" She slid out of the seat. "I should have known. You don't look a day over forty-five." She slammed the door as he continued to scowl at her.

She was fucking with him. He knew that. But she was so damn good at it.

The woman knew exactly what to say and do to rile him up and did it at every opportunity. Unfortunately, she seemed to be figuring out how to rile him up in more than one way, so hopefully she managed to make the call to Heidi. Then they could meet up with Rico at the closest airport and get back to Fairbanks.

Back to everything that waited for him there.

He scrubbed one hand down his face, already tired at the thought. The weight.

The guilt.

He watched from the camper, keeping his focus on Courtney to avoid letting it get stuck on more difficult things. Things he couldn't actually do anything about.

At least here, he could fix shit. He had the skills to get Courtney out of Florida. Could change her life in a way that would hopefully be for the better. It was a marked contrast to all he couldn't fix in Alaska. It didn't matter how strong he was. How capable. How much money he threw at it, the problems he faced there would never go away.

They would only get worse.

Courtney pressed one hand over her mouth as she made a beeline for a young guy loading bags into the trunk of his Mustang. She reached him, shoulders hunched, looking small and broken. Her other hand came out to rest on his arm as they spoke. Within seconds he was digging into his pocket and pulling out his cell phone, passing it over without hesitation.

Reed shook his head. "You've got to be fucking kidding me."

Apparently, Courtney could be quite convincing when she needed to be, because this guy looked ready to do whatever it took to help her. He dug through his trunk, pulling out a bottle of water and offering it up with a bag of chips as she dialed his phone.

Reed gripped the steering wheel a little tighter as the guy moved closer, invading her space.

Nothing would happen. Courtney was completely safe, he knew that. The distance between them was small enough that if the guy made one wrong move, he would be on him before the asshole knew what hit him. But he still didn't fucking like how close he was to her. The desperate way she looked at him, like he was her savior.

Courtney stood a little straighter, her eyes darting his way for just a second as her lips started to move into the cell phone. Hopefully she gave Heidi enough information to make it possible for one of Intel's hackers to get into the cell lines and figure out exactly where they were. Unfortunately, that meant the call would last a little longer than he cared for.

Especially since the guy was now rubbing her back like he was trying to soothe her.

He narrowed his eyes, zeroing in on the point of contact. "Fucking guy."

After nearly five minutes of conversation, and five minutes of that asshole touching her, Courtney finally ended the call and passed the cell phone back, offering up a sweet smile.

Phone guy didn't seem interested in letting her get away

that easily. As she backed up, he walked toward her, talking and gesturing at his car.

Courtney shook her head, waving him off with one hand before turning and skipping back to the camper. She jumped into the passenger's seat and locked the door before turning to him. "Let's get the fuck out of here before that guy decides I owe him for using his cell phone.

"I'll kick his fucking ass." His words carried a little too much of an edge. One that gave away more than he'd like.

But Courtney didn't seem to notice as she sank further into her seat. "I would let you." She let out a little breath as he pulled out of the parking lot, leaving the confused-looking cell phone lender with his arms out as he watched them retreat.

"What did Heidi say?" Reed tried to get Courtney talking.

He needed information. Needed to think about something other than his responsibilities in Alaska, that fucking guy, and the way Courtney's legs felt wrapped around him.

"She said she's going to hook us up with a cell phone but we have to pick it up at a store around the corner. Then she said we should go to a campground instead of a hotel since fewer people will see us there because there aren't as many cameras."

Reed snorted. "Heidi wants us to go camping?"

Heidi had asked him to do a lot of things when he was out on jobs or missions, but spending the night in a nineteen seventies motorhome with the daughter of a Colombian drug lord might take the cake.

Courtney turned to him, lifting her brows. "What's the matter, Sexy Pants? Not much of an outdoorsman?"

He had to laugh at that. "I grew up in Alaska, Princess. Everyone's a fucking outdoorsman there." He turned at the light, heading in the direction Courtney pointed. "I'm worried about you. You're used to the finer things in life. I can't imagine you'll be too comfortable roughing it for a night."

Courtney motioned to her filthy T-shirt and messy hair. "Do I not already look like I can handle some shit?" She grabbed the wrapper from her energy bar and chucked it at him. "At least give me a little goddamned credit."

Reed turned to face the road. "I will admit, you have done surprisingly well under the circumstances."

"Under the circumstances?" She pointed at his forehead. "At least I duck under bridges, Mr. Outdoorsman." She wasn't willing to give him an inch. Probably because he hadn't done it for her.

And unfortunately, he was starting to like it as much as he hated it. "I guess we'll just have to wait and see how you handle being a nature girl for an evening." He lifted one finger in the direction of a freestanding cell phone store. "Is that where we're headed?"

Courtney glared at him a second longer before turning away. "Probably."

"What do you mean, probably? You don't know?" His irritation flared to life, making him relax a little. It was infinitely safer than any of the other emotions trying to tie themselves to the woman beside him.

"Do I look like a fucking GPS to you?" Courtney crossed her arms.

There was no way to stop the smile spreading across his face, no matter how much he wanted to. "What you look like, is a pain in my ass."

CHAPTER ELEVEN

COURTNEY

"THIS PLACE IS way nicer than I expected." Courtney looked around their campsite, taking in the trees and the grass and the quiet. After hours of driving, they'd finally not only made it out of Florida, but also through most of Georgia. And while the weather was a hell of a lot cooler, the fear pushing her to keep running was finally starting to ease.

Reed finished opening one of the collapsible camping chairs they'd picked up after meeting with one of Heidi's contacts to collect the money she'd wired them. He'd passed along not only the cash, but also a few prepaid cards to use for gas, along with an offer of assistance. He'd seemed a little on the dangerous side so she'd been relieved when Reed politely declined.

"It's decent enough, I guess." He hooked the bag that came with the chair over the back before going to work on the second chair. "I mean, it's not as nice as the national parks in Alaska, but I can't imagine Georgia is a hot destination for outdoor enthusiasts."

Courtney smiled, relaxing a little more at the peace and

quiet of the nearly empty campground. "Is that what you are? Not just an outdoorsman, but an outdoor *enthusiast?*"

Reed glanced up at her as he worked on expanding the other chair they'd snagged at her new favorite store while picking up warmer clothes and food. "My dad's family has lived in Alaska for as long as any of them knows, so I'm pretty sure being an outdoor enthusiast is in my DNA."

She wasn't surprised to hear that Reed's family was Alaskan to their core. He was clearly at home in the cold and unforgiving climate, frequently showing up coatless for his shifts when she was in the cabin. "Is your mom Alaskan too?"

Reed finished with the chair and moved on to the fire pit, dropping in a few of the logs from the bundle they bought at an unmanned stand in someone's front yard just outside the campground. He went to work lining them into place. "No. My mom's Korean."

She inched closer, eager to learn more about the mysterious man who kept his personal life close to his chest. "Does that mean you speak Korean?"

Reed chuckled as he spilled some charcoal briquettes around the wood. "Only when I'm in trouble." He glanced up at her. "She has a harder time being mad at me then."

Courtney lowered into one of the chairs, watching as he added a squeeze of lighter fluid and started the fire. "She sounds fun."

Reed shook his head, his smile holding, eyes watching the fire. "She's something all right."

The warmth of the fire had her wanting to inch closer. To learn as much as she could while Reed was in a chatty mood. But the annoying itch of her scalp made it hard to sit still. And her dirty hair might not be the worst of what she had going on. She ran her tongue across the front of her scummy teeth, cringing a little at the texture. "Do you think they have bathrooms here?" Her eyes drifted to the trees around them. "Or is this a 'go in the woods' sort of outdoor experience?"

Reed's focus came to her, one dark brow cocking. "You would go in the woods?"

Courtney waved her hands around them. "Where else am I gonna go? I can't hold it forever."

Reed studied her for a second before returning his attention to the fire. "Today's your lucky day then, because most campgrounds have bathrooms *and* shower houses."

That had her springing to her feet. "I could take a shower?"

She'd done her best to scrub Reed down before bandaging him up, but there simply hadn't been time to waste on her own filth.

Reed gave her a nod as he continued working on building up the fire. "The closest one is at the end of this loop. Why don't you go do that while I make us something to eat."

He didn't have to tell her twice. The words were barely out of his mouth before she was rushing into their little camper and digging through the bags of items she lawfully purchased from the local Walmart. After packing a plastic bag with travel size bottles of body wash and shampoo and conditioner, along with a fresh set of cheap clothing, she rushed back out, giving him a wave over her shoulder as she flip-flopped her way along the blacktop.

She'd expected to be bathing with bottled water and doing nothing more than a tops and tails sort of thing, so the thought of a hot shower felt like a freaking luxury at this point.

But her version of hot, and the campground's version of hot turned out to be two very different things. Still, a lukewarm shower was better than nothing. She scrubbed hard at her skin and hair, rinsing away the muck left from their hike through the swamp, and the bit of Reed's blood still lingering under her fingernails from where she cleaned his feet and head. Once every inch of her was squeaky clean, she wrung out her dark hair and stepped from under the water.

To discover she had not brought a towel.

Didn't matter. She didn't care. She shook off her arms and wiggled around to try to knock the bulk of the remaining water loose before pulling on her bulk bag panties, fleece joggers, and an oversized T-shirt emblazoned with the words There Better Be Coffee. After collecting her toiletries, she stepped out of the building and shivered. A towel wasn't all she forgot. Her thin T-shirt did nothing to stop the chilly air as it cut through the trees, making her hustle her way back to the campsite, ready to pull on a sweatshirt and get warm.

A glorious scent wafted through the air as she rounded the front of the camper to see Reed cooking over the flame. "What are you making?"

He turned to glance her way, doing a double take that lingered, his eyes drifting down her freshly cleaned frame.

She followed suit, looking down to see what was so attention-grabbing about her outfit, outside of the words printed across her shirt.

But it may not have been the corny text printed across the front that caught his attention.

Reed's sudden focus might have had something to do with the fact that the wetness from her skin soaked into the thin, lightly colored fabric, leaving very little to the imagination. The coolness of the weather made her shiver, and her nipples were pulled more than tight, poking at the cotton fused against them like a second skin.

Reed quickly snapped his eyes back to the fire, but not

before she saw the tiniest hint of lust lingering in their dark depths.

She pressed her lips together, smothering out a smile. It seemed like maybe she was growing on him. And that was an opportunity she wasn't going to waste. Even if it meant freezing her ass off a little longer.

Dropping the plastic bag of items at the door, she grabbed her chair and pulled it to the other side of the fire pit. Sitting directly across from him, she positioned herself so her damp, unmissable tits were looking him right in the eye. "You didn't answer me. What are you making? It smells amazing. I can't wait to put it in my mouth."

Reed's eyes lifted to her mouth, lingering a second before snapping to the cheap skillet they'd picked up where a pile of meat, vegetables, and noodles were cooking together. "This is a version of my mom's japchae recipe, so I'll make sure I tell her if you like it."

Courtney shifted in the seat, discreetly pushing her tits out a little more. "Technically, I'm moving to Alaska, so I could tell her myself."

The thought of meeting Reed's parents was intriguing. Seeing what sort of people combined to create the man in front of her would definitely be interesting.

"We'll see." He pulled the pan off the fire and came to her side, dragging the second chair along with him before sitting down and holding the food between them. He dug into his pocket and passed off a plastic fork. "The noodles are wrong, and it's better when there's kimchi to go with it, but it should be decent."

Courtney's stomach was growling as the savory scent hit her full force. All she'd had since crawling away from her burning home was a couple of energy bars and drinks. And while they did help her power through, they weren't very satisfying.

She snagged the offered fork and went to work twisting some of the prepackaged noodles before stabbing a hunk of chicken and a carrot and shoving the whole thing in her mouth. It was salty and slightly sweet and like nothing she'd ever had before. She moaned around the mouthful, eyes rolling closed as she chewed through the bite. "This is fucking amazing."

When she opened her eyes, Reed was watching her, that same simmering intensity in his dark gaze. "I'm glad you like it. It's all I really know how to make."

She gave him a little smile as she went in for another bite. "It's more than I know how to make, so I'm not one to judge." She shoved in another mouthful, unable to stop herself from moaning again. "I'm not sure how anything would make this better, even—" Her eyes went to his, "I forget what you said would make this better."

"Kimchi. It's fermented cabbage." Reed finally took a bite, looking unaffected by the deliciousness of the meal. Probably because he got to eat shit like this all the time.

"What's kimchi taste like?" She worked up another bite, not even bothering to pretend she wasn't starving.

"It's a little spicy. A little sour. It adds freshness to this and a little crunch." Reed's eyes dipped to her mouth again. "My mom always has a big vat of it at her house and we eat it with pretty much everything."

Courtney relaxed back into the chair, her plans of taunting Reed with her diamond hard nipples completely overshadowed by the deliciousness of the dinner he made. "Now I definitely want an invite, because I can't imagine anything better than this, and I love pickled foods." She chewed through her latest mouthful. "Is that all you do with kimchi? It's just sort of like a condiment?"

Reed shook his head. "You can use it for all kinds of shit. It's good in fried rice. Great in these savory pancakes called kimchi-jeon." His head tipped to one side. "I think my favorite way to eat it is this soup my mom makes. Jjigae."

She waited for him to elaborate, and when he didn't, she prompted him. "What's Jjigae like?"

He pursed his lips, hesitating just a second. "It's made with over-sour kimchi, tofu, and usually spam or hotdogs." His eyes skimmed over her face before darting away. "Not exactly gourmet, but..."

Was he embarrassed? Did he think she would judge him for the way his mother cooked?

Probably. He seemed to have all sorts of ideas about who she really was.

Technically it was her own fault. She had spent most of her time around him acting spoiled and stuck-up and demanding.

"That sounds really good." Courtney jabbed the plastic tines of her fork into a hunk of zucchini. "Spam is that sort of canned ham stuff, right?"

He continued watching her, like he was gauging her reaction. "Right. It's cheap and shelf stable and super salty, so a little goes a long way."

His explanation marinated as she chewed, bringing a realization that might explain a few things. Reed's family might not have had a lot when he was a kid. They still might not have a lot. Was that why he judged her for being so ungrateful for everything she had? Because he didn't know how much she *didn't* have.

"I might actually want more than one invitation, so I can get real friendly with your mom and learn all her culinary secrets." She gave him a little smirk. "Or maybe your dad's the easier mark."

Reed's chin tucked, but not before she caught the hint of a smile working across his lips. "My dad is definitely the easier mark."

Courtney nodded, trying to look earnest. "That makes complete sense. You must have gotten your sweet disposition from him."

Reed barked out a loud laugh, seeming to relax a little. "He always tells me I'm too serious. That I need to relax."

Her lips flattened a little. "Life can be serious, so I get it." She poked at the food, losing a little of her appetite. "It's nice that he cares enough to worry about how you are."

Reed's eyes came her way. "That's what parents do."

She smiled in spite of the pain threatening to steal the tiny bit of joy she'd found in the last few minutes. "Not all parents."

Reed held her gaze for a few seconds longer, the amount of focus it carried making her feel exposed. Vulnerable.

"I should probably get things organized inside." Courtney stood up, hurrying to the door of the camper, pausing to glance back his way. "Thank you for dinner."

She yanked open the door, desperately in need of an escape. A little breathing room. Something to help her get away from the pain always nipping at her heels. Because it was bad enough that, outside of how it would affect him, her father didn't give a shit what happened to her.. Treated her like a liability. Something that could, and would, be used against him at any time. Making her an inconvenience he resented having to deal with.

But he'd still done more than her mother, who'd dropped

her off on his doorstep right after she was born, refusing to have any link to him or his family.

Even if that link was her own flesh and blood.

Courtney grabbed a few of the bags from the seat of the dinette and headed back to the bedroom. After pulling on the clearance rack Christmas hoodie she forgot to take to the shower house, she dumped out the blankets and pillows she'd insisted on buying. Peeling each from their plastic wrapping, she assembled the full-size bed that took up the bulk of the back end of the camper. A camper she was starting to feel a little fondness for. Yes, it was cramped. And yes, it could break down at any moment. But it felt safe. Like no one would ever know who she was or give her a second glance in it.

And, after a lifetime of everyone knowing who you were and judging you because of it, being inconspicuous was freeing as hell.

Once the bed was put together, she went back to the bags, digging out a toothbrush and the toothpaste. She used a bottle of water to brush her teeth, rinsing the foam down the sink and crossing her fingers it didn't simply dump out onto the cement below. But what would it matter if it did? No one was there to care except for Reed, and he'd judged her enough already. She was sort of immune to it at this point.

Once her teeth were handled, she finger combed her hair before working it into a braid and tying off the end with a cheap rubber band that might have been wrapped around the green onions in their dinner.

As finished as she was going to be with the abbreviated version of her nightly routine, she poked her head out the door, ready to face Reed again. "Are you staying up?"

He sat in one of the folding chairs, but his gaze was still

just as intense and focused as it was when she ran away earlier. It brought back that uneasy feeling of really being seen, though it didn't feel quite as uncomfortable as it had before.

"For a while. I want to make sure everything's okay."

Her heart skipped a beat in spite of the way his gaze made her feel. He was looking out for her. Making sure no one was lying in wait to finish what they started.

Sure, he'd done it before. But that was when she was handing over an exorbitant amount of the money her father threw her way to avoid having to deal with her. Money she no longer had, which meant Reed was looking out for her because he wanted to.

And it was almost as uncomfortable as the way he looked at her.

Courtney nodded, forcing on a little smile. "Okay. Be careful." She started to back into the camper, ready to close the door and hide under the covers, but Reed's voice stopped her.

"Princess?"

The warmth in his tone snaked through her, trying to soothe the raw edges of the always present ache she carried. "What do you want, Sexy Pants?"

Reed's sinfully perfect lips slowly lifted at the corners. "You better not be a bed hog."

The tease made her relax a little. Helped her settle back into something that felt normal and safe. She lifted her chin, standing a little straighter. "You better not be a cuddler."

Reed was still laughing as she closed the door, a smile quirking her lips. Not because she was amused with herself. But because she was almost positive the man sitting outside, making sure it was safe before he would go to sleep, was most definitely a cuddler.

CHAPTER TWELVE

REED

HE WAS A COWARD. That wasn't anything he ever expected to say about himself, but right now there was no denying it.

He was fucking exhausted. Between lack of sleep, lack of food, a head injury, and the stress of the past two days, he needed sleep. Desperately. Yet, here he was, sitting outside alone around a dying fire, pretending to keep watch for a threat that didn't currently exist.

They were safe. Without a GPS, Courtney had taken one hell of a convoluted path north, and landed them in a spot no one who might be trying to follow them would expect. Add on that they hadn't had cell phones or bank cards to leave a digital trail, and the odds they'd be found dropped even more.

But he still couldn't make himself go inside that camper. Because while the threat outside it might have been neutralized, the threat *in it* was real.

He'd spent every minute since meeting her thinking he and Courtney were like oil and water. But after those few minutes in the rest stop bathroom, he had no choice but to admit he was wrong.

They were like fire and gasoline. Combustible. Explosive. Dangerous.

Being in bed with her would lead to nothing good. It was a huge conflict of interest, and he'd already broken so many of his own rules in life. Adding that one to the list felt like he'd be completely giving in. Abandoning the man he grew up believing he would be and acknowledging how far he'd fallen.

Courtney was a job. A woman he was paid to protect. The lines between them were perfectly clear, but he'd already seen how willing he was to ignore them.

How easily she tempted him.

Reed leaned back in his chair, scrubbing one hand over his burning eyes as he considered his options. He could stay up all night, but then he wouldn't be as sharp as he needed to be in the morning when they got back on the road. He could sleep outside, propping his feet up on the other chair to get as much rest as the cold and uncomfortable position allowed.

Or, he could pick up his balls, go in the camper, and lay down next to Courtney.

Courtney who drove him absolutely fucking insane. Courtney who was snippy and defiant and more than happy to break the law. Courtney who was also turning out to be loyal and selfless and a little more broken than he ever could have anticipated.

She'd been so invested when he talked about his parents. And the hurt in her eyes when he made an offhand comment about the way people should be with their kids was palpable. It was threatening to make him see her in a whole new light. Again. One that illuminated the shadowy parts of his own choices, highlighting decisions he tried his best to ignore.

"Fuck me." Reed grabbed Courtney's chair and yanked it

closer, kicking his feet up onto the seat before sliding down. He couldn't go in that camper. It would be all sorts of bad.

Dropping his head against the canvas back, he folded his hands in his lap and settled in as much as possible. Luckily, exhaustion was on his side and he was drifting off almost immediately, falling into a blissfully ignorant state where life could be easy and choices were simple. He was so relaxed that when the new cell phone Heidi sent them to retrieve started to ring in his pocket, the chair nearly tipped over as he jerked awake.

Managing to get one hand out, he barely caught himself before fully hitting the dirt. After shoving himself upright, getting all four feet of the camp chair on the dirt, he connected the call.

"Hey." Dutch's voice on the other end surprised him.

Reed swept his surroundings, suddenly unnerved. "What's wrong?"

This was why he needed to get Courtney to Alaska and off his hands. She was a distraction in so many ways. One that limited his ability to do his job.

And he prided himself on doing his job and doing it well. It wasn't a job he necessarily wanted, but he still did everything in his power to be as good at it as possible. Even when he didn't believe the people he was put in charge of deserved protecting.

Which was a position Courtney once occupied.

But now…

Dutch sighed into the phone. "I've got some bad news."

Reed was on his feet almost instantly, regretting he hadn't tried to get his hands on a weapon while they were stopped for money, supplies, and a phone. "Do I need to start moving?"

"No. Nothing like that." Dutch paused. "We just got word that Courtney's father was killed a few hours ago."

He stared into the darkness as Dutch's words sank in. They weren't what he was expecting to hear and it took his brain a second to circle around the bite of adrenaline driving his thoughts. "What?"

"Yeah. I guess there's some sort of turf war happening down there. A couple different groups fighting for control of imports, if you know what I mean."

Reed raked one hand through his hair, turning back to face the camper before lowering his voice. "You're sure?"

He'd only just begun to see a different side of Courtney, and already knew enough to realize this was going to fuck her up.

"Positive. We sent a contact to confirm before I called you."

"But we thought the same thing about Courtney, and she's real fucking alive." He was searching for hope. Some chance he might not have to go into that camper and tell the woman inside the father he suspected let her down over and over again wouldn't have the opportunity to let her down again. Or the opportunity to change.

"We wouldn't have confirmed Courtney dead until we had actual proof." Dutch hesitated. "I take it this news isn't going to go over well?"

Reed worked his jaw from side to side. "Does it ever?"

There were probably some instances of people not caring when they learned about a family member's death, but it wasn't often. Most people were upset, either because of the connection they had or because of the connection that would never be. Courtney was likely to fall into the latter.

"I'm sorry you have to be the one to deal with all this. Just keep moving. Get to Kentucky so Rico can pick you up. Then you won't have to fuck with it anymore."

Dutch thought he was reassuring him. Freeing him of the burden that was Courtney. But her presence wasn't feeling quite as oppressive as it once did. Not just because she saved his ass, proving she wasn't exactly what he thought, but also because he was realizing how wrong it was to put her father's misdeeds on her shoulders.

It shouldn't have ever happened, but it definitely needed to stop now.

"It's fine. I'll handle it." He thanked Dutch before turning to the camper door, taking one final bracing breath before grabbing the handle and stepping in.

It was dark as hell inside without the glow of the moon or the fire, and it took his eyes a second to adjust. Once he could make out the shadowy lines of the interior, he flipped the lock and made his way to the back of the small RV. He'd been in a number of campers in his life, but the quarters of this particular model were about as tight as it got. It left very little room to move around as he kicked off his shoes, peeled off his sweatshirt so the heavy scent of smoke wouldn't taint the sheets, and climbed in beside her, laying on top of the covers.

"Princess?"

Courtney shifted, rolling toward him, her shadowy eyes open and showing no sign of sleep. "Who was on the phone?" Her voice was soft. Barely a whisper.

His stomach clenched, the thought of telling her there would be no more opportunities for her father to redeem himself twisting his insides. "It was Dutch. It was about your father."

She softly sniffed, lips pursing as they worked first to one side than the other. "He and I are really different." Her fingers toyed with the edge of the blanket. "He always believed he was untouchable. Smarter than everyone. Invincible." Her voice was sad, displaying an amount of emotion he'd never heard from her before. "But I always knew how much I lacked. I grew up knowing I was nothing more than a weakness. A weapon people would use against him. And for a long time I pretended like it didn't matter." She took a shuddering breath. "But it always did." Her fingers smoothed down the bit of blanket between them, the tips barely brushing against his skin. "Once I got older, I discovered being his daughter was more than just a liability for him. It was one for me too."

The ache in his chest got tighter, making it impossible to lay idle when she was in so much pain. He raised his hand and gently brushed back her hair, smoothing the strands that fell loose from her braid. "What does that mean?"

Courtney's lips lifted into a sad smile. "It means that all anyone ever saw me as was his daughter. They either used me for it or avoided me because of it. I could never have real friends. Real relationships. Anyone who didn't see me through an Emiliano Vasquez colored lens."

Guilt compounded the ache in his chest and the twist in his gut. It brought out an admission he should have made earlier. "I did it."

Courtney lifted the shoulder not pressed into the aging mattress. "Don't feel bad. Everyone does." One of her fingers left the blanket and lightly traced across his chest. "I try not to take it personally. I know it's a lot to get past, and I'm not necessarily the easiest person to like."

The fact that she was making excuses for his bad behavior only made everything worse. "You're not hard to like."

She huffed out a little laugh. "You're not a good liar, Sexy Pants."

Her comment cut into the sore spot he always carried. Because he *was* a good liar. And a frequent one. Dished them out daily to the people who trusted him most.

But he wasn't lying now, and the ramifications for that were getting more and more difficult to avoid.

"It's not a lie." Reed forced his focus to her instead of the list of untruths he hid behind every day. "You're starting to grow on me."

Courtney's finger continued sliding over his skin as she offered another soft smile. "I'm sure you say that to all the girls."

Her tease eased a little of the emotional hurricane battering him from the inside out. "I have been told I'm pretty charming."

Courtney snorted. "By who?"

Reed toyed with a dark strand of her hair. "Careful, Princess. You might offend me."

Her head tipped, pressing deeper into the pillow as she cocked one brow. "I'm sorry. Did we decide we were going to stop offending each other? Because I'm not sure I want to make that deal."

He let out a low laugh. "That does sound pretty boring, doesn't it?"

"It sounds fucking miserable." She went quiet for a minute, eyes dropping to where she continued touching his skin. "How'd it happen?"

He wasn't surprised she already knew what the call was about. Courtney was more perceptive than most people. Maybe even him.

He shook his head. "I don't know."

She nodded, pressing her lips together. "I always knew it would probably happen, but part of me hoped—" She stopped.

"I know." His fingers moved from her hair to her face, brushing over the soft skin of her cheek. "I wish he could have been what you needed him to be."

Courtney's eyes came to his. "Me too."

He wanted to ask more. Dig deeper into the ways her father had let her down. Find out who else had fallen short of being what she deserved. Friends. Family. Learn everyone who forced this woman to believe she was not just unlikable, but unlovable. Made her into someone who behaved in a way that proved them right so she didn't have to risk feeling like it was genuinely true.

Because that's what Courtney did. She used carefully crafted words and performative actions to build a wall, so that when it crumbled she could remind herself it was fake. That it wasn't really her everyone always let down because they didn't even know the real her.

It made him want to be someone she could count on. Someone she could trust.

"If you want, we can call and get more information later." He didn't offer to do it now because she deserved the right to rest. To wrap her head around this new information and let it digest before trying to shove more down her throat. "Once you've had time to recover from the last couple of days."

Courtney's lips lifted at the corners. "Okay. That sounds good." Her eyes moved over his face. "Thank you for looking out for me." She leaned in and brushed a soft kiss across his mouth.

It was sweet and chaste and gentle. So many things he didn't think she was capable of being.

He'd been so fucking wrong about her on so many damn levels and every new one he learned about sent him places he shouldn't go. Made him consider things he shouldn't entertain. Made him do things he shouldn't do.

Like letting his fingers continue sliding across her skin, tracing a line along her jaw before following the column of her neck. "Thank you for looking out for me." His eyes held hers, locked in by a connection he couldn't explain. "Most people would have left me where I laid."

"I almost had to." Courtney's hand lifted to his arm, giving his bicep a light squeeze. "I didn't think I could get you into the RV."

She brought up an interesting point. "How did you get me in here?"

She blew out a breath that buzzed her lips. "Determination."

It was yet another characteristic he didn't expect her to have. Not like this anyway. "Why were you so determined?"

Courtney's touch moved over his shoulder before sliding down the center of his chest, one finger pausing to flick against his nipple. "I wanted the chance to look you in the eye and say, I told you so."

CHAPTER FIFTEEN

COURTNEY

REED'S EXPRESSION TIGHTENED in the dim bit of moonlight peeking through the threadbare curtains. "I deserve it."

That was… surprising.

She wasn't expecting agreement from him. Ever, really. But he probably felt guilty. Bad that her father was dead. She should probably feel bad about it too, but it was almost a relief. His existence tainted her whole life. Her whole self. Made it so no one cared who she was, only about her connection to him.

They also never judged her for who she was. Only who he was.

Just like Reed had.

"My father and I were never close. We didn't have anything in common." She continued tracing across his chest, following the hard line of muscle there.

"You might be a little alike, considering how comfortable you are taking things that don't belong to you."

Reed's comment was a reminder that he still believed, at

least partially, she was an apple who hadn't fallen far from the family tree.

"If you're trying to compare some petty criminal shit I learned how to do—thinking it would get him to notice me—with trafficking billions of dollars' worth of drugs into the country, then you can fuck all the way off."

Reed opened his mouth, but quickly clamped it closed again.

It was a smart move.

But then his lips parted a second time and he took a deep breath. "I wasn't trying to be an ass. I thought maybe you were sad you were nothing like him and I was trying to find some sort of connection that might make you feel better." His dark eyes moved over her face. "But if you want the truth, I don't see any similarities." His fingers went back to toying with her hair as he continued. "Even at your worst, you're nothing like the Emiliano Vasquez I knew."

She wasn't sure what part of that had her chest tight. The fact that Reed genuinely didn't think she was like her father, or the fact that he'd tried to make her feel better. The attempt failed, but he still tried, and that was more than she could say for anyone else in her life.

"I wasn't close with my dad. Ever." The words came out as a soft whisper. A shameful admission she'd always thought said more about her than it did the man who contributed to her DNA. "He was never interested in me or concerned about getting to know me in any way. He just threw money my way and assumed I would take care of myself."

"It seems like you did." Reed's deep voice helped ground her in the moment instead of the past. It made it easier to face her mistakes. Her bad decisions. Her failures.

"I think saying I took care of myself is a stretch. I mostly just acted out and tried to get him to pay attention to me any way I could. It didn't matter if he was mad or disappointed or frustrated. All I cared about was that he noticed me. Remembered I existed." She pressed her lips together, trying to smother out the wave of emotion threatening to make her voice wobble. "But it never lasted. He would pay whatever it took to make what I'd done go away and then he'd move on. Sent me back to whatever house I was living in with whatever adult he'd hired to be in charge of me."

She'd been through a string of nannies and babysitters and even bodyguards. Every one of them got tired of her bullshit and walked away. She couldn't blame them. Sometimes she drove herself a little crazy. When she finally figured out nothing would get her father's attention, she moved on to finding friends. Buying herself company and community. Her life had always been transactional, so the fact that her friendships were also paid for didn't chafe the way it probably should have.

"What about your mom? Wasn't she ever around?" Reed's question reeled her back in. Stopped the spiral of self-loathing she easily fell into.

Reminded her there was a reason she was the way she was. Two reasons, actually.

"My mother didn't want to have to deal with my father. The minute she left the hospital she drove me to his house and left me on his doorstep." The story sounded unbelievable, but it was true. "Literally. She literally left me in a car seat on his doorstep and never came back."

Reed stared at her a second, unblinking. Like he was shocked. Most people were, but for her it was old news. A wound that she'd carried her whole life.

"That's fucked up, Courtney. You know that, right?" Reed's words were sharp. Almost angry.

"It was smart. If I could have gotten away from him, I would have." She paused. "I did, I guess."

Her mother's abandonment hurt. Always would. But that didn't mean she didn't understand. Especially as an adult, seeing what her mother would have gone through. What it would have cost her. As much as it fucked her world up, her mother had done the right thing. At least someone had been spared.

But Reed was already shaking his head, the motion rocking his skull against the pillow. "No. It's fucked up. Mothers don't leave their babies on a drug lord's doorstep and walk away."

She chewed her lower lip for a second, letting what she was seeing sink in. "You sound angry."

"I am fucking angry. It's bullshit." There was venom in his voice. "It shouldn't have fucking happened. You shouldn't have had to grow up the way you did. It—"

Anything else he was going to say was sealed off when her mouth hit his. The move was unexpected but not unwarranted.

He was angry for her. Pissed at the life she'd been given. He actually gave a shit about what she'd been through. All she'd lost. Everything that had been taken. And it drew her closer, chasing the connection he offered. The empathy he showed.

The closeness.

She'd never been close to anyone in her life. Never had anyone interested in her feelings or her thoughts. Never had anyone share theirs with her. And it made her want to share more with him. Made her greedy. Desperate for just a little more.

Reed's hand came to her face, gently holding her in place as he leaned back, breaking off their kiss. His eyes held hers. "I don't think you really know what you're doing right now, Princess. You're emotional—"

That made her laugh. "Have you met me? I'm always emotional."

She scooted a little closer, sliding one leg along his. "I'm also not the kind of girl who does anything she doesn't want to do."

A lot could be said about her. A lot had. Little of it cast her in a good light, which she probably deserved. But that didn't mean there was nothing good about her. Nothing worth being proud of.

She was honest. Determined. Confident in spite of all she'd been through. Braver than most people would suspect. She knew what she wanted, and she went for it.

And it was becoming very hard not to want Reed.

Hooking one knee over his hip, she used the connection to lock his body to hers. "I know it's hard to believe, what with you being such an asshole and all, but I'm starting to be fond of you."

Reed's unwavering stare held, but one corner of his mouth twitched. "Did you just say you were *fond* of me? How old are *you*?"

Courtney smiled, the expression genuine and easy. She loved the way he liked to bicker with her. Loved the verbal sparring always happening between them. "I was trying to be thoughtful. You seemed so offended when I offered to suck your dick, so I was trying to explain how I felt in a more palatable way. But if it makes you feel better," she leaned closer, pressing against the grip of his hand on her face, "I wouldn't be against you sliding your cock against my tongue."

She expected him to be just as irritated by her forward behavior as he was before, but Reed's reaction this time was very different.

"Careful, Princess." His nostrils flared as his eyes dipped to watch as his thumb skimmed across her lips before pressing between them, sliding into the wet well of her mouth. "You keep making that offer, I might take you up on it. Give this mouth something better to do than give me shit."

Holy hell. She was no virgin, but any dirty talk she'd experienced up until now was severely lacking. Borderline hilarious. There was nothing funny about the words coming out of Reed's mouth. A mouth she now suspected could be quite filthy when properly motivated.

Courtney pursed her lips, curling her tongue around his thumb as she sucked, taking it deeper, her eyes staying on his. She hadn't been touched in God only knew how long, and right now she was desperate for some sort of contact.

If she considered it too long, it would probably be apparent that it wasn't general contact she was interested in, but contact from a very specific source. That would have to be a problem for another day. She learned long ago that living in the moment might be the only way she could ever live, and it had always served her well. But something told her tonight wouldn't remain in this moment. She wouldn't want it to.

Reed watched, his focus completely on where her lips wrapped around him, as she flicked her tongue against his skin, hollowing her cheeks in the way that made most men shoot their wad in a matter of seconds. It wasn't so much about how it felt. It was about how it looked. Men were visual creatures, and she was more than happy to put on a performance. That was what her whole life had been after all.

Reed slowly withdrew from her mouth, popping his thumb

free with a wet sound that hit her between her thighs.

For some reason, the thought of sucking him off was appealing as hell. It could be easy to think it was because she would be on her knees and at his mercy, but that wasn't the way that particular act worked. The power dynamic actually worked in the opposite direction. That was likely why she was so hyper focused on it. The thought of being in control of a man like him fed the weakest parts of her. The bit that never had power. Was never in charge of her own life or her own destiny.

Holding someone as in control and strong as Reed in the palm of her hand made her both heady and horny. A combination that was not so easy to ignore.

Reed dragged his wet digit across her lower lip. "You are determined to always be a problem, aren't you, Princess?"

"I don't know many men who would classify a woman offering them sexual favors as a problem." She was starting to wonder how it was so easy for him to turn her down. Especially when it was becoming more and more obvious he was just as interested as she was.

"I'm not in the market for favors, Courtney." His tone almost sounded chastising, and it got her hackles up.

"Fuck you then. I take it all back." She planted both hands on his chest and shoved, grunting in frustration when he didn't budge. "Oh my freaking God. Why are you so hard to move?"

Reed didn't even have the decency to look upset by her outburst. "Maybe I'm not the issue, Princess."

She scoffed, the sound snorty and indignant. "You're always the issue, ass."

Reed grabbed her hands, stopping her increasingly aggressive shoving. "I think maybe we're both an issue." His thumbs stroked along the insides of her wrist in a touch that stole all her focus and pulled her gaze to the point of contact. "I'll admit I'm an ass, but you are absolutely a brat."

"I must not be that big of a brat." She pushed out her lower lip, giving him a pout. "Because you still haven't spanked me."

Reed's lips pulled into a slow smile as his fingers kept stroking her skin. "You are definitely that big of a brat." He lifted her hand to his mouth. Her breath caught as his lips brushed against the angry bruise still blooming across her thumb. "Bratty enough I'm sure one day my palm will warm your ass, but not right now." His tongue flicked across her skin, teasing the sore spot with a gentle touch. "Right now you need something else."

She struggled to breathe as he continued teasing across her skin. "What do I need?"

"You need someone to be nice to you. Because I'm starting to think that hasn't happened much." His lips moved to the inside of her wrist, sliding over the sensitive spot his thumb just stroked.

"And you're the one who's going to do it?" She watched him with rapt attention, barely managing an unbelieving snort. "I'm not sure that's in your wheelhouse."

"I can be sweet." His lips traveled up her arm, pausing at the crook of her elbow—a spot she didn't know was as sensitive as it was until he nipped it with his teeth. "Just like you can be patient."

"Patience isn't my strong suit." The words were breathless as he continued tracing a path up her arm with frustrating slowness. "I would think you'd have noticed that."

Reed's lips shifted to a smile as his eyes lifted to hers. "I guess it's time to learn then, Princess."

CHAPTER FOURTEEN

REED

THE SOFT SOUND of sheets rustling carried in from the back portion of the RV where Courtney was still tucked into bed. Reed glanced down the minuscule hallway just as she sat up, dark hair rumpled, the side of her face pink and lined from where it pressed into the pillowcase.

His gaze lingered longer than it should, but eventually he pulled his eyes back to the cooler he was sifting through. "Good morning."

Courtney made a grumbling noise. "It's not morning. This is still night. Why are you awake?"

That was a good question. One that had a number of answers, but only one he was willing to offer to her. "It's hard to sleep with you snoring in my ear."

Courtney's eyes widened and her mouth dropped open. "I have a deviated septum, you ass. I can't help it."

He couldn't resist looking her way again. "They can fix that, you know."

Courtney's hand flew to cover her nose. "They have to

break it. You know what it sounds like when a nose is broken?"

"I do, actually." He snagged one of the glass bottles of premixed coffee from the melting ice before dropping the cooler's lid into place, shaking the drink as he walked her way. "Mine's been broken more than once."

Courtney's eyes zeroed in on his nose. "That explains why it looks the way it does."

Reed yanked the coffee drink back just as she reached for it. "I thought we were trying to turn over a new leaf here, Princess."

Courtney's lips hinted at a smile before she pressed them flat. "You said I needed to learn to be patient. You didn't say anything about being sweet." She snatched the drink away, popping the seal on the lid before taking a drink. Her tongue skimmed across her lower lip, wiping away the bit of liquid clinging there in a move that pulled all his attention to her mouth. "And we both know I was just giving you shit." She lifted her free hand and motioned at his face. "You obviously have a perfect nose."

He crossed his arms as she continued to drink. "Obviously."

Courtney downed half the bottle before raking one hand through her messy hair, obliterating what was left of the braid it started in last night. "I'm assuming you're awake because we're leaving?"

"That's the plan. You said you wanted to get to Alaska. We need to meet Rico at an airport in northern Kentucky. And considering what we're driving, I'm not sure how long that will actually take."

He'd asked Heidi for a new vehicle. Begged, actually.

She shot him down. Explaining no one would be looking for the daughter of a wealthy drug dealer in a piece of shit RV.

He'd reminded her it wasn't simply a piece of shit RV, but a *stolen*, piece of shit RV. And it stood out like a sore thumb, making it significantly more likely they would get pulled over. Or just break down again, possibly attracting even more unwanted attention.

But again, Heidi was two steps ahead of him and everyone else.

"I can't believe that guy didn't ask any questions when someone showed up to buy his missing RV." Courtney glanced around the tiny bedroom. "I know it's not much, but he definitely was not the kind of guy who liked to get rid of things."

"Everyone has a price, Princess. You know that."

When her expression hardened, he knew he'd said the wrong thing.

"That's not how I meant it." He was still adjusting to this new place he was with Courtney, and it left him flailing a bit. "You know anyone would have sold you out for the right price. That's just the way the world works."

Courtney's shoulders seemed to relax a bit. "I know." She bobbed her head from side to side, rolling her eyes upward. "Obviously, since someone blew my house up."

"At any rate, we are now the proud owners of a decrepit RV that probably won't make it to our destination." He resisted the urge to reach out and smooth down her hair. To touch her. It was the same urge he resisted last night, and it was only getting harder to accomplish.

He thought their moment at the rest stop was simply driven by adrenaline. A collision created by stress and frustration. But last night there was no adrenaline. No stress. No frustration. And his desire to put his hands on her was still just as strong.

Maybe stronger.

Discovering the truth about who Courtney was and the life she'd been born into was turning out to be a significantly bigger problem than he anticipated. One that was growing with every minute they spent together. With every whispered confession that passed through her full lips.

"Are you hungry?" He tried to reel his thoughts back in. Narrow his focus where it belonged. Ensuring Courtney made it to Alaska safe was his only task. One he was being paid to accomplish. One he had no intention of failing.

Courtney's eyes met his, her chin lifting as one corner of her mouth curved. "Are you offering to give me something to put in my mouth?"

The fact that her continued innuendos no longer irritated him was yet another problem he needed to deal with. Almost as big of a problem as the fact that her suggestive tone had his dick hardening almost immediately.

"You know what I mean, Princess."

Courtney smirked up at him. "One of these times you're going to take me up on my offer, and then you'll regret not doing it sooner."

He shouldn't let her reel him back into this conversation. Nothing good would come of it.

But then again, nothing good seemed to come from any of their conversations.

"You're awfully obsessed with sucking my dick." He'd spent time with women. Had a handful of short-lived relationships he knew from the beginning would never go anywhere. His lifestyle wasn't conducive to attachment, and it had nothing to do with his job.

But not a single one of the women in his past had been quite so focused on that particular act. Sure, they'd do it if it was requested, but not a single one of them had offered it up. Not once, let alone multiple times.

"And you're awfully resistant to taking me up on my offer." Her eyes drifted down his body, locking in on where his obvious erection tented the front of his knit pants. "Especially considering you are clearly interested in it."

"I'm resistant to it because I know you're up to something. I know you're not offering just to be nice."

Courtney's smile turns mischievous. "You're smarter than most men. Less led by your dick."

"I can't afford to be stupid. It could end badly for me." He couldn't stop staring at her mouth. The wicked smile lingering on her lips.

He tried to taunt her last night. Teasing her with a hint of what she was suggesting. But when she eagerly pulled his finger deeper into her mouth, he'd struggled to rein in the lust telling him to give her exactly what she wanted. To put her on her knees and feed his cock between her warm, willing lips.

Courtney's head tipped to one side, her brows pinching together. "I'm not plotting your demise, Reed. That's not what it's about."

He reached out to slide his finger along her jawline, unable to stop himself from touching her any longer. "Then what is it about?"

"Power. Control." She admitted her motives so freely, and without any shame. "I haven't had much of that in my life, so I take it when I can."

"If that's what that act brings, then maybe I'm the one who should've been making offers. Because you aren't an easy woman to keep under control, Princess."

Courtney's eyes darkened as they stared up into his, her nostrils flaring, full lips parting. "Then that's where we're different, because I would absolutely take you up on that offer."

"Yeah?"

She slowly nodded, her eyes never leaving his. "Yeah."

He couldn't pull his gaze from hers even though he should. They needed to get moving, but his motivation to leave was suddenly lacking. The thought of driving down the highway didn't hold a candle to the thought of Courtney's thighs clamped around his ears.

She was right when she said her offer was about power and control. He understood her desire to grab them with both hands whenever the opportunity arose. He was the same way.

And right now that opportunity was impossible to ignore.

Every interaction they'd ever had turned into a fight. A war for the upper hand. Never once did he manage to get it, but this could be his opportunity. His chance to put Courtney where she belonged. Show her who really ran the show.

He tipped his head toward the pillows. "Then lay back."

Her sharp inhale shot straight to his dick, making it strain against the lackluster confines of the cheap pants he'd grabbed in every color. "You better not be fucking with me, Reed."

He didn't react to her thinly veiled threat. "You're wasting my time, Princess. Wait too long and I'll change my mind."

As much as he wanted to pretend her window of opportunity was closing, it was not. Now that he'd decided what he wanted, there was no way he wouldn't have it.

Have her.

Courtney eyed him a second longer before scrambling back across the small mattress and dropping her head to the pillows.

She looked too fucking good laying there, her cheeks already pinking up. Eyes glassy as they watched him. The urge to lick his lips in anticipation was strong, but this was about gaining the upper hand.

Nothing more.

"Take off your pants."

She immediately hooked her thumbs in the waistband and skimmed them down her long, tanned legs, tossing them to one side.

His cock was already throbbing, the ache in his balls impossible to ignore as he focused on the cheap cotton still hiding her lower half. "Panties too."

Again, Courtney didn't even hesitate. Her panties were gone in a heartbeat, dropped into the growing pile beside her. A pile he intended to add to.

"Shirt next. Then your bra." He didn't need her naked for this, but he wanted it. Wanted every inch of her smooth skin exposed to his gaze.

Courtney gripped the hem of her shirt, arching her back as she worked it over her head, leaving her in nothing but a stretchy sports bra that fought her as she tried to free herself of the compressing material.

Once she was completely bare, he slowly worked his gaze down her frame, taking in her barely browned skin. Her tits were full and plush with large, pillowy brown nipples that had his tongue sliding across his teeth. He could practically feel the way they would pucker in his mouth and it had him reconsidering how streamlined of a process this would be. Because, whether he wanted to admit it or not, this wasn't just about trying to gain power. It wasn't about control. He was smart enough to know no one would ever control the woman in front of him.

But if it wasn't about either of those things, then it would have to be about something else. And that wasn't a possibility he was interested in facing. Especially not when he could focus his attention elsewhere.

He took in the soft curve of her belly and hips before settling on the perfectly groomed crop of hair between her thighs. "I thought you said you had a Brazilian, Princess."

Courtney gave him a slow smirk as she pulled her knees up and let them fall open, one hand sliding to the bare lips of her pussy. "I didn't expect you to want a specific description of how I groom myself." She teased along her slit before parting herself to reveal every inch of her to his gaze. "But since you seem so interested, I leave a little in the front but everything else is gone." Her fingers slid across the flushed pink skin, teasing across her clit. "But maybe you should check just in case. See if they missed anything."

He took a slow breath, trying to calm the bite of lust pumping through his veins. For the first time he wasn't as mad about the turn his life took when Pierce crossed his path. Because if his life had gone the way he'd planned, what was happening right now would be a huge problem.

There were no lines when you worked for Alaskan Security. It was something that frequently kept him up at night and sat like an albatross around his neck. But what was once his main source of frustration and guilt finally presented an opportunity.

"I'm not in charge of your grooming, Princess." He rested one knee onto the mattress, leaning forward to drop his hands to the sheets. "I'm here for one reason and one reason only."

Courtney's glistening fingers continued tracing a path around her clit. "To show me you're in charge."

He offered a single nod. "That's right."

Her chin barely lifted. "You're wasting a lot of time for a man who wants to be in charge."

"It's not wasting time. It's called being calculating." He lifted his other knee to the questionable mattress. "I think that's something you know more about than you want to admit."

She held his gaze, looking unbothered by his assessment. "I'm more than willing to admit to being calculating." One brow lifted. "Are you willing to admit you're stalling?" Her expression was challenging. "Because if you wait much longer I'm going to finish the job myself."

"No you won't."

The hand working between her legs stopped and her eyes barely widened. "I won't?"

He slowly shook his head. "No."

She huffed out a laugh. "Why not?"

"Because I said you won't."

Her next laugh carried more weight. "What makes you think I'll do what you say?"

Reed leaned down until his lips nearly brushed hers. "Oh, you'll do what I say. Because if you don't, I'll suck on that sweet little clit of yours until you're desperate to come." He grabbed the hand between her thighs and lifted it to his mouth, sliding her wet fingers between his lips and letting his tongue glide over her slippery skin before setting them free. "And then I'll stop."

CHAPTER FEFTEEN

COURTNEY

REED DIDN'T LOOK like he was prepared to follow through on that threat. Right now he looked like a man with a singular focus.

And that focus was her.

It was a heady realization. One that made her want to push him just to prove it was true.

She grabbed his face, fingers digging into the rasp of hair covering his jaw. "You talk a good game, Sexy Pants, but I have yet to see you play."

Hopefully he was ready to play in more than one way. She was getting addicted to their back-and-forth. Not only because she loved to challenge anyone who came up against her, but also because Reed always bit back. He always stood his ground. He never just walked away. Didn't blow her off. Didn't abandon the conversation because it was too much work. He put in effort. Even if that effort went into fighting with her, she was willing to take it.

"Is that what you want to do, Princess? Play?" Reed continued to taunt her, but he had yet to touch her in any sort of meaningful way outside of their little collision at the rest stop.

The moment was branded in her memory. It carried just as much heat and combustion as whatever exploded in her basement and took her house to the ground.

And this might do the same thing. Reed might flatten her. Ruin her and leave behind only fragments of what she once was. But she would finally know what it felt like to be wanted, even if it was just for a short time.

"I'm not the one playing." Courtney slid her free hand down his front to grip the hard line of his cock. "I'm more than ready to put my money where my mouth is." She leaned closer, running her tongue over her lower lip. "Among other things."

Reed closed his eyes and sucked in a breath, the air hissing between his teeth as his jaw clenched tight. His reaction made her bolder. Made her want to chase more of this feeling.

"Do you want me to stop?" She ran her hand up and down his length, gripping as tight as she could through the layers of fabric. "Or do you want to suffer through allowing me to touch you?"

His eyes opened and narrowed on her face as his hand came to shackle her neck the same way it had the night she'd crept into his room. "You are a fucking menace." His free hand cupped her pussy hard, squeezing with a possessive grip. "Someone needs to put you in your place."

She gasped as his finger pressed into her slit, putting pressure against her clit. "Probably, but I'm not sure you're the man to do it."

She couldn't stop herself from taunting him. From pushing Reed the way she always had. From seeking any reaction she could get.

He leaned closer, his lips moving against hers as he spoke. "Is that right?"

She whimpered as his warm finger pressed deeper, sliding against her already drenched flesh. "That's right."

Reed's nostrils flared as his touch skimmed over her clit once more before sinking into her body, offering the first penetration she'd had in forever. "It doesn't seem like you really believe that." He worked his fingers in and out of her, grinding the heel of his hand against her clit. "Do you hear that?" He groaned, the wet sounds of her body sucking him in becoming louder and more obscene with each stroke. "You're not this wet because you think I can't handle you, Princess." He pinched her lower lip with his teeth, sucking it between his lips before dragging free. "You're this wet because you know I can give you exactly what you want."

She was struggling. Struggling not to come. Struggling to keep her wits. Struggling with the fact that being pinned down and fingered within an inch of her life clearly did something for her.

But, even though Reed was using the control he so easily took to give her exactly what she wanted, it was still hard to completely comply. To allow it to happen.

Because where would she be once it was over? Alone and on her own again with no one who gave two shits.

It took every bit of focus she had to work her fingers into the waistband of his pants so she could yank them down to free his more than sizable cock. She held his gaze as she fisted him tight, running her thumb through the wetness collecting at the tip of the flared head before pumping root to tip.

To her surprise, he thrust into her hand on the next pass, fucking her palm as his fingers continued fucking her pussy.

It was too much. Forced her to latch onto him in every way

she could. She gripped his face, her nails pricking his skin as she clenched around him, hips rocking against his palm as the first crest of climax crashed through her, making her forget what she was doing.

And Reed clearly wasn't going to let that happen.

His hand left her neck, strong palm coming to wrap around her grip on his dick, squeezing tighter than she ever would have on her own. His eyes stayed locked on hers, dark and intense. Like he was daring her to look away as his thumb dragged out the orgasm possessing her. He watched every breath. Every shudder. Every twitch and every jerk as he buried his fingers into her body over and over.

It was the hottest thing she'd ever experienced. And it only got better when his cock jerked in her hand and hot streaks of cum splashed across her belly as he groaned. The head of his dick dragged against her skin, leaving a path of wetness in its wake. And even then his eyes held hers.

It should make her feel exposed. Vulnerable.

Instead she felt seen. Connected.

The moment left her at a loss for words, which didn't happen often. It also left her confused about what to do next. Did she lay there and wait for him to say something? Did she find a towel to wipe his jizz off her stomach? Did she ask how long it would be before he was ready for round two?

Her vote was definitely for the last one because Reed was more than right. He *could* handle her. In pretty much every way.

His hand slowly eased from her body, fingers sliding free and leaving her feeling surprisingly empty. Empty enough to pull a whimper from her lips.

He pointed one of those wet, wicked fingers at her face. "No. None of that." He whipped his T-shirt over his head and went to work cleaning her off. "If you keep making noises like that we'll never make it to Kentucky."

She pressed her lips together, suppressing a smile. "I didn't do anything."

Reed stayed focused on where he was cleaning her. "Like hell you didn't do anything." His voice was gruff but his touch was gentle.

"You started it." She wiggled one finger in his direction. "Maybe you're the problem."

Reed finished cleaning her up before grabbing her clothes and tossing them onto her face. "Not likely."

She yanked the pants and shirt away, catching his smile as he turned toward the front of the RV. "Ass."

"Brat." He didn't stop. "Get dressed so we can get this show on the road."

"YOU REALLY AREN'T gonna let me drive anymore?" Courtney stared across the cab at Reed from where she sat in the passenger seat, her feet kicked up on the dashboard.

"No." There was no hesitation in his answer.

And also no explanation after it.

"Why not? I'm the one who stole it." She snapped off a bite of the Slim Jim she picked up at their last pitstop.

"Which I massively appreciate. But I'm willing to bet you don't have any sort of advanced training in maneuvering something this size at high speed." He glanced her way, lifting his brows like he expected an answer. Confirmation he was right.

Which he was. But she wasn't going to admit it. "As far as you know I have."

"And as far as I know you haven't. So we're going to stick with me in the driver's seat because I absolutely have had that advanced training." His eyes went back to the road, but he looked significantly more relaxed than he had up to this point.

Probably because of the orgasm.

The reminder had her thighs clenching tight, as if her body wasn't satisfied with the morning's activities. It should have been. It was the first time she'd been touched by someone else in too damn long.

It was also probably the first time she'd been touched by someone who didn't have ulterior motives for doing it.

That was probably why she wanted more. It was also why she was sitting here irritating Reed in the hopes that he would get aggravated enough to give her more. Maybe even that spanking she'd worked so hard to deserve.

It was weird how appealing that particular act was. Especially considering she'd never been spanked in her life. No one ever cared enough to put the effort into reprimanding her.

And maybe that was the appeal. Maybe she wanted someone to give a shit enough to tell her when she was being a bad girl.

"So I guess that means Alaskan Security teaches everybody to be a super good driver?" She watched him for his reaction. "Because if they did, I'm gonna make sure they know you haven't been using your turn signal when you change lanes."

His head snapped her direction. "Yes I fucking have."

She gave him a sweet smile. "As far as they know you haven't."

Reed glared at her for a second, but then started shaking his head, huffing out a laugh as he faced the road once more. "Are you always this difficult?"

"Probably." She took another bite of her meat stick. "Are you always this grumpy?"

His lips pulled into more of a smile. "Probably."

She considered arguing with him a little more, but decided not to be a total pain. "So now we just drive to Kentucky?"

It was what she wanted. Technically.

Her whole plan had been to convince Reed to take her to Alaska so she could build a new life. Start over where nobody wanted to use her and she might actually find people who genuinely gave a shit that she existed.

But the process of getting there was turning out to be a little more enjoyable than she expected.

"*Hopefully* we drive to Kentucky." Reed looked over the gauges on the dashboard. "I'm not convinced Bernadette here is going to make it."

Courtney choked a little on her Slim Jim, making a horrifying snorting and slightly gagish sound as a shocked bark of laughter tried to break loose. But instead of coming out, it sent her straight into a coughing fit as she tried to clear her airway of the heavily preserved snack. She managed to get enough loose to talk and wiped the tears from her eyes as she squinted Reed's way. "Did you name the camper?"

He didn't look at her. "It didn't seem like *you* were going to name her."

Why did it seem weird that he named the camper? Maybe because Reed was always so uptight and by the book she almost assumed he had no feelings and no personality.

But that was clearly not true. It took a hell of a lot of personality to name a camper Bernadette.

"So are you going to call her Bernie for short?" Courtney turned to peer back through the dated furnishings. "Because I think Bernie might be a little more fitting."

"Don't give her a hard time. She can't help the way she looks." Reed continued talking about the RV like it was a whole-ass person. "She just needs a little bit of a facelift."

He almost sounded like—

"Are you planning to keep this thing?" She wasn't as surprised by the possibility as she would have been two minutes ago when she didn't know Reed had already named their primary mode of transportation and temporary home.

He lifted one shoulder and let it drop in a shrug. "Might as well. I bought her."

Courtney pursed her lips, sifting through the words he just said. A few in particular. "I thought you said Alaskan Security bought the camper."

He just shrugged again.

Courtney opened her mouth to say something snarky, but clamped her lips back together. There was something about the set of Reed's jaw and the way he was pretending to be so casual that made her think his decision to buy Bernadette was anything but. "Why?"

"What do you mean, why? I had to buy her because you've got sticky fingers and I didn't want the police to come after us."

She continued watching him, unconvinced by his explanation. "Seriously. Why did you *really* buy her?"

There was more to the story. Something that sat right on a nerve and she wanted to know what it was. Not because she wanted to use it against him like she would have before, but because Reed's reaction to the conversation was so different. Almost like he wanted to lie, but couldn't make himself do it.

"I just told you why I did it." Reed glanced her way, his eyes lingering long enough to give a little more away. There was an amount of emotion there. Closely guarded, but there nonetheless.

She chewed her lower lip, trying to come up with a reason Reed might be behaving that way. But it wasn't easy to pick apart another person, especially one like him.

Her own reasons and motivations were not normal, she knew that. Her life hadn't offered the kind of connections and experiences most people had. People like Reed. People with parents who loved them.

"Did your parents have an RV like this?" It was an obvious leap, which was probably the only reason it came to her. Anything more specific would be far outside of her scope of understanding.

Reed was quiet for a minute, the muscle in his jaw ticking in a way that made her think she might actually be close. Finally he let out a breath, the tightness of his shoulders dropping the tiniest bit. "No."

Well, shit. She really thought she was onto something there for a minute. That Reed finally might open up to her the way she'd opened up to him the night before. But apparently—

"But they always talked about it. Had all these plans for what they would do when my dad retired. All the places they would go visit." Reed paused, his hand gripping the wheel a little tighter before relaxing. "They even looked at RVs at one point. Had the model they wanted all picked out and everything."

Courtney turned in her seat again, looking over the worn paneling and threadbare upholstery. "And they picked this one?"

Read chuckled. "No. I think this is the only RV of its kind in existence."

Courtney stayed sideways in her seat, letting her temple rest against the back as she faced him. "That's because Bernadette's special."

Reed stayed quiet, but he was still clearly holding onto more. It seemed like maybe he'd been holding onto it for a long time. The same way she had.

"Why didn't they do it?"

Reed's head tipped, jaw working from side to side. "Why didn't they do what?"

He was stalling. He knew darn well what she was asking, but if he needed a minute she'd give it to him. "Why didn't they buy their RV and go see all the places they wanted to?"

Reed watched the road, lips pressed together like he was used to keeping this conversation in. Finally he offered up an explanation she wasn't expecting.

"Because my dad decided it would be more exciting to have a stroke the week after he retired."

CHAPTER SIXTEEN

REED

VERY FEW PEOPLE knew about his father's condition. Telling them what happened might lead to more questions he didn't want to answer. Didn't want to face.

Courtney was quiet for a second, but her big brown eyes never left his face. He waited for the normal words most people would offer.

That's terrible.

I'm so sorry.

How is he doing?

But instead, her lower lip pushed out in an expression he was beginning to realize she used as more than just a pout. "That fucking sucks a bag of dicks."

The unexpectedness of what she said had him laughing without even realizing it. It eased the tension discussing his father's situation always brought. "You have no idea."

She tipped her head against the rest of her seat, continuing to sit sideways so she could watch him. "You're right. You should explain it to me."

He huffed out another laugh, thinking she was still trying

to lighten his mood. But when he glanced her way, Courtney's expression was earnest. Honest. Like she genuinely wanted to know about what he was going through.

And, after facing it alone for so many years, he considered telling her. God knows she was in no position to judge him for the choices he'd been forced to make.

"I never planned to work at Alaskan Security." He started at the beginning, gripping the wheel tighter as he struggled with old emotions.

The sadness. The disappointment. The fear.

"Where did you want to work?" Another genuine sounding question. Soft and sweet. Gentle in a way Courtney didn't usually act.

And that surprisingly sweet and gentle tone had him offering a confession. "I was going to be a cop."

Courtney immediately nodded. "That makes sense."

Something odd warmed his chest, bringing his hand to rub against it. "It does?"

She sat a little straighter. "Absolutely. You're grumpy and uptight and a stickler for the rules. You would have been an amazing cop." Her lips lifted in a lopsided smile. "I would have definitely robbed a store just so you'd have to frisk me."

Another laugh broke free at another comment that eased the tension normally accompanying this conversation. The few times he'd had it anyway.

Courtney blew out a sigh, dropping against the back of her seat again. "I bet working for Alaskan Security pays way more than being a cop though, huh?"

Her ability to zero in on the crux of the matter would have surprised him a few days ago, but not now. Every second he spent with her it became more clear that the Courtney he thought he knew was nothing more than an act. An exaggeration of her personality designed to get all the things she'd never had. Attention. Protection. Hell, even conversation.

And right now he didn't mind offering it to her. "Pierce definitely pays a hell of a lot more than the force would have." He paused, expecting shame to hold him back, but it didn't. "He approached me right after I finished the Academy and not long after my father had his stroke. I was already trying to help my parents with medical bills because Medicare isn't the greatest, so I knew just how bad things were going to get for them."

Courtney rubbed her lips together, looking a little distressed. "I don't know what any of that means."

Of course she didn't. She was the daughter of a drug trafficker with more money than he could count.

A *former* trafficker who *used* to have more money than he could count.

But for the first time he didn't hold it against her. "Medicare is the insurance the government offers to people over a certain age. It covers some things, but not everything, and even a supplemental plan leaves a lot of my dad's prescriptions and physical therapy unpaid."

And that was just the absolute basics. If they wanted his father to have any special therapy that might help him regain some of what he lost, that came out of their pocket. *His* pocket.

That's why he had to make them as deep as possible.

Courtney's eyes moved over his face, warm and expressive in a way he'd never noticed. "I wish I could help you." She paused, lips pursing as they twisted to one side. "But you probably wouldn't let me since all the money I had was from..." Her voice drifted off like she didn't want to remind him.

And it made him feel like an ass. He'd done to her exactly what everyone else in her life had. He judged her. Refused to look beyond the mask to see that she was more.

"I'm sorry." They were words he owed her long before now. "I put shit on you I shouldn't have."

She gave him a soft smile. "Don't be sorry. I gave *you* shit I probably shouldn't have." Her smile faltered. "I didn't know how much you had on your plate."

"I won't hold that against you. No one really knows how much I've got going on." It was yet another admission that was difficult to make. He'd always been close to his parents. As an only child, conceived after many years of trying, he'd been their whole world. And he'd known it. So he always worked hard to be present in their lives. To stay close even after he became an adult.

But then his dad got sick and the tables were reversed. His parents became his whole life. Everything he did was for them. To help them. It left him more isolated than he wanted to admit, and more resentful than he expected.

"You haven't told anyone that you work with what's going on?" Courtney seemed surprised. "I always got the impression you guys were really close."

"We are." Outside of his parents, they were the only people he spent any amount of time with. On the rare occasion he socialized, it was always with them. "I didn't want them to know I don't necessarily love working for Alaskan Security."

It was yet another layer of guilt he dealt with. There were any number of people who would be thrilled to work for the company. Between the pay and the benefits, there weren't many other jobs someone with his background would find that could compete.

Did he put his life on the line on a regular basis? Yes. But he was planning to do that anyway. At least at Alaskan Security he could do that and give his father the best chance at a full life.

"Your secret is safe with me." Courtney lifted one hand to her lips, cranking an imaginary key before tossing it away. "Do I get to meet your parents when we get to Alaska?"

His brows lifted in surprise. "You want to meet my parents?"

Courtney's open expression shattered. She lifted one shoulder and let it drop. "I guess not. I just thought—"

He was fucking up again. Putting her in a box she might not belong in. "My mom would probably really like you." He faced the road, oddly amused by the thought of his mother and Courtney interacting. "She will expect you to cook though."

Courtney's eyes widened. "Cook?"

He grinned, even more amused as he imagined the way that meeting would play out. "If you go over there she's going to want to feed you, but she's also going to expect you to help her in the kitchen. That's just how she is."

Courtney stared at him a second, her lips pressed together. A tiny hint of a smile worked its way onto her lips. "That might not be too bad."

He'd almost forgotten that her father wasn't the only parent Courtney had lost. "She tries to mother everyone, so you probably want to brace yourself."

Courtney's smile lifted a little more. "I will."

He settled into the possibility more, imagining Courtney joking with his parents. Brightening up the struggle of their lives with her teasing but warm personality.

"How is the RV gonna get to Alaska?" Courtney's question pulled him away from his thoughts.

He checked the dashboard at her mention of the RV, making sure nothing too terrible was going on. "I'm going to drive it there."

Courtney's mouth pulled into the pout he was so familiar with. "You're not flying back with me?"

Her obvious disappointment pleased him in a dangerous way. "Not if I want to get Bernadette home."

Courtney pursed her lips, shifting around in her seat, looking uncertain. "What if I just went with you?"

He huffed out a laugh. "You would rather spend days driving across the country than a few hours on a plane?"

She chewed her lower lip, that uncertainty lingering. "I don't mind it so much. And now that we have money, we could sort of spruce the place up a little bit." Her eyes fixed on his face. "Unless you don't want me to go with you."

She was about to make him admit yet another thing he'd intended to hold onto. "I guess I could suffer through your presence a little longer."

Courtney's smile was bright and immediate. "Okay. You'll definitely regret it."

He couldn't stop the smile working on his lips. "You're supposed to tell me I won't regret it."

Courtney rolled her eyes. "We both know that's not true."

And just like that, she eased him away from a conversation he normally avoided like the plague and into lighter territory. "But, before I make any promises, we should check in with Heidi and the rest of Intel. Make sure it's safe for you to stay with me."

Courtney's eyes widened and her skin paled, making it clear she'd fully believed they were out of the woods. "You think they would follow me all the way here?"

"Honestly? No." He glanced in the side mirrors even

though he knew no one was following them. "But I think it's worth double checking."

Courtney's eyes went to the mirror on her side of the cab. "How will Heidi know? She's all the way in Alaska."

He grinned. "You would be amazed at what Heidi knows." He settled into his seat, relaxing a little more. "Plus we have connections all over the planet. She's been collecting all the information she can get her hands on about what's going on in Miami." He hesitated, but decided if he could talk about his difficult topics, she could talk about hers. "That's how I knew about your dad."

Courtney stiffened the tiniest bit at the mention of her father. "I should probably ask what happened to him, huh?" She didn't sound particularly interested in his answer.

"Only if you genuinely want to know. I won't judge you if you don't." He'd done enough judging of this woman already. And, after finding out about the way both of her parents had treated her, he was more likely to put blame on them than her for anything and everything he could.

Courtney was quiet for a second before softly admitting, "I don't really think it matters to me." She smoothed back the bits of hair coming free from the fresh braid she'd styled before they left. "Not just because he obviously didn't care about what happened to me, but because I didn't really know him. He wasn't someone I was ever close to."

Her voice was sad. Filled with disappointment and a little regret.

It irritated him. Not because of her, but because of the people who'd let her down. The people who should've loved her. Offered her affection and understanding. Instead, they'd abandoned her. Left her on her own. Her father threw money at her like she was a problem that could be solved if he just spent enough.

And it was an approach Courtney picked up. She'd done the same thing with Alaskan Security and anyone else who found their way into her life. But she learned it didn't work a whole lot faster than her father did, and was willing to give it all up for a fresh start.

A chance to live a happy life.

"It's his loss." The confession seemed to surprise them both, and sent him backpedaling the tiniest bit. "You're pretty hilarious when you want to be."

If Courtney was bothered by his half-assed retraction, she didn't show it. Her smile was bright and immediate. "*Finally*. I've been trying to tell you I'm funny."

"And I've been trying to tell you you're a pain in the ass." His smile held like it wasn't planning to leave anytime soon. "Seems like neither one of us is a very good listener."

Courtney leaned toward him, bracing her elbows on her knees, stretching the limits of her seatbelt. "That's where you're wrong. Because I absolutely know I'm a pain in the ass."

He couldn't stop his eyes from finding her again. "I guess they always say to go with your strengths."

One of her dark brows angled. "Is that why you're always so grumpy?"

She wasn't going to give him an inch. And maybe that was part of the reason he was finding himself less and less annoyed by her. Courtney always held her ground. Always came right back at anything and everything he tried to dish out.

She might not have had anyone to fight for her, but she was always ready to fight for herself.

The thought was sobering and had that warmth in his chest turning to an ache. "I don't mean to be."

"Liar." She continued smiling, the expression reeling him in more with each passing second. "You love being a crab." She reached across to poke at his bicep. "But it's okay. I kinda like it. I always know where I stand."

His brows pinched together in confusion. "Where you stand?"

She toyed with the hem of his sleeve, smoothing it out and flattening it against his arm. "Most people are fake around me. They try to act a certain way so I keep buying drinks and paying for meals." She focused on where her fingers brushed against him. "Even if they don't like me, they pretend to so they can keep being around me. So people will think they're important or connected." Her eyes finally lifted to his. "Not anymore though, I guess."

He shook his head, glad she was finally getting away from that life. From the people who either used her or abandoned her. "No. Not anymore."

CHAPTER SEVENTEEN

COURTNEY

"WHAT IN THE hell do you have in there?" Reed looked over the packed cart she was pushing.

"What do you mean, what do I have?" She looked over the items stacked into the bright red buggy. "If you're keeping the RV, then we might as well make it comfortable. Especially since we'll be in it for another week." She poked one finger into the plastic-wrapped queen-sized pillows she'd carefully selected. "I got you a side-sleeper pillow and I got myself a back-sleeper pillow so you don't have to listen to me snore all the way to Alaska." She moved her poking finger to the sheet set beside them. "And I got a nice set of flannel sheets so we don't abrade all the skin off our bodies with the shitty ones I stole from Walmart." She moved on to the next item. "I also got a duvet with a removable cover, so when we get up to where it's crazy cold neither of us will turn into an ice cube." She lifted her hand into a shrug. "That's all. It looks like way more than it is, but it's just so we can be comfortable while we sleep."

Bernadette was definitely growing on her, but the bed in

the back was terrible. The mattress was old and uncomfortable and barely big enough to fit both of them.

Maybe she didn't hate that second part so much. Especially since she'd been right and Reed turned out to be a cuddle bug the second he fell asleep. Having his heavy arm draped around her waist and his warmth baking into her back went a long way in making their current sleeping arrangement more tolerable.

And now it would be even better. As long as he didn't make her put everything back.

Reed turned from where he'd been perusing windshield wipers, the frown curving his mouth softening a little. "Why is everything so pink?"

She was ready for that question. Saw it coming a mile away. "Because Bernadette's favorite color is pink."

He'd started this whole let's name the RV thing, and now she was going to run with it. Use it to get something to brighten up the dreary seventies interior while they drove through equally dreary weather.

Reed crossed both arms over his broad chest. "Is it now?"

Courtney nodded, keeping her expression serious. "Absolutely. She also mentioned she was fond of gold accents." Once she found out Reed planned to keep the RV, she'd started looking at it a little differently. Seeing it for its potential instead of for all it lacked.

It was small, but the layout wasn't bad. Sure, it was cramped, but it had everything you could need. A bed big enough for two people who didn't hate each other. A little kitchen that would be great for cooking once they made sure it wouldn't blow up. A table to eat at or work at. The thing even had a toilet and a tiny shower, though neither of them felt confident using it until it got the same look over as the kitchen.

It was cozy, and would be even cozier filled with fluffy blankets and comfortable sheets. And maybe if they painted the cabinets white. Added gold hardware. Possibly even painted the walls. Not pink, but something bright. Something cheery. Bernadette was a cheery bitch.

"You're thinking about this awfully hard, Princess." Reed's voice sounded grumpy, but there was no hiding the hint of a smile on his lips.

"I guess that's good since you clearly haven't thought about it all." She pointed at his empty cart. "You're supposed to be picking stuff out too."

Reed looked pointedly at the pink sheets and duvet cover in her cart. "I was supposed to be finding what we need to keep Bernadette up and running, not making her look like a little girl's birthday party exploded."

He was teasing her, she knew that. But his jab hit a little close to home. Close enough to bring out yet another humiliating admission about her sad little life. "I never had a birthday party when I was a kid, so maybe I'm trying to live vicariously through Bernadette."

Reed took a deep breath, his head tipping back toward the ceiling as one hand came to scrub over his face. "You really know how to make me feel like an ass, you know that?"

"I wasn't trying to make you feel like an ass. I just thought maybe it would explain some things." Like why she was a little needy. Why she was a little difficult. Why she had taken more than a slight interest in making Bernadette feel like a home.

Reed turned back to the wipers, shaking his head. "The more you explain, the more I want to punch somebody in the face."

She perked up a little bit. "Really?"

His head came her way as he looked her up and down. "The fact that you sound excited about that worries me."

She reached out to adjust the pile of linens filling the cart. "I don't know that anyone has ever been pissed *for* me before." She lifted her eyes, watching as his jaw clenched tight. "I just liked that you were angry on my behalf."

Reed sighed, his focus going back to the rows of wipers in front of him. "Go find more shit for the camper. Pick out anything you want."

He was trying to get rid of her by giving her what she wanted, but it didn't feel like it was because she was annoying him. It seemed like Reed was sending her away because her birthday admission made him feel things he didn't quite know how to handle. It made her want to lighten his mood. Take away some of the upset she'd accidentally caused. "Can it be pink?"

Her tactic worked. Reed's tight posture immediately relaxed and he huffed out a laugh. "Sure. Go crazy."

She beamed at him, gripping the handles of her cart. "Okay." He didn't have to tell her twice. She was more than happy to find all sorts of things for Bernadette.

Courtney headed across the Target store they'd stopped at after reaching Kentucky. It was in a pretty posh area, so the selection was top tier. And definitely better than what she'd come across at Walmart. No shade to Walmart—the place was kind of growing on her. Their bedding selection sucked, though.

She made a beeline for the center of the store where all the home and decor items were located, and went to work packing as much into the cart as possible. She grabbed towels. She grabbed washcloths. She loaded in throw pillows and fuzzy blankets. Then it was on to housewares for a couple pots and pans to add to the single one they currently had. Some more cooking utensils that might encourage Reed to make her another batch of japchae. A tiny coffee maker and a couple of mugs.

Paper goods was next. She stacked in disposable plates and plasticware. Paper towels and tissues. She started to leave, but caught a whiff of laundry detergent and rounded to the next aisle, grabbing a small bottle of Gain and some dryer sheets before collecting an array of cleaning products and plastic gloves.

If they were going to spend the next week in the camper, she'd have plenty of time to give Bernadette a good scrub down. And everyone felt better after a good scrub down. After adding on a broom and a couple of brushes, she headed toward the registers.

Her steps barely slowed as she passed cosmetics and, for a second, she considered stopping to collect a few things to maybe make her look a little less—

Rough.

But the thought of slathering on makeup and styling her hair seemed ridiculous. Especially since she was simply going to be spending her days in the passenger's seat of the RV next to Reed, who didn't seem to mind her makeupless with messy hair. If anything, he might like her better that way. Undone. Free from who she used to have to pretend to be.

It was one thing they had in common—she liked herself this way better too. And after a year of isolation and fear, it was nice to feel a little settled. A little safe.

A little liked.

And Reed had definitely liked her that morning.

Her cheap sneakers came to a squeaking stop right in front

of the pharmacy. She chewed her lower lip, staring at the counter, brain working a mile a minute as she focused on the final item she very much wanted to add to her cart.

There was no way she'd be able to sneak any of her purchases past Reed, and he didn't appreciate it when she helped herself, so not paying for something wasn't an option. But he also seemed to like her forward nature a little more than he initially admitted, so maybe she was overthinking this.

Courtney turned the cart down one of the aisles, going straight to the counter and making her request before dropping the box in her basket and going to the registers. Reed was already there, waiting with his own very full cart.

She lifted her brows. "You look like you've been busy."

"An old camper has a lot of needs." He motioned for her to go ahead of him in the line.

She tipped her head. "Thank you." She went to work loading up all her items, filling the belt more than once due to the sheer bulk of all she'd picked out. As she expected, Reed watched everything as it stacked up. So when she set the final item onto the belt, she turned back to meet his gaze, lifting her chin.

Daring him to say something.

Hoping he would.

And he didn't disappoint her.

"That's a big leap, Princess."

She picked up the box of condoms, unashamed. "Not that big. Only got a twelve pack." She waited, watching his expression so she could gauge his reaction.

See if he was thinking the same thing she was.

They were about to be locked in the camper together for a

week. And if the opportunity presented itself, she didn't want there to be any reason she couldn't take it.

Twice.

Twelve times.

Reed tipped his head toward the belt. "Put them down."

She gave him a little smile as she dropped them into place. "Yes, sir."

Courtney smiled at the checkout girl as she pushed past with her cart, grabbing the loaded bags and piling them in as Reed added his own selections to the belt. It took just as much work to get everything in the second time, so she nearly missed seeing all he'd picked out.

Almost.

When the final item passed across the scanner, she stared at it, unable to look away as emotion tightened her throat. "What's that?"

The checkout girl blinked, looking from side to side, clearly believing Courtney was talking to her. She lifted up the plastic container as if seeing it better might help the identification process. "It's cupcakes."

She pressed her lips together, swallowing hard as her eyes dropped to the bag in front of her. Inside was a pack of candles.

He bought her birthday cupcakes.

Her eyes found Reed. "It's not my birthday."

He met her gaze, expression just as focused as it always was. "I know." He turned to the cashier, passing over a stack of bills. "I figured you had a lot to make up for, so you might as well get started."

She was speechless, which wasn't a normal thing for her.

Reed finished cashing out, collecting his change and the

receipt before turning to her. He lifted his brows, expression stern. "Time to go, Princess."

She blinked, trying to work herself out of the stupor his shockingly sentimental purchase had put her into.

It must not have happened quickly enough, because he gripped her hips, spinning her away from him and toward the handles of her cart, urging her forward until she grabbed them and started to go. He snagged the front of his own cart with one hand as he leaned into her ear. "Good girl. Keep moving."

Cheese and rice. Did he just follow-up buying her birthday cupcakes with calling her a good girl?

The only thing that might make this day better is if he dished out birthday spankings. The possibility had her stomach flipping and her legs clenching tight.

Then she stepped out into the frigid air, losing her breath a little at how fucking cold Kentucky was. She'd made it all the way through Georgia and Tennessee sort of assuming maybe winter wasn't as bad around here as she'd heard. It couldn't be anywhere as cold as Alaska, right?

But for some reason, it felt like a fucking tundra as she pushed her way across the parking lot, huddling deeper into her brand-new coat and scarf. They'd had to park at the back end of the lot since the camper took up more than one space, so the hike there felt like it took forever. By the time they reached the door, her teeth were chattering and every inch of her skin was tight with goosebumps.

Reed opened the door and urged her in. "You stay there. I'll pass the bags up to you.

"Th–thank you." She grabbed the first bag, recognizing the pillows by their squishy feel and tossing them down the short hall onto the bed. "Did it get colder while we were shopping?"

Reed's eyes lifted to the sky. "Maybe. The clouds look a little closer, so it might be getting ready to snow."

She made a disgusted sound while catching the bundle that contained the duvet then chucked it on top of the pillows.

Reed laughed, the sound rich and deep. "Are you regretting your decision to drive across the country?"

"No." She caught the next bag, this one holding the sheets. "I just need to get used to it. And it's probably better if I'm introduced slowly instead of flown in and dropped into the middle of Fairbanks." She threw the sheets onto the bed. "I probably would've been a human popsicle by the time you got there." She turned to face him, wiggling her brows. "You would have had to warm me up."

She'd always flirted with Reed, but most of it had been harmless. Done for no other reason than to irritate the shit out of him. But the hungry way Reed looked at her now made it clear her flirting affected him in a completely different way.

A way that made her glad as hell she bought that box of condoms.

He continued passing in items, emptying out her basket before moving to his. He handed part of them her way, including the cupcakes and candles, but kept a few in the cart. Closing the door halfway, he paused to look her over. "You stay in here. I'm gonna go change out our wipers and fill up the fluids. I've got a feeling we're going to need it."

She jumped a little when he closed the door, almost like she was jolted by the separation. And maybe she was. She'd gone her whole life without anyone to rely on. Having no one who genuinely cared about her. No one who listened when she talked. No one to get mad over the bad things that happened.

No one to buy her birthday cakes or candles.

Now there was, and it would make sense that she might get a little too attached a little too quickly.

But hell if she knew how to stop it from happening.

She blew out a breath, smoothing back her windswept hair. "Shit." That was a problem she would think about later. Right now she needed to get things situated so they could get moving.

While Reed worked under the hood, she went to work putting away the loose items. She opened up one of the blankets, shook it out and draped it over the rough weave of the couch. Then she added a couple of the cute throw pillows, placing them carefully even though the couch was even more uncomfortable than the bed. Hopefully they sold something similar so it could be replaced. If not, maybe it could be reupholstered and—

Courtney groaned, letting her head drop back as her eyes closed. "Shit."

She was absolutely getting too attached, and not just to the man under the hood. This was Reed's RV. Whatever he did with the upholstery would be his choice. Sure, he let her pick out some blankets and pillows, but that was probably because he felt bad for her.

Maybe most of what he did was because he felt bad for her.

And that felt gross. Disappointing and gross.

The tightness from earlier clenched her throat again, this time bringing an ache. It'd been so nice to feel like she mattered. To feel like somebody cared. The thought that maybe it was driven by nothing more than guilt hurt.

She jumped a second time as the side door opened and Reed stomped in. His eyes went to her face almost immediately. "What's wrong?"

She swallowed, the act much more difficult than normal.

"Nothing. I'm fine." She pointed to the couch, hoping to redirect his focus. "I'm a little disappointed about how bad the pink looks with the green."

Reed stepped closer, smelling like the cold outside air and the fresh Old Spice body wash she'd picked out during one of their Walmart trips. He shook his head. "No. You're not going to do this."

She blinked, unfazed by his gruff tone, but definitely affected by his nearness. "Do what?"

"Lie." He kept coming, crowding her space. "I don't mind you being a brat. I don't mind you being a pain in the ass. I might even fucking like it." His big body came close. "But don't lie to me."

She swallowed hard, caught in a cluster of opposing feelings. "I didn't mean to lie."

He continued to watch her. "Then why did you do it?"

She considered lying again. Telling him she didn't know. But she did. "Because I don't really know how to tell you how I feel."

Reed's hand came to her hip, holding with a firm but gentle touch, the heat of his palm sinking through the fabric of her knit pants. "Try."

She struggled to breathe. This was harder than she expected. All her life she wanted someone to care about her feelings, but now that she was faced with having to actually admit them, it felt uncomfortable. Significantly more so than admitting her feelings about her father. "I just thought maybe you've been nice to me because you feel bad for me."

Reed's dark eyes continued to hold hers, pinning her in place and making it nearly impossible to catch her breath. "Is that what you thought?"

Is it? She shook her head. "I don't know, but I was afraid

that maybe—" She managed a shaky breath before trying again. "Maybe it was why—"

"Why I touched you this morning?" He finished for her.

She wanted to break the tension, but her brain couldn't scrounge up anything even remotely amusing to say, so she was stuck with, "Kinda?"

Reed's nostrils flared, making him look almost angry. "I didn't touch you this morning out of guilt or pity, Princess." He pushed against her, backing her up until her butt hit the edge of the tiny countertop, pinning her between it and the hard line of his body as his free hand came to grip the braid at the back of her head. "I touched you because I'm having a hell of a time thinking about doing anything else."

CHAPTER EIGHTEEN

REED

SHE WAS KILLING him. Breaking his heart in ways he never expected. And it was causing a hell of a lot of problems.

"Really?" Courtney's question was breathless. The look on her face a little skeptical.

It was yet another part of her he never saw coming. The almost shy, insecure, broken bit that struggled to believe someone, anyone, would genuinely want her.

Seeing it both pissed him off and drew him in at the same time. It made him want to be closer to her. To be close enough she would see the truth of what she'd done to him.

It also made him want to throw shit. Rip apart the line of people who'd let her down. Left her alone.

But he'd have to tear himself away from her to do that, which was becoming harder and harder to accomplish. Especially when she put that wide-eyed, vulnerable gaze on him. Like she was now.

"You've got to stop looking at me the way you do." He was on edge. In a position where he might not make the best decisions. The smartest choices. Not about her, but about her safety.

Courtney barely shook her head, dark eyes staring up into his. "I'm not doing it on purpose."

That was part of the problem. He'd seen how she acted on purpose. Knew that her teasing and flirting and brazen sexual innuendos were done with purpose. This new bit of her was not, and it called to his protective nature in a way that was impossible to ignore.

For all her brashness, Courtney was unbelievably delicate. Afraid to even consider she might have the possibility of being genuinely cared for. And she fucking deserved to be genuinely cared for.

He looked over her face, the hope and the fear there. The raw need bathing in the pool of her gaze. It was unmissable and unignorable. Just like so much else about her.

"I know you don't mean to." He gripped the tab of her coat's zipper, yanking it down before pushing the heavy fabric open. "But if you don't figure out how to stop, it's gonna take us fucking forever to get to Alaska." He gripped the waistband of her pants, unhindered by the normal concerns about interest and consent. He knew Courtney was interested. Knew she wanted anything he was willing to give her. She'd made it abundantly clear on a number of occasions, and right now he was grateful as hell for it. Because it meant nothing stood between them outside of the clothes he was quickly removing.

He yanked her pants down to the middle of her thighs, taking panties and all before grabbing her by the waist and hefting her up onto the counter, the bare skin of her ass resting on the cushion of her coat as he dropped to his knees, dragging her pants down with him. He got them to her ankles, but abandoned the tangle when it caught on her shoes, choosing instead to lift her feet over his head, letting them fall against his back as he leaned in.

"What are you do—" Her breathy question ended in a strangled sound as he took his first taste of her, running the flat of his tongue up the heated slit of her pussy. As promised, her skin was soft and hairless with the exception of a tiny patch just above her pubic bone. Without the hindrance of hair, it was easy to tell how unbelievably soft she was here. How unbelievably slick. Unbelievably warm.

"Oh." The word rushed out on a breath as she gripped the counter, her feet digging into his back as she balanced herself on the edge.

The need to make her happy, to show her he touched her by choice, was driving him to be a little rougher than normal. More focused. More determined.

He gripped her thighs, fingers sinking into her flesh as he held them wide, pinning her in place as he rolled his tongue against the bead of her clit. Working it relentlessly as she started to pant above him. He thought about teasing her. Edging her until she was begging to come. Return a little of the torture she'd so happily dished out during their time together. But now wasn't the time for that. Right now he needed to sate both her need and his.

Hopefully it would help him refocus.

Courtney rocked against him, one hand releasing the counter to grip his hair, fisting tight as she made soft, needy sounds that had his cock straining against his jeans.

But those enticing sounds quickly turned into words. Words that he would fucking remember forever.

Her head dropped back against the upper cabinets, chin tipped high, dark eyes closed. "Fuck, you're good at that." Her heels dug into his back as she worked her hips against him. "I knew you'd be like this. Knew you'd be able to make me come so hard." She gripped his hair tighter. "Just like that. Just like that. Don't stop." Her words pitched higher. "You have the best tongue."

He'd never dealt with a woman who was so vocal. But, then again, he hadn't dealt with anyone quite like Courtney. So he shouldn't be surprised that even in a moment like this she was determined to make him lose his mind. And he wanted nothing more than to return the favor.

While his tongue continued teasing against her clit, he found the well of her pussy and eased in a finger, nearly moaning himself as a ragged groan passed through her perfect lips. He kept his strokes slow and deep, curling his finger to add pressure where it would serve him best. The first pass had her hips raising up off the counter. The second had her legs clamped around his ears.

And she still didn't stop talking.

"Fuck. I should've known you'd be able to find that spot." Her head banged back against the cabinets as she continued moving. "You're going to ruin me. No one else is ever going to be able to touch me again."

Those words shouldn't have been as satisfying as they were. Shouldn't have made him try harder in the hope they might be true.

But he did. He added a second finger, filling her a little more and offering more pressure against the spot that had her writhing beneath him.

When her legs started to shake, he pursed his lips, wrapping them around the hard bud of her clit and offering a gentle, pulsating suck.

"*Reed*." His name came out on a wail, long and drawn out,

as her pussy clamped around his fingers and wetness coated his palm.

Every inch of him wanted to stand up and sink into her. To take her hard and fast. To show her all he was capable of offering. But he was still sane enough to know that would be a really bad idea. Not that what he'd just done was a great idea, but he had to draw the line somewhere.

And the somewhere he was picking meant that box of condoms she picked up was going to stay sealed until they got to Alaska. Then they'd have the chance to reevaluate things when they weren't forced to share a tiny camper.

Courtney panted above him, her fingers still laced in his hair as she stared down at him. "You surprised me, sexy pants." She took another shuddering breath. "I didn't expect you to be the first one on their knees."

He hadn't expected a lot of things from her and it was nice to finally be on the other end of the surprises. "Good." He pressed a kiss to the inside of her thigh. "But we need to get moving." He carefully ducked under her legs, keeping her balanced before helping her slide to the floor.

Courtney made no move to adjust her clothing. Instead, she pushed out her lower lip, leaning into his chest as one hand gripped his aching length though the denim of his jeans. "I'm sure we have enough time for me to return the favor."

He gritted his teeth, loving and hating how forward she was. It left him clear where she stood on things, but also made it very hard to keep his head. "That wasn't a favor, Princess. That's not how shit like that works." He crouched down, partly because they really did need to get moving, but also to get her hand away from his cock before he proved how weak he really was.

Courtney held still as he found the waistband of her pants

and panties, lining them up before carefully working both up her legs. She watched his every move, her lower lip pinched between her teeth. "You should probably know I don't really know how shit like that *is* supposed to work."

Of course she didn't. She'd been surrounded by people whose interest in her only went as far as who her father was. Because, like she said, good or bad, that was what people saw when they looked at her.

"Then I guess you'll have to learn." He got her clothing back into place, making sure everything was as it should be before taking a step back. Literally, and figuratively. "And that's why we won't be fucking until we get to Alaska and figure this," he motioned between them, "out."

Her eyes fixed on his hand before lifting to his face. "This? Does that mean we're something?"

He wasn't ready to answer that. Not yet. "We're sure as hell not nothing." He glanced around the RV. "But right now we're in an extreme circumstance. One that might have us acting in ways we normally wouldn't."

Courtney nodded like she agreed. "I see what you're saying." She stepped forward, closing the gap between them, her hands fisting in his coat. "Because normally I would have absolutely sucked your dick by now."

He was trying to be serious. Trying to be reasonable. Trying to be logical.

But just like always, Courtney managed to lighten him up. Remind him that even though life was serious, it didn't have to be so intense.

"It doesn't mean you're not still a pain in my ass." He managed to say it, but the fact that he was smiling probably meant it didn't come across the same as it used to.

Courtney laced her arms around his neck, tipping her

head. "And you are still as grumpy as ever."

Before he knew what he was doing, his arms were around her back, holding her close. It was easy to do and felt like a completely normal thing. Like he'd done it a thousand times.

Courtney chewed her lower lip, eyes on his. "So, when you say we can't fuck—"

"I mean no fucking, Princess." He palmed her ass, pulling her a little closer, the press of her belly against his cock feeling way better than it should. "I think we need to be sensible about this. Not get ahead of ourselves."

Courtney tipped her head from side to side, eyes lifting to the ceiling. "I think I can work with that."

He was a little surprised she was agreeing so easily. Especially since she was the one adding condoms to their order. But Courtney was turning out to be way more easy-going than he remembered. Adding to the laundry list of ways she was not at all what he thought.

Courtney backed up, carefully shucking her coat and tossing it onto the couch. "I guess we should get going then."

Maybe what he was seeing now wasn't Courtney being easy-going. Maybe what he was seeing now was Courtney when she was up to something. She was being too agreeable. The fact that she hadn't given him a hard time at all was suspicious as hell.

And a little disappointing. As much as he gave her a hard time about it, he loved her attitude. Loved how feisty she could be. He might even do shit specifically to bring out that side of her, much like he suspected she goaded him. Courtney grabbed a bag of pretzels from the table, fished a bottle of water out of the large pack beneath it, and dropped into her seat without a word of complaint.

Yeah. She was definitely acting suspicious.

But he wasn't going to argue. Not now anyway. They really did need to get on the road, especially if the weather was going to be shit. And it looked like it was.

He'd been able to get new tires put on the camper at one of their stops, but he still wasn't completely confident the thing was going to make it all the way to Fairbanks on its own. But if he had to pay a tow truck to take it the rest of the way, then that's what he would do. Until then, he was going to enjoy the ride his parents would never get to take. Grabbing a bottle of water for himself, he climbed into the driver's seat, starting the engine and testing out the new wipers before pulling out of the lot.

The rest of the day passed quickly, with occasional stops for gas, bathrooms, and stretching breaks. By the time they got to the campsite Heidi reserved for them, the sun was long down and his ass was starting to drag.

But Courtney seemed just as full of energy as she always was. She practically leapt from her seat, going straight to the back of the camper. "Heidi said this campground was supposed to have a laundry room and really nice showers." She was already peeling open the new sheets and duvet cover, shaking them out before shoving them into the large tote bag she bought to keep her things collected in. "I'm gonna go load these in the washer and take a shower." She turned to him, her expression sweet and innocent. "What about you? What are your plans?"

He moved toward the bedroom, pausing at the closet to collect some fresh clothes and his small bag of toiletries. "I could use a shower too."

They'd stopped to grab dinner on the road, so there was no need to start a fire or try to cook anything, which was great because the farther north they went, the more difficult it would be to do that anyway. Courtney's new pots and pans would have to wait for another trip to be used.

Shit. Now he was already planning another trip. With her. Even more proof they had to keep their heads. This close proximity was making it easy to get carried away.

"We can go together then." Courtney slung her bag over one shoulder, giving him a sweet smile as she opened the door, climbing out the side of the RV and immediately yelping. "What the fuck?" She wiggled around, trying to grab the hood of her coat to get it yanked up over her head, but between the bag and the positioning of the hood itself, her arm wasn't quite capable of reaching.

Reed hurried out behind her, closing the door before grabbing what she couldn't and settling it over her head. He pulled the ties at the front, bringing it down tighter so less wind would break through. "We need to get you a hat."

Courtney's eyes lifted to his own bare head. "Aren't you cold?"

"I've lived my whole life in Alaska, Princess." He grabbed her by the shoulders and turned her toward the bathhouse. "This is nothing."

He put one arm around her, making sure she moved quickly down the lane, watching for any spots that looked slick. There was no snow on the ground, but sometimes ice was worse. Luckily, everything seemed dry enough that it wasn't a problem. And when they stepped into the laundromat portion of the main building, the humid air felt like a sauna.

Courtney let out a long breath. "Oh my gosh this feels so much better." She went to one of the washing machines and dropped in their new items, adjusting them around the barrel. Once the lid was dropped in place she looked over the slots on the side. "I hope you know how to do this."

Reed smiled, realizing it was ridiculous as fuck that being able to help her with this felt like an accomplishment. "Lucky for you I've visited a few laundromats in my day." He went to the change machine, feeding in a five before bringing the quarters back and loading them in. Then he added an appropriate amount of detergent from the small bottle Courtney picked up during their Target trip.

Courtney watched his every move. When he was finished, he turned to her and she wiggled her brows at him. "I didn't know watching a man do laundry could be sexy." She leaned into his chest, her voice practically a purr. "But I'm starting to realize I think just about everything you do is sexy."

He tapped her on the end of the nose. "We're still not fucking, Princess. No matter how sexy you think I am when I do laundry."

Courtney's mouth dropped open, like she couldn't believe he'd already figured out what she was up to. "What about how sexy I find it when you go down on me?" She moved in a little closer, gripping the front of his coat. "Or when you shove your fingers in my—"

The door swung open, letting in a blast of cold air along with an older woman carrying an overflowing laundry basket. She stopped a few feet in, looking them over with a frown. "You two weren't about to fuck in here, were you?"

Her blunt question was shocking to him.

But not so much to Courtney who immediately huffed out a breath and pouted. "No. Unfortunately."

The older woman's eyes came his way, looking him up and down. She gave a little shrug. "I guess I can't blame her." She went to one of the washers and dropped her clothes in. "Do what you want, just don't get anything nasty on my underwear."

CHAPTER NINETEEN

COURTNEY

"I THINK SHE liked you." Courtney grinned at Reed, wiggling her eyebrows as he yanked open the door to the shower house.

Reed offered her a smile, looking more relaxed than he normally was. "I think she has to get in line."

Courtney grinned as she walked past him into the building. "I'm not worried. I'm pretty sure I could take her." She held her bag against her chest with one elbow as she took a fighting stance, holding both her fists up. "I'm scrappy."

"You're something." Reed looked down the line of doors running up each side of the hall. "This is different."

She had to agree. She hadn't been in many shower houses, but so far they'd each had a men's side and a women's side. This one did not. There also didn't seem to be a separate shower area and toilet/sink area like normal.

Reed pushed the closest door open and flipped on the light, his brows jumping up. "Holy shit. Heidi did find us a nice place to stop."

Courtney stepped in close, peeking into the room. It was a

complete, self-contained bathroom. It had a toilet, a sink with a mirror, and a shower all together. It even had a little wood stool and a wire rack hooked over the shower head for shampoo and body wash. "Damn. This is really nice." She stepped in, gripping his coat as she went. "There's plenty of room for both of us in here."

Reed didn't budge. "I don't know if that's a good idea, Princess."

For some reason his reluctance gave her a little thrill. "Because you're positive you won't be able to control yourself around me?"

He was silent.

That made her pause, realizing she might actually be right. And it sent a tiny thrill blooming into something bigger. Something that was more than arousal.

"What if I promise to be good?" She held up one hand, extending her pinky. "No P in the V. Pinky swear."

He looked at her finger before moving his eyes to her face, dark brows lifting. "P in the V?"

She tipped her head, a little shocked that he couldn't figure that out on his own. "Penis in the vagina." She wiggled her pinky. "I promise I won't try to get you to fuck me."

He was quiet a second longer before finally lifting his hand to hook his pinky through hers.

She curled her digit around his, linking them together. "Now, if things get all slippery and it accidentally slides right in there all on its own..."

Reed's lips twitched, hinting at a smile, and she knew she had him. He liked being grumpy and serious. It seemed to be his natural state. But he definitely liked that she could break him out of it. Even if it was only for a minute.

She might have also liked it a little. Knowing she could

help him take a breath and stop being so serious. Relax the tiniest amount.

Reed used their connected fingers to spin her toward the shower before swatting her on the ass with his free hand. "No accidents, Princess."

She groaned dramatically, pushing out her lower lip in a pout. "Fine. I'll be very careful so I don't accidentally slip and fall onto your dick."

He chuckled behind her, the sound deep and rich and something she was beginning to crave. There was something about being the one to make him laugh that made her feel special, and she chased that feeling. Wanting, maybe needing, as much of it as she could get.

Courtney crossed to the tiny bench, setting her bag on it before peeling off her coat as Reed locked the door. She hung it on one of the hooks lined down the wall before peeling her shirt over her head. Reed didn't move a muscle. Didn't reach for his own coat or seem like he had any intention of stripping down.

She lifted a brow at him as she folded her shirt. "It's easier to take a shower if you're naked, Sexy Pants."

His eyes drifted down to the stretchy sports bra confining her tits. "I'll get undressed in a minute. Right now I'm watching you."

Well then.

She might not be getting boned anytime soon, but it seemed like Reed was more than happy to dish out other services. Who was she to question his strategy?

"Does that mean I get to watch you?" She grabbed the waistband of the knit joggers she'd become a little too fond of, working them past her hips and thighs before letting them drop to the floor.

Reed's dark gaze moved down her belly and over her completely unsexy cotton panties. "That can probably be arranged."

"I guess we have a deal then." Courtney toed off her sneakers, continuing to watch Reed's face as his eyes moved over her body.

He might want to believe their attraction and connection was based on circumstance, but, if anything, their circumstance should have prevented it from happening. Neither of them was at their best. Stress had brought out the worst in her and him both. They were also both looking a little rough around the edges. Her outfits were about as unsexy as it got, right down to her underwear. She hadn't styled her hair in days, and there wasn't a stitch of makeup anywhere on her face.

But Reed didn't seem to care. Right now he was looking at her like he could swallow her whole. Like she was the sexiest thing he'd ever seen. Like it was taking every bit of control he had to keep from throwing her down and fucking her senseless.

And she wasn't even completely naked yet.

Courtney quickly shucked her panties and bra, kicking the stack of clothes away before pulling the rubber band at the end of her braid free. She worked her hair loose, letting it fall past her shoulders to curl along her tits. "Your turn."

She'd seen Reed naked before, but was a little distracted both times. Having the opportunity to take him all in at once, without pretending she wasn't looking, was making her antsy as he finally peeled off his coat.

She held her breath as he worked his shirt over his head, revealing a ridiculous set of abs and a perfectly smooth chest. His nipples were dark and tightened almost immediately at the cool air of the room, making her wish she was close enough to give one a little pinch.

Reed kicked away his shoes before shoving down his pants, taking jeans and underwear all at once. He gathered the pile and dropped it onto the counter of the sink before straightening in front of her, looking a little proud.

As well he should. The chill of the room didn't seem to be affecting the rest of him, because the line of his cock jutted toward her, hard and straining. Reminding her that only one of them had gotten off earlier.

She could remedy that situation.

Desperately wanted to remedy that situation.

He'd mistaken her earlier offer. Seemed to think she felt she owed him. But that wasn't it. Not by a long shot.

She wanted it. Was starting to get a little desperate to look up at him while she swallowed him down. Ready to see if the way she imagined him reacting to the heat of her mouth was correct. Wanted to know if he would lace his fingers into her hair and pull her onto him. If Reed would thrust deeper into her throat. Take charge of the act the way he took charge of everything else.

She really fucking hoped so.

Everything about him was powerful. From the lean muscle covering every inch of his body to the commanding way he held himself. It was appealing for a number of reasons, but primarily what all that strength and control would be like when it was unleashed on her.

Hopefully that happened at some point.

But tonight would not be that point.

"Seems like you work out a lot." She should drag her eyes away from him, but that was easier said than done. The more she looked, the more she wanted to continue looking.

Wanted to touch.

"On occasion." Reed was unflinching as she drank him in, looking her fill.

His body was ridiculous. Freaking insane. Definitely capable of pounding her into a mattress.

The thought had her pussy clenching, reminding her it would not be filled anytime soon. Somehow, Reed believed they were going to lay next to each other every night without screwing, and right now that seemed highly unlikely. Not because she was going to try to derail his plan. She wouldn't do that. He seemed concerned that they weren't making smart choices, and she certainly didn't want him believing anything that happened between them was a bad idea.

But they weren't so good at keeping their hands off each other. The push and pull between them was constant, and eventually the rope snapped and they crashed together. It had happened before and would no doubt happen again.

Reed tipped his head toward the shower. "Start the water for us."

Courtney forced her eyes back to his, struggling to both breathe and string together words. "Yup. Yes. I can do that." She reached in and twisted the knob, cranking it a decent amount before holding her hand under the faucet. The water trickling out of the shower head was plenty warm, but the pressure left a lot to be desired, so she cranked it up more, managing to get little more than a weak stream that would make it hard as hell to rinse her hair.

But at least it was warm.

She glanced Reed's way. "I think this is as good as it's gonna get." She stepped into the basin, immediately positioning herself under the water, back to the spray.

Reed was right behind her, sliding the curtain into place

before standing directly in front of her. "You're hogging the water, Princess."

"You could've gotten in first." She closed her eyes and leaned back, letting the water dribble onto her hair, managing to finally get all of it wet before stepping forward and wiping her eyes.

Reed still stood exactly where he started, watching her with a hooded gaze. No one had ever watched her shower before, and while she felt a little exposed, she also felt a little sexy. Especially since Reed almost looked angry. Like he was pissed he couldn't stop himself from getting close to her. And it made her feel powerful. Desired.

Wanted.

She squeezed out some shampoo into her palm and worked it through her hair before rinsing it out in a painstakingly slow process. Once all the studs were finally gone, she moved on to the conditioner, stroking it down the ends of her long strands before backing under the spray. While it rinsed out, she added body wash to her palm, working it into suds before smoothing it over her arms and down her front, spending a little more time than usual on her tits.

Reed watched every second of it. Focused on each move she made. By the time she got to the spot between her legs, he'd eased in close enough the tip of his cock barely brushed her skin.

"I think you're teasing me, Princess."

Courtney widened her eyes as she cleaned her most delicate parts. "That doesn't seem like something I would do."

Reed's mouth crooked into a smirk. "That seems exactly like something you would do." He backed up just a hair, so his body no longer touched hers. "Finish up. I'm ready for my turn."

There was something in the way he said it. Something that made her think maybe they weren't just talking about the shower. And it lit a bit of a fire under her britches. She rushed through rinsing off the soap before squeezing out her hair. "I'm done."

Reed gripped her hips, holding tight as he switched their places, putting his back to the weak spray. He leaned into it, eyes still on her as the water ran over his hair and down his face, slicking his body. He scrubbed down, working his big hands over his arms, his chest, his stomach. And finally—

Her lips parted as he fisted his cock, gripping it tight as his free hand went to his balls, cupping them as he continued working his cock.

Courtney swallowed hard, bringing her eyes to his. "I'm happy to do that for you if you'd like."

Reed stroked himself again. "I'm more than capable of washing myself, Princess."

Courtney licked her lips, itching to get her hands, and her mouth, on him. "I wasn't so much talking about the cleaning." She held his gaze as she slowly went to her knees.

And waited.

Reed stared at her, nostrils flared, jaw set. He didn't move for a few seconds and then he slowly backed away.

That was disappointing. What did a girl have to do to suck a dick around here?

She was just about to stand, feeling a little embarrassed and slightly rejected, when Reed moved in close again, bringing the head of his freshly rinsed cock against her lips. "Open."

She didn't hesitate. Didn't give him a second to reconsider. Courtney immediately parted her lips, sticking her tongue out just a little as her hands came to rest on the solid mass of his thighs.

Reed's hand went to her wet hair, curving around the back of her head before gripping into the soaked strands. "Good girl. Just like that." He traced the tip of his cock across her upper lip. "Stick your tongue out a little more for me."

Again, she immediately did as he asked and was rewarded when he tapped the underside of his dick against it with a few light slaps. It was definitely a sexy move, but she wanted more, so she tried to lean forward. Attempted to take what she wanted.

But Reed's hand held tight to her hair, keeping her in place as he slapped his cock against her tongue again. "Greedy girl."

He wasn't wrong. She was more than a little desperate for this. Somewhere along the line, her offer had turned to a request, possibly a need, and she wasn't mad about it.

Because she trusted him.

Was he occasionally an ass? Yes.

Was he overly serious? Double yes.

But he'd also proven he would always watch out for her. That he cared about how she felt. That he listened.

And that made her want this moment just as much as he hopefully did.

When Reed eased closer her heart skipped a beat and her stomach flipped in anticipation. He'd barely slid past her lips when someone started banging on the door hard enough to rattle it on its hinges.

By some grace of God, she didn't accidentally bite him as her whole body tensed up and she scrambled back, trying to put as much space between her and the door as possible.

Heidi said they were in the clear, but what if she was wrong? She was all the way in Alaska and they were still nowhere near there. It wasn't a complete stretch to think the men who tried to kill her once had moved in to finish the job.

And now they would kill Reed too.

Somehow that was almost more upsetting.

The fear that they might take away the first person who genuinely gave a shit about her had Courtney back on her feet, grabbing the wooden stool and slamming it against the floor as the banging continued.

The stool, a little rickety from the constant humidity in the room, easily broke into pieces, one of them sporting a wickedly sharp edge. She gripped it tight, pointed end coming out the back of her clenched fist. When she turned toward the door Reed was staring at her with wide eyes.

"Are you feral?"

She nodded. "I think so."

He gave her an approving look. "Good." He stepped close as whoever was on the other side got even more aggressive, hooking one arm around her waist and pulling her in for a quick kiss, his lips hard and demanding as his tongue slicked against hers before disappearing too soon. His dark eyes held hers. "Do whatever it takes to get out of here." His expression was as serious as she'd ever seen it, which was saying something. "That includes leaving me behind."

She knew him well enough not to argue, but there was no way she'd go without him. So she broke the one rule he gave her and offered up a lie she'd apologize for later when they were both safe. "Okay."

CHAPTER TWENTY

REED

IF SOMEONE HAD asked him a year ago whether or not Courtney would have his back in a dangerous situation, he would have laughed in their face. But seeing Courtney, dripping wet and naked, holding a spike of wood like she was ready to fight, didn't surprise him now. Over the past few days he'd learned she was brave and determined and, honestly, way more dangerous than he'd ever given her credit for.

That still didn't mean he would let her put herself on the line.

He grabbed one of the big towels she'd bought from Target and tossed it her way. "Wrap that around you in case you have to run. I don't want you freezing to death."

Courtney caught the towel, but instead of putting it around herself, she motioned at him. "What about you?"

He grabbed the second towel and wrapped it around his waist, tucking it as tight as he could before holding his hands out. "Better?"

It would figure she'd still want to argue with him in a situation like this.

Courtney nodded, wrapping her own towel into place. "Better. I don't want your dick to get hurt before I have the chance to fully enjoy it."

Christ. Was she making a joke at a time like this?

Of course she was. She would probably crack a joke while he was balls deep inside her too. The woman definitely didn't understand timing.

He held one finger to his lips, turning to the door. He took one quick breath before flipping the lock and whipping it open, hoping to catch whoever was on the other side at least a little off guard.

They were safe. He knew that.

Probably.

But he still let out a sigh of relief when he saw who was raising absolute hell outside the door.

The woman from the laundry room stared at him, looking bothered by his presence. "Your washer finished. I switched your stuff over to the dryer."

That was what she nearly beat the door down for?

He exhaled, relief sagging his shoulders. "Thanks."

She lifted her brows, holding one hand out. "You owe me three-fifty."

Holy hell. He might have actually found someone who was a bigger pain in his ass than Courtney.

Reed turned to where his jeans were tossed on the counter, digging in the pocket to pull out a five. He passed it off. "Keep the change."

The woman looked him up and down. "Don't get jizz on the shower curtain." Then she turned and walked away, leaving him staring after her, heart still pounding, adrenaline still dumping into his system.

He never reacted like this. Always kept his cool in any

circumstance. It was part of the reason Pierce chose him over everyone else in his graduating class. Not only did he know most of Alaska like the back of his hand, but he stayed calm in any situation.

Almost any situation.

He closed the door, re-locking it before turning to find Courtney still standing with the chunk of wood in her hand. She wiggled it back and forth, shooting him a grin. "Want me to go stab her anyway?"

Fuck if he didn't laugh. There was no way not to. The whole situation was goddamn ridiculous. "Put that down and get dressed."

Courtney pushed out her lower lip in the way he was becoming familiar with and partial to. "Are you serious?"

"As a fucking heart attack." He grabbed his own fresh clothes and started putting them on. "You want to sleep on nice sheets, don't you?"

Her pout held. "Well yeah, but I also wanted to suck your dick."

She sounded disappointed, which had his temporarily relaxed cock perking backup. But right now he wanted to get out of this windowless room more than he wanted to see her on her knees again. This place was a fucking trap. And the thought of leaving Courtney in here a second longer made his skin crawl. She needed to be somewhere he could keep her safe. Somewhere they could make a break for it if they had to.

He crossed the small room, stopping in front of her to cradle her face in his hands. "I fucking love how eager you are, but now isn't the time and this clearly isn't the place."

Courtney huffed out a breath, rolling her eyes toward the ceiling. "Fine."

As usual, he couldn't help but smile at her pouty, bratty

reaction. He leaned in and pressed a chaste kiss to her lips. "You'll thank me when you're curled up on your nice comfortable sheets."

Courtney groaned, but didn't argue, making it evident the lure of nice sheets was greater than he expected.

They finished dressing, collected their things—along with the destroyed stool—and hustled out of the bathroom. He took her straight back to the RV, getting Courtney safely inside and making sure she locked the door, before he went back to retrieve their sheets and blankets. He'd planned to run the towels through the laundry also, but those would have to wait for another day. Right now he wanted her locked up tight and right next to him.

He got back to the camper, giving the door a quick knock. Courtney opened it without checking to make sure it was him. He scowled at her smiling face. "I could have been anybody. You've got to be careful."

It wasn't like him to act like this. To be so wound up when he knew rationally there was no reason for it. They were a thousand miles away from Miami. Far enough that the chances of anyone finding them were practically none. But when that old woman knocked on the bathroom door, he was ready to kill anyone who tried to get Courtney. Thinking of all the ways he would do it with his bare hands. What else he could do to make sure she had the chance to get away.

"Who else would it be?" She huffed out a breath. "Maybe the old lady again, but that's it." She took a slow breath, like she was trying to calm herself down. "Heidi said we were fine. That's why I didn't have to fly to Alaska. She said they knew I wasn't dead, but had no clue where I'd gone."

Reed studied her. Took in the uncertainty in her expression. "Are you trying to convince me, or yourself?"

She let out a shaky breath, her lips shifting into an awkward smile. "A little of both."

He dropped the sheets and blankets onto the sofa before snagging her and dragging her close, pinning Courtney against his chest as he tucked his face into the wet drape of her hair.

She linked her hands around his middle, pressing her face into the crook of his neck. "I thought I was gonna have to stab somebody with a hunk of wood. It was about to be prison rules in that bathroom."

He smoothed one hand through her damp hair, working a few tangles free. "You weren't going to stab anybody." He needed her to understand the way things had to be. "If anything happens, your only job is to get as far away as you can, understand?"

Courtney leaned back, her dark eyes meeting his. "No."

He didn't expect her to immediately agree, but he also wasn't expecting her to refuse so adamantly. "Did you just say no?"

Courtney's chin lifted. "I'm not going to just leave you."

"Yes, you fucking are." He gripped her chin with his fingers as he leaned closer, hoping she understood how serious this was. "You are to run. Get your sweet little ass out."

She held his gaze, full of defiance. "No."

"Yes." Why was she even arguing this? He knew how to handle himself, she didn't. Sure she knew how to steal some shit, but when it came to actual hand-to-hand combat? No way was Courtney capable of holding her own. Especially not against armed men.

She jerked her chin from his grip and stepped back, but her gaze didn't leave his. "No." Then she turned and walked away, going straight for the bedroom.

He followed right behind her. "Yes."

Courtney shook her head. "Not happening." She reached the bed and turned to face him. "You told me not to lie to you, so I'm not gonna lie to you. If shit goes down, I'm going to be in the middle of it."

"Like hell you are." The thought of her putting herself in a dangerous situation made it impossible to stand still. Difficult to breathe. He raked one hand through his damp hair, trying to find the focus and the calm he needed. "You will get out of there, or else."

Her dark brows lifted, but she looked completely unintimidated. "Or else what? You'll spank me for being bad?" She snorted out an indignant laugh. "I don't think you have it in you."

She was goading him. Pushing him like always in an attempt to get her way.

This time, she just might accomplish it.

He tipped his head to the bed. "Bend over and we'll see what I have in me."

Her sharp intake of breath shot straight to his cock, reigniting the ache still lingering in his balls from the shower interaction that was cut short.

Courtney stared at him for a heartbeat, lips parted, pupils dilated.

"I don't have much patience right now, Princess." He grabbed her face with one hand, the tips of his fingers sinking into the soft skin of her cheek. "The longer you make me wait, the redder that pretty little ass is going to be."

"Holyshitonacracker." The muddle of words rushed out of her lips on a breath. "That was so fucking hot."

Her reaction cooled the edge of his anger. Of the helplessness he felt when he thought someone might try to hurt her.

But he wasn't going to tell her that. Not when it was clear Courtney wanted this so much.

Maybe she even needed it. He was willing to bet she'd never been disciplined in her life. No one took the time to care if she was making the right choices or not. No one put in the effort to help her choose the right directions. If she needed to know he cared enough to hold her accountable for her actions, then so be it.

Courtney immediately spun away and dropped to the bed, bending at the waist, her upper half pressed against the cheap blanket still covering the mattress.

He stared down at her, still struggling with all the emotions warring inside of him. After years of having only one focus, her presence had him a fucking mess. "Pants and panties down. I want you to feel my hand on your skin."

Courtney shifted, grabbing the waistband of her fresh knit pants and shoving them over her presented ass, leaving them bunched at her knees.

He nearly groaned at the sight of her tanned skin and curved cheeks. He hadn't expected to be so turned on at the sight of her like this, but it felt almost like they were coming full circle. Like she was offering herself up for him to collect. And after everything she'd done over the years, she certainly deserved a swat or two.

He pressed one palm to the center of her back, pinning her in place as the other moved along the full curve of her ass, petting the soft, golden hue of her skin. Then he pulled back and gave it a sharp smack, the fullness of her cheek bouncing from the impact. Her flesh immediately pinked up as she let out a tiny whimper.

He lifted his hand again before bringing it down against the other cheek, fascinated at the way her ass moved when his hand connected. At the flush immediately creeping over her skin. At the sounds she made. Sounds that absolutely were not from pain.

He swatted her again, feeling the connection in his cock. Another, this one making her moan. "Is this what you wanted from me?" Another swat. "You wanted me to prove I cared enough to make you behave?" Swat.

Courtney made a whimpering groan, but that wasn't what he wanted to hear.

Swat. "I want an answer, Princess."

"Yes." The word came out as something between a yell and a sob.

He leaned down, pressing her into the bed with his weight as his chest met her back, his palm smoothing over her heated skin. "Now that you got what you wanted, are you going to behave?"

Courtney turned her head to the side, cheek smashed where it pressed against the blanket, and her eyes met his. She was breathing heavy, damp hair sticking to her forehead as she held his gaze. "Absolutely not."

He didn't fight his smile. "I didn't think so." Swat.

Her moan was loud and long and her legs were shaking, possibly from the stinging in her ass, but more likely from something else. He ran his palm down the crack of her ass, feeding his fingers between her legs. A groan of his own slipped free when he was met by her drenched folds. "You're soaked." He wedged his hand further, forcing her to spread her legs. Her whole body shuddered when he found her clit and started to work it under the flat of his fingers, rubbing side to side as he kept her pinned in place. "You just don't know how to behave, do you, Princess?"

She was rocking against his palm, desperate for everything he was willing to give.

"I guess it's a good thing I don't mind punishing you when you're bad." He worked her faster, needing to give this to her as much as she needed to get it.

A ragged moan ripped from Courtney's lips as she bucked against him, wetness coating his palm as she came against it.

He cupped her pussy, holding it tight as she continued twitching intermittently. He smoothed back her hair, pushing it away from her face before pressing a kiss to her temple. "Stay here. I'll be right back."

She groaned again as he got up. "I don't think I could move if I had to."

He adjusted the line of his cock, trying to find a comfortable position as he went to the closet, looking for anything that might be useful. He snagged a bottle of her lotion before going to the cooler and pulling a bottle of water free. When he got back to the bedroom she had actually listened, and had not moved.

"Up on the bed." He grabbed her around the waist and hefted her fully onto the mattress, ass still in the air. He settled down beside her, squeezing a little lotion onto each cheek before gently smoothing it into her reddened skin. "Did I hurt you?"

Courtney's face was pressed against the pillow, the pressure smashing her lips into a protruding pout. "Yes, but in a good way."

He carefully finished rubbing the lotion in before working her panties into place and resting the water bottle on one cheek. "I didn't know there was a good way."

Her brows pinched together, face still distorted from how she laid. "Really? Because you're pretty fucking good at it."

He moved the cool bottle to her other cheek. Offering her a smirk. "You should probably keep that in mind before you give me shit."

Courtney sighed, looking relaxed in spite of what just happened, or maybe because of it. "I absolutely will."

CHAPTER TWENTY-ONE

COURTNEY

COURTNEY PEERED OUT the RV windows at her new hometown. After over a week of travel, they'd finally arrived, and she was doing her best to take it all in. Every dark, snowy, frigid bit.

Reed glanced her way. "Does it look the way you remembered?"

She couldn't stop the smile spreading across her face. "It looks better than I remembered."

Last time she was in Fairbanks, she didn't appreciate the freedom it had offered her. The ability to be whoever she wanted to be. Free of judgment and expectations.

Sort of.

The man beside her had offered up plenty of both. But now she understood why, and that changed the way she viewed it in hindsight. Hopefully he'd learned enough about her that his own views of their past had changed a little.

It certainly seemed like they had.

Because while Reed hadn't touched her in any sort of sexual way since the unbelievably hot interlude after their slightly scary shower incident, he had done plenty of touching in other ways. Ways that she almost liked more.

Almost.

Reed brought Bernadette to a stop at a traffic light and turned her way, reaching across the gap between their seats to curve her loose hair behind one ear. "Are you warm enough?"

She nodded, leaning into his touch. "I think the trip here gave me plenty of time to acclimate to the cold weather." They'd made fantastic time, and part of her had to believe it was because Reed wanted to be home. Back where he felt comfortable. Back where he could make sure his parents were as okay as they claimed to be during one of his many phone calls to them.

She felt the same way. Even though each day made it more evident no one was following them, Fairbanks still felt like a safe haven. A place she wouldn't have to constantly be looking over her shoulder. Worrying that the men who blew up her house and killed her father would decide they needed to finish the job on principle.

"I know you're tired and probably want a real shower and some decent food, but we have to go to the offices and meet with Pierce first." His expression was apologetic. Like he knew just how unexcited she was about facing down the owner of Alaskan Security.

Hindsight hadn't only changed her view of Reed. It had also made it a little more difficult to come to terms with her past bad behavior. Were there reasons she acted the way she did? Absolutely. Did they still feel like as great of excuses as they once had? Definitely not.

"I would feel better about meeting with him if I could throw some money at him to make this all better." It was yet another thing she was going to have to get used to. Up to this point her life had revolved around her ability to pay for the things she desired. Clothes. Makeup. Fancy meals and late-night drinks.

Also friends and for people to give a shit about her well-being. Her past was a double-edged sword, but she was tired of being cut to achieve any sort of happiness.

Reed held her gaze. "It will be okay."

She nodded even though she didn't quite believe him.

Pierce was even more intimidating than Reed had once been. With Reed she felt like she had a little bit of footing because he was single, and single men were usually swayed by flirting and sexual opportunities. Pierce was as unsingle as it got. He was madly and desperately in love with his wife Mona, but even if he hadn't been, she was pretty confident his interest in her would have been zilch.

She couldn't really blame him. The feeling was mutual. Pierce did absolutely nothing for her. Never had. Just like most of the men who'd been charged with babysitting her.

The light turned green and Reed maneuvered the RV along the nasty roads. The drive had gotten increasingly stressful as they'd hit colder, snowier climates, but he was wickedly good at navigating them. Probably because he'd spent his whole life in Alaska.

But the treacherous conditions brought up another thing she was worrying about. "I'm guessing I'll have to learn to drive in the snow, huh?"

"If you want to go anywhere you will." Reed shot her a quick glance, his eyes moving over her face before going back to the road. "But don't worry about that either. I'll teach you."

It sounded good in theory, but more and more of her future was dependent on him. Right now she was completely at his and Alaskan Security's mercy. She talked a good game back in Miami—claiming she was more than capable of starting over—but now that it was happening, the logistics of it were much more daunting.

She had no job. No car. Nowhere to live. No friends. No family. Hell, she didn't even really have an identity at this point unless she wanted to lead the assholes who tried to blow her up right to her new front door.

And the thought of that was terrifying, especially since the door technically didn't belong to her.

So she was back to balancing on a double-edged sword, this one colder and snowier than the last, but just as intimidating.

Her stomach clenched as they pulled up to the gates of Alaskan Security, pausing long enough for Reed to punch in a code. He waited, but nothing happened. Instead, the box beside his window let out a long, angry sounding beep.

A second later a static sound came out of the small speaker next to the keypad. "Go ahead with your order when you're ready."

Reed didn't laugh, but the set of his jaw softened a little. "Did you change the code?"

"Things have been exciting while you've been on your sightseeing journey across the United States." The female voice on the other end paused. "The code to the gate changes every morning and sometimes at lunchtime now." The box beeped again, but this time the gate lifted. "Please pull to the next window for your order."

Reed rolled up his window, all the tension he'd had from before coming back in an instant. Plus some.

"What's wrong?" His reaction made her uneasy. Made her worry that Fairbanks wasn't going to be as safe as she hoped.

Reed turned her way. "Just work stuff. Nothing you need to worry about."

Courtney sat with his response for a minute before deciding to do exactly as he said. She had enough of her own shit to worry about, there was no way she was going to add Alaskan Security's problems to the list.

The narrow road leading back to the main campus was flanked by trees, making it feel more isolated than it was from the commercial office park at the edge of the property. By the time the trees parted and the massive campus came into view, it almost felt like they were somewhere different. An isolated city of its own.

Reed pulled alongside the collection of buildings instead of parking right in front where she'd entered last time she was here. Courtney took in the massive expanse of the place as they drove alongside it and turned up the back. She'd been here before, but only to the main entrance. And even then, she'd only made it to Pierce's office before being whisked away and hidden in a cabin outside of town. It felt strange to be seeing this side of it. Like she was no longer a client.

Technically she wasn't since she didn't have the money to be a client. A twist of worry tightened in her gut at that thought, forcing her to take a deep breath to try to make it relax.

A tall garage door lifted as they approached and Reed went right in, pulling the RV up to a glass vestibule where a man stood wiping his hands on a rag. They were in some sort of parking garage, filled with SUVs and cars and even a few vans. A number of random model vehicles sat apart from the more uniform black of the SUVs.

Reed shut off the engine and climbed out but didn't say what she should do. Was she supposed to follow him? Stay there and wait until he came back? Right now everything felt so uncertain and it made her uncertain. Uncertain and anxious. And she wasn't on her best behavior when she was uncertain and anxious.

Courtney was just about to get out of the RV, primarily because her nerves made it impossible to sit still, when Reed came back from the vestibule, rounded the front of Bernadette and opened her door, extending one hand her way. "We're all set."

She turned back to where the man in the vestibule was hanging the keys to the RV on a line of hooks just outside the door. "Are we just leaving Bernadette here?"

"For now. Artie's going to look her over. Fix everything that needs fixed and make sure her engine is the best it can be." He stopped waiting for her to take his hand and instead took hers, using the hold to pull her out. "Once he's finished, she'll go to an RV shop to be updated and overhauled."

Courtney turned to look over the camper. It initially served as nothing more than a means of escape, but over the past week it had turned into a sanctuary of sorts. Somewhere she felt safe. And the first place she ever felt appreciated.

She reached out to rest one hand on the filthy metal side. "How long will that take?"

"I don't expect it to be a quick process. I want some pretty major changes, so we probably won't get her back for at least three or four months."

Why did that make her feel so emotional? It was ridiculous. She didn't even get this upset over her house and car being blown up, but here she was considering crying over an RV being gone for a few months. "I guess we can't really take her out right now anyway." She took a deep breath, trying to rationalize her oddly out of control thoughts.

"Exactly. She's going to be sitting in storage here anyway, so I figured we might as well put the time to good use so she'll be ready to go when the weather breaks."

She didn't miss how Reed continued saying *we*. Like she was included in his better weather plans.

Oddly enough, that didn't surprise her. Sure, this whole situation with him had been completely different from any interactions she'd had with men in the past. Not just because of how it started, but because they'd been in very close quarters for days and days and hadn't even come close to having sex. Yes, they'd done just about everything except that, but in her experience, most men went straight for penetration.

In her experience, most men were also full of shit, and she'd bet her whole ass Reed wasn't. It just wasn't in his nature. He was grumpy and occasionally an asshole, but he wasn't manipulative. If he said something, he meant it. And that left her feeling shockingly secure with where she stood.

But it was still terrifying.

She gave Bernadette a little pat. "I guess I'll see you soon, sister." It was harder than it should have been to take her hand away. Even harder to walk with Reed across the garage and leave her behind.

Courtney slowed her steps. "What about all our stuff?" She wasn't trying to come up with a reason to go back, really she wasn't. But she desperately wanted to go back. To hide in the first place that had ever felt somewhat like a home to her.

"I'll make sure we get everything out and pack it up." Reed kept walking, not slowing down a bit as he led her across the garage and through a heavy metal door.

She stopped short, jumping back when she nearly ran into a giant man in all black. He had a whole freaking arsenal strapped to his body and a frown almost as sharp as Reed's.

He stopped when he saw them, looking her over before turning to Reed. "When did you get back?"

"Just now." Reed's dark eyes moved to where a group of men dressed exactly like the one in front of them stood at a set of double doors. "What's going on?"

The man shook his head, frown deepening. "Nothing good." He looked ready to murder someone. "Somebody took out one of our fucking cabins. Blew the whole goddamn thing up."

Courtney stumbled back, the skin of her face going cold. "They blew it up?"

There was no way. No way anyone from Miami would come all the way up here to blow up one of Alaskan Security's cabins.

Reed's arm looped around her waist, holding tight as he pulled her into his side. His grip was firm, but his voice was calm when he asked, "Any idea who it was?"

The man shook his head. "Somebody with some fucking skill. They managed to knock out all the cameras we had on the place before it happened, so we've got absolutely nothing to fucking go on unless we find something there."

Read continued holding her tight. "I wish I could go with you, but—"

The man held one hand up. "You just got back. Get your shit together and then we'll talk. See if there's any place you can think of in that area we should check."

Reed gave him a nod. "Will do."

The man turned and joined the rest of the group as they filed out the doors and into the back of the waiting van, piling in with shocking efficiency before pulling the doors closed and taking off.

"You need to breathe, Princess." Reed leaned into her ear,

his nose buried in her hair. "That had nothing to do with you. No one is coming all the way here to bother you. I promise."

She relaxed a little because she believed him. He wouldn't tell her that if it wasn't true. Both his integrity and his temperament combined to make him honest and realistic to a fault.

She managed a smile. "I guess I'm just a little jumpy." And, like she always did when things got to be a little more tense than she wanted, she cracked a joke. "Plus, I definitely don't want to deal with Pierce if he thinks I'm responsible for his shit getting blown up."

Reed's expression barely hardened. "Pierce won't think you're responsible for anything."

She almost laughed. Pierce was absolutely going to pin quite a bit of shit on her, and she probably deserved it. She'd been a huge pain in the ass, but she planned to be better. To be a slightly smaller pain in the ass.

She'd dealt with any number of scary men in her life, most of them employed by her father, but this was different. Right now she had no one's name to protect her. Sure, her father never purposefully protected her, but his name and their connection offered a certain amount on its own.

Not anymore.

Reed pressed one hand on her lower back, guiding her down the hall. He turned, directing her into an open door on the right.

Pierce sat behind his desk, fingers steepled in front of him. Mona, the tiny blonde woman he married, was perched on the edge of his desk, looking more than a little agitated.

Fuck. Even Mona was pissed at her?

She'd met a handful of people from the company, and Mona had been the kindest. If Mona was angry then—

Pierce motioned to the chairs across from him. "Sit down." It wasn't a request and he didn't sound even a little nice.

Courtney started to do as he asked, because what the fuck else was she supposed to do? He'd spent no small amount of money getting her here, and she had absolutely no way of paying him back, so right now she was sort of at his mercy.

It was not a fun place to be.

But Reed caught her just as she started to move, one hand splaying across her hip to drag her close and pin her at his side. It was a move both Pierce and Mona noticed, their eyes snapping to where the warmth of his hand burned into her skin like a brand.

"We can stand. We've been sitting for a long time." Reed's words sounded reasonable enough, but the tone he said them in was clipped and short.

Pierce leaned back in his seat. "Very well." His eyes came her way, pinning her in place. "It appears you were finally telling the truth about your situation, Ms. Vasquez."

It was unsurprising to have her past misdeeds thrown in her face. She saw it coming. Knew it would happen. It still stung.

Courtney opened her mouth, ready to apologize since that was her only option, but Reed cut her off.

His gaze was sharp as it landed on Pierce. "Watch your fucking tone."

CHAPTER TWENTY-TWO

REED

COURTNEY STARED AT him like he'd lost his fucking mind.

So did Pierce.

The only one in the room not looking at him like he had two heads was Mona, whose mouth was tipped up in a knowing smile. She turned to her husband as she slid off his desk to her feet. "It seems like I'm not needed here, so I'm going to get back to work." She turned away from him without another word, her cool blue eyes fixing on Courtney as she passed. One closed in a conspiratorial wink.

When the door closed behind her, Pierce let out a long sigh, tipping his head back to stare at the ceiling. "Is there anything I should know about?"

Reed shook his head. "Nope."

Again, Courtney and Pierce's eyes found him. But this time it wasn't shock in their gazes. Courtney looked a little hurt and Pierce looked confused as fuck. He didn't give a shit about how Pierce felt, but he sure as hell cared about her.

Reed kept his focus on the owner of Alaskan security as he explained his answer, primarily for the benefit of the woman beside him. "What I do in my free time isn't really your business."

Pierce's brows lifted. "I don't disagree that your free time is your own to spend as you wish, but when you spend it with one of Alaskan Security's clients, my interests come into play."

Reed stared him down. "Then I guess it's good I didn't spend any time with a client of Alaskan Security." Courtney's jaw dropped open in his peripheral vision. He caught her hand with his, but he didn't stop doling out the truth of who funded their trip. "Not a cent of Alaskan Security's money was spent getting Ms. Vasquez from Miami to Fairbanks. I explained to her we would no longer be helping her as I was directed to do, and I was not paid for any of my time from that point on."

He'd worked the logistics out with Heidi since he needed her help to access his bank account, and adjust his paycheck, but it appeared she hadn't filled Pierce in, because one of his eyes was twitching the tiniest bit as he stared them down across his desk. "Is that so?"

"It is." He'd made it halfway through the trip before realizing the huge conflict of interest that was happening. He'd abandoned enough of his principles as it was. Having a physical relationship with a woman he was being paid to take care of wasn't one he was willing to cast aside. It'd happened more than once at the company, and at the time he'd passed judgment on the men who did it. His opinion of their actions and reasonings had changed, but it still wasn't anything he was willing to do himself.

"Well." Pierce pursed his lips before running his tongue across his teeth. "It would appear there's nothing for us to discuss regarding the situation then."

Reed agreed. "Not a thing."

Pierce brought his eyes back to Courtney, folding his hands

on his desk and giving her a tight smile. "Welcome back to Fairbanks, Ms. Vasquez. I hope you enjoy your stay."

Courtney stood silently, eyes shifting from Pierce to him before going back to Pierce. "Thanks?"

Pierce took another long breath, his shoulders lifting and dropping as he refocused on Reed. "Once you're settled, you should be briefed on what happened while you were gone."

"Understood." He needed to find out what was going on, but he needed to get Courtney situated first. She'd obviously been nervous about meeting with Pierce, probably because she expected a confrontation. So when the owner of Alaskan Security came at her right out of the gate, he couldn't keep his mouth shut. Didn't want to.

He had a point to make to both people in the room.

He turned to Courtney, tipping his head to the door. "Come on."

Giving Pierce one more glance, she angled her body at the door and let him guide her out. She stayed completely silent as he led her down the hall of offices, through the glassed-in entryway, and along the walkway connecting the main building to the rooming house where he stayed when he was on duty.

Heidi was standing outside his door when they got there, holding up a brand-new badge. "Figured you might need this."

He snagged it and used it on the door, planning to go straight in, but Heidi stepped in his path. Or more accurately, Courtney's.

"Pierce wasn't an ass to you, was he?" Her hands went to her hips as she studied Courtney. "Fuck. It looks like he was an ass to you." Her lips twisted into a scowl. "I swear to God—"

Courtney shook her head a little. "He wasn't really an ass."

Heidi tipped her head, lifting a brow. "Are you sure?"

Courtney gave her a small smile, nodding. "I'm sure. He just welcomed me back to Fairbanks."

Heidi's eyes narrowed in suspicion, but she didn't argue. "Huh." Her eyes came Reed's way, moving over his face before going back to Courtney. "Are you going to be staying in Fairbanks?"

Courtney's already weak smile faltered a little more. "I'm not really sure yet. A lot is still up in the air."

The fact that she didn't immediately say she was staying in Fairbanks grated on him. Not because she couldn't do as she pleased, but what she pleased should be staying in fucking Fairbanks. She knew people here. Could have a support system. Could have people looking out for her.

"Fair enough." Heidi stepped closer, resting her hands on Courtney's shoulders. "Whatever you decide to do, I will help you with whatever you need." She leaned in, speaking in Courtney's ear low enough he couldn't hear what she said. Then she leaned back, gave her the same kind of wink Mona had, then turned and grabbed his cheek in a stinging pinch before disappearing down the hall.

"Looks like you're making friends already." Reed held the door wide as Courtney stared at Heidi's retreating form.

He waited for her to go in. She was exhausted. Worn down from both the road trip and everything that preceded it. She needed a shower. She needed to be fed. She needed sleep.

But Courtney didn't budge. She stood there, almost transfixed as she watched Heidi leave.

"Come on, Princess. Time to go get comfortable."

Courtney's eyes finally came his way. "Do you really think so?"

Her confusion didn't quite make sense. "Do I think you need to rest? Fuck yes, you need to rest."

Courtney's head barely shook. "No. Not that." She turned to glance back down the hallway. "You think she really might want to be my friend?"

The hope in her voice made his chest tight. And pissed him off yet again over the way she'd been treated.

"The two of you are a lot alike. So, yeah, I'm pretty sure you're going to end up best friends." He didn't tell her he was also suspicious Mona would soon be her friend too. And Harlow. And Eva. And Bess. And all the other women who had infiltrated Alaskan Security over the past few years. Every single one of them was a pain in the ass in their own way. They would understand her. Give her the grace he hadn't for too fucking long.

Courtney turned to face him, a hesitant smile on her face. "I guess we'll see."

She didn't want to get her hopes up, and he couldn't blame her. She'd been used her whole life by people claiming to be her friends. Unloved and unwanted by her parents. It would make sense she didn't have high hopes. It was why he backed off after their overly intense night where things got a little out of hand. Figuratively, and literally. Courtney would easily believe she was being used, because that was how it had always been. And the fucked-up thing was, she probably wouldn't even mind. She'd dished out money, gifts, and favors in exchange for companionship her whole life. It was all she knew.

He didn't want her to believe that's what was happening with him. She needed to see that this thing between them wasn't transactional.

Easier said than done. It was a constant fight to keep his

hands off her. To keep his mouth away from her skin. To resist the constant urge to give her exactly what she'd asked for so many times.

But that was how Courtney believed things worked. She offered something, be it money or her body, so she could get what she wanted in return—a connection. Even if it wasn't real.

And even though he hadn't openly admitted it, it was clear what they had was real. It wasn't pretty and it wasn't sweet, but it was honest.

Reed tipped his head into the room. "Come on. Get moving."

Courtney took one final look down the hall before doing as he said, entering the first-floor room he'd put half his shit in when he first came to Alaskan Security.

He let the door swing closed behind them, resting one hand on her back to urge her toward the bathroom since it seemed like she needed a little help to keep her feet moving. "Bathroom's in here." He flipped on the light, nudging her onto the tile floor before reaching in to start the shower. "Your stuff should be here soon, but I'll get you a T-shirt and some sweatpants to wear until then."

He turned away—going to the closet to collect both items —returning moments later to find her standing exactly where he'd left her. He wasn't quite sure how Courtney would react to being back in Alaska, but he didn't expect her to look so shellshocked. If anything, he'd prepared himself for her to be mouthy and confrontational and aggressive.

But the woman standing before him looked lost.

He closed the door, setting the clothes on the sink before stepping close. "Arms up."

She lifted her hands toward the ceiling, eyes on his face as he peeled her sweatshirt up and off. He moved to her knit pants, working them down to her ankles before slipping off her shoes and socks, followed by the pants. When he stood up, her eyes met his.

He wrapped his arms around her, fingers going under the elastic edge of the back of her sports bra. "What?"

"Why didn't you let Pierce yell at me?"

It was a good question. One that would be easy to blow off —to pretend was nothing—but they both obviously knew it was important. "Because you don't deserve to be yelled at." He lifted his chin. "Arms up again."

Again Courtney's hands lifted to the ceiling. "Yes I did. I was awful when I was here before. I wasted everyone's time. Alaskan Security's resources. Money."

Reed carefully worked the fitted garment past her full tits before skimming it up her arms, doing his best to ignore the way her dark nipples puckered when the cool air hit them. "I don't give a fuck if you wasted a million dollars and a year's worth of man hours." He took a steeling breath before hooking his fingers into the waistband of her panties. "You just wanted somebody to give a shit about your existence and the only way you could make that happen was to pay for it."

There was no way to temper his tone. No way to keep from sounding as pissed off as he was. It was bullshit. Bullshit that she'd been left to fend for herself for so long, the only real way to get anyone at her side was with money. No wonder she was so needy. So desperate.

He skimmed her panties down to the floor, pushing back to his feet without setting his eyes on what he'd revealed. "In the shower."

Courtney's feet didn't move, even though she was starting to shiver. "You didn't have to do that."

"Yes I did." There was no way in hell he would let her believe he was one more person who didn't have her back. Not just because she'd had his on more than one occasion. But because even if she hadn't dragged his unconscious ass through a swamp, or broken a bench so she'd have something to help fight with, Courtney deserved to have someone stand up for her. Someone to cut the shit and make sure she was treated right.

Someone to protect her from a world that had unleashed nothing but shit on her head.

He rested his hands on her shoulders, urging her back, holding her steady as she stepped into the walk-in basin. He tried to step away, but her hand jumped to his chest, fisting into the fabric of his shirt. "Don't go."

He brought one hand to hers, ready to loosen her grip. "I'm not leaving. I'll be right outside the door."

Courtney shook her head, fingers gripping tighter. "I need you to stay."

He searched her face, looking for some explanation of why she was acting the way she was. He'd been at her side since they got out of the RV, but maybe he missed something. "Did somebody say something to you?" His hand clenched into a fist at the possibility. If anyone had upset her he would—

Courtney shook her head. "Nobody said anything." Her eyes moved over his face. "This is about what *you* said. What you *did*." Her fist relaxed, but one finger reached out to jab him in the center of the chest. "You're the problem."

His chin tucked in surprise. "I'm the problem?"

Courtney's chin lifted as water cascaded over her skin. "Yes. You're the fucking problem. You were just an asshole to your boss for me." She flung her hands out, slinging water droplets through the open glass door, hitting him and the wall beside him. "You need this job. You have to take care of your parents. You can't go around being a dick to Pierce. You should have just let him yell at me."

Reed almost smiled. There was the woman he knew. The woman he was already too fucking attached to. Her sudden outburst brought them back to more familiar territory. Unfortunately, it was also more combustible territory.

"Fuck. That." He enunciated each word, so she knew exactly where he stood on this. "I don't give a shit about Pierce."

He stopped short of finishing the thought. But it was clear from her expression that Courtney knew exactly what he wasn't saying.

That he didn't give a shit about Pierce, but he *did* give a shit about her.

Her hand came back to the front of his shirt, grabbing hard and yanking him into the shower. Their bodies collided, her arm looping around his neck as his mouth hit hers, lips bumping, her back hitting the tile wall as water soaked his clothes.

She grabbed at his shirt, fighting the waterlogged fabric as she shoved it up his chest, wrestling it over his head before letting it drop to the basin with a heavy slap. "We're back in Alaska now, so you need to fuck me."

CHAPTER TWENTY-THREE

COURTNEY

SHE'D BEEN DESPERATE for many things in her life. Attention. Affection. Connection.

But this was different.

It was different because she had attention. She had affection. She had connection. Reed offered all of them.

But instead of being satisfied, thrilled that she finally had so much of what she always wanted, it made her greedy. Made her want more. More of this thing she couldn't have even imagined. Especially not with him.

But she wasn't the only one who seemed to want more.

Reed came easily when she pulled him in. His hands hit her with just as much need as her own. And, since there were no clothes in his way, the heat of his palms immediately went to areas that distracted her from the task she'd started.

His mouth was hot and hungry as it found hers, fingers plucking at her already tight nipples as he spoke against her lips. "You make me fucking lose my mind, Princess."

"Good." She clung to his shoulders as he rolled the puckered point, sending a jolt of sensation to her already aching pussy. "I like you best when you're a little out of control."

Now that she considered it, she always had. It was why she pushed him. Said all the things she knew would piss him off and irritate him to the point he bit back. Because he'd never treated her like everyone else. He'd never fed her what she wanted to hear, hoping she would do something for him. He always told her exactly what he thought of her. Even if it wasn't good. She always knew where she stood with him.

That's why when this thing between them started to change she believed it. Because Reed had never fed her shit and he wouldn't start now. Especially since she had nothing to give him.

His hand curved around the weight of her tits, smoothing across her water-soaked skin before sliding up over her collarbone to cup her face as the weight of his body pinned her to the shower wall. "That's good. Because you seem to bring out the worst in me."

The weight of him pressing into her was indescribable. Made it difficult to keep her train of thought. "That's a matter of opinion. I think I bring out the best in you."

Reed's lips curved against hers as the warmth of his laugh fanned across her skin. "You would." He skimmed his hands across her shoulders and down her back, sliding south to curve against her ass as he pulled her tight against him, grinding the hard line of his cock against her lower belly. Reminding her he was still dressed from the waist down and all of it was now drenched.

She grabbed at the waistband of his jeans, fighting the wet fabric as she flipped the button and unzipped the fly. Getting them down was next to impossible, and she let out a frustrated grunt as the fabric refused to give way.

"You make everything so goddamned difficult." He snagged her hands away, shoving at his pants aggressively, forcing them down his hips and thick thighs before fighting off his boots. He slapped at the faucet, shutting off the water. "Impatient as hell. Can't even wait five minutes."

Courtney smiled at his grumbling. "I think you might be the only man in the world to complain that a woman is so desperate to have his cock inside her that she can't wait any longer."

Reed's dark eyes came to her as he kicked away the remainder of his clothes, leaving the draining mass on the shower floor. One hand braced on the wall next to her head and the other went to the jutting length of his dick, fisting it tight in a smooth stroke. "Is that what's wrong, Princess? Is that why you're always so fucking difficult?" Another firm stroke. "You need me to fuck some patience into you?"

She expected Reed to be intense. Knew he would be focused. Hoped he would be as driven to perfection in situations like this as he was in everything else. What she didn't expect was that fucking mouth.

And that fucking mouth might be the death of her.

"You didn't answer me." Reed's tone was sharp. Commanding.

Courtney couldn't look away from where he continued stroking his cock. "I forgot the question."

She did *not* forget the question, she just wanted to hear it again.

Reed's nostrils flared as he cornered her in the rapidly cooling stall. "I asked if you needed me to fuck some patience into you."

Holy shit. It sounded just as hot the second time.

She nodded. "You might have to do it twice to get it all in there."

"Only twice?" Reed's dark gaze pinned her in place. "I've known you for a while, Princess. I think it's gonna take a hell of a lot more than twice."

She was struggling to breathe at the closeness of his body. The impending fucking she was about to be on the receiving end of. "*Oh no*." Her sarcasm was clear, but breathless. "That sounds awful." She pressed her lips together, eyes dropping to where his hand still gripped his length. "How will I ever survive?"

When her eyes lifted back to Reed's face she was met by a smug smirk. Like he knew just how much she was looking forward to this. He jerked his chin toward the door. "Go."

Courtney scoffed. "Where am I going?" She thought they were doing it right there. That it was finally going to happen.

Reed's big shoulders lifted in a little shrug. "I guess as far as you can get before I catch you, because when I do—"

She didn't give him a chance to finish. Rushing out of the shower, Courtney snagged a towel as her feet hit the rug on the other side, whipping it from the bar before yanking open the door and rushing out, fully planning to launch herself into the center of the bed so Reed could properly pound her into the mattress.

And possibly next week.

But Reed was fast as hell. He had her before she was three steps into the room. Strong arms wrapped around her body, one bracing across her chest between her tits, hand clamping on her shoulder, the other over one hip, wide palm cupping between her thighs. His front slammed into her back, the collision sending them a few feet forward before landing her face down on the mattress, legs hanging over the edge. His hard cock pressed against the crack of her ass, sliding along her cheeks as he ground against her. "I thought you would make it farther, Princess."

"Really?" She moaned as his fingers started to work her clit. "Because I kinda considered not running at all."

Reed chuckled, low and deep in her ear. "What would be the fun in that?"

She fisted the comforter, gripping tight as he thrust against her ass again. "It probably would've pissed you off. And you are really fun when you're pissed off."

"Am I?" He nipped at the shell of her ear. "Does that mean all those times you pissed me off you were just trying to get me to fuck you?"

Why was he still talking? Asking questions he knew damn well she was going to struggle to answer. "That sounds like me."

"It definitely does." He reached for the nightstand, stretching to get his hand on the pull before yanking the whole fucking thing out and letting it drop to the floor. "I'll remember that the next time you're a pain in my ass." He snagged a condom from the pile of what probably used to be orderly paperwork and chargers. "I can't imagine I'll have to remember for long."

Courtney twisted her head so she could glare at him. "Ass."

Reed's mouth lifted in a smile. "Brat."

Her heart skipped a beat at how easy this was. How real. "Maybe. But I'm your brat."

Reed's eyes held hers. "Does that mean I'm your ass?"

She pushed her lower lip out as she considered. "It doesn't quite have the same ring, does it?" Her breath caught as he slid against her again. "I guess I'll have to think about it then. Decide whether or not I want you."

Reed's gaze narrowed. "Like hell, you will." The head of his cock pressed against her, lining into place before he buried the thick length to the hilt in one swift move that stole her breath and sent her eyes rolling back in her head.

"Oh." All the air rushed out of her lungs at the sensation of being filled to capacity. It had been a while since she'd done this, and the stretch was a little surprising.

But then Reed's hand was back on her pussy, skilled fingers working her clit as he started to move, fucking and fingering her relentlessly with a single-minded focus that had her head spinning almost immediately. They'd danced around this moment for so long, edged each other in just about every way possible, and it was almost a relief that it was over. That they'd finally reached this point and could now move forward.

Whatever that meant.

Reed leaned into her hair, his voice rough. "Talk to me, Princess. You're being too quiet."

She grunted as he stroked into her again, the pressure exactly what she wanted but almost too much at the same time. "I can't talk. I'm pretty sure my mouth is full from how deep you're going."

Reed paused, but didn't stop completely. His body shifted, the drive of his hips turning shallower. "Is this better?" He was barely teasing her now, offering nothing but the tip. "I thought you wanted to be pounded into the mattress."

She tried to push back against him, hoping to reclaim a little of what he'd stolen. But Reed's hand gripped her hips, pinning her in place. "Careful. You might hurt yourself."

She growled in frustration, aggravated by the tiny, barely penetrating movements he was offering. "You're an ass."

"We've established that. We've also established that I'm

your ass, so it seems like you need to start talking so I know exactly how you prefer to be fucked."

Courtney tried to push back against him again. And again, Reed held her in place.

"You said you didn't want all of me. I don't want to give you more than you want." He nipped at her shoulder before sucking hard at her skin. The pinch of pressure was enough there would be a mark later, and knowing there would be proof of this moment had her pushing back again. Seeking all he had to offer.

Suddenly Reed's palm connected with her ass. It wasn't overly hard, but the jolt was surprising and made her yelp. "I know we've got a dynamic that works for us, but that dynamic won't be as useful when we're fucking." His hand soothed across the spot he'd just slapped. "You might be joking, but I'm not taking that risk. Understood?"

She managed a nod as her pussy clenched around the hard length of him, trying to hold onto as much of him as possible. "Understood."

Reed's palm slid up to press into the small of her back. "So let's try this again." He carefully pulled out before slowly rocking back in, finally giving her all he had. "Tell me how you want to be fucked."

Her eyes slid closed at the thorough way he was moving into her. "Often."

Reed made a deep sound of approval. "That's a good start." His palm slid up her spine, pressing down when it came to rest between her shoulder blades. "What else?"

What she wanted was easier to confess than she expected. "I wouldn't be mad if someday you wanted to hold me down while you fucked me." She swallowed hard before adding on the rest. "Like you want to be sure I won't get away."

It sounded kind of fucked up, and in the wrong situation probably would be. But the thought of a man, of Reed, needing her so badly he held onto her like his life depended on it, sent a flood of heat pooling in her insides and her pussy clamping tight.

Reed groaned as she clenched around him, the palm at her back pressing hard, pinning her to the mattress. "What else?"

"Deep." Her eyes closed as he thrust hard, hips bouncing off her ass. "I want to feel it even when we're done." She wanted to carry a reminder of him. Of what they'd done. Of what they were.

Needed it like air.

She wanted to ache from how well he took her. Wanted to remember it every time she sat down.

Reed's arm snaked under her belly, hefting her up from the mattress. She squealed in surprise, completely caught off guard. "What are you doing? Things were just getting good."

Reed crawled onto the mattress, depositing her in the center before shoving her head down to the blankets so she was face down, ass up.

"I figured you wouldn't mind if it got a little better." His fingers tangled in her long hair, twisting tight as the other gripped her shoulder, making it impossible to move. "Hold on tight, Princess."

She grabbed the blankets, fisting her fingers into the fabric as he started to move. Each stroke was brutal. Unforgiving. Hard and fast. The hand on her shoulder ensured there was no escaping each stab of his body into hers.

It was fucking perfect. Had her struggling to breathe in seconds, body winding tight as he filled her to the limit over and over and over again.

When his hand shifted from her hair to slide under her

belly, fingers expertly finding her clit, she was gone, bucking against him as unintelligible words poured through her lips.

She'd just started to come when his hand clamped tighter on her shoulder and lifted her up from the bed, bringing her back to his front, his strong arm bracing across her collarbone as he continued driving into her. "Is this what you want, Princess? You want me to fuck you like you're mine? Like I want to make sure no one else will ever be good enough to touch you?"

She continued babbling, unable to form anything coherent. Mostly spitting out rambling words like *yes* and *don't stop* and some version of his name, but it seemed to appease him.

Reed's lips moved against her ear, his voice a deep growl. "Because that's what you are. You're fucking *mine*."

Her body clenched again. Was it possible to come while you were coming? Because that's what it felt like was happening as he continued fucking the hell out of her and strumming her clit, pinning her body to his as he took everything she was more than willing to give.

His breathing was ragged, voice raspy as his movements became sharper. More erratic. "I want to fuck you with nothing between us, Princess. I want to fill your pretty pussy until it can't hold anymore." He grunted against her skin. "And then I'm going to fill that pretty little mouth you keep promising me."

He drove deep into her, the grip at her shoulders and pussy keeping her body to his as he groaned into her hair. The size of him swelling as he jerked inside her dragged her to what felt like yet another climax on a climax.

It was too much. More than she could handle. And it sent her slumping back against him, unable to hold herself upright as her body continued to spasm.

Reed carefully eased his body from hers, the loss of him surprisingly distressing, but she didn't have enough energy or focus to complain. His touch gentled as he laid her on the mattress, peeling the covers down, working them under her body. He carefully tucked the blankets around her as she slowly blinked, suddenly hit by all the exhaustion that had been chasing her for over a week.

He leaned down to press a kiss to her forehead. "You sleep. I'm gonna go talk to Pierce. And when you wake up, we can see if your definition of often is the same as mine."

CHAPTER TWENTY-FOUR

REED

PIERCE OPENED THE door of his apartment, balancing his daughter on one hip as he studied Reed with a wary gaze. "Should I take her to Mona?"

"As long as you don't plan on crossing the line when it comes to Courtney, we won't have any issues." He didn't expect Pierce to welcome her with open arms, but he wouldn't tolerate anyone, including Pierce, treating her like shit after all she'd been through.

Pierce studied him a second longer. "I take it your trip went well then?"

"I'm not sure I would say it went well, but it changed some things." Reed shook his head, ready to end this conversation before Pierce could dig any deeper. "But that's not what I'm here to talk about. You said I needed to be briefed, so that's what I'm here for."

Pierce probably intended for him to wait until tomorrow, but that wasn't the way he handled things. He liked to know what was going on and prepare. Work everything out in his mind so he was ready for what came at him. That meant Pierce was going to have to deal with him tonight.

"Fair enough." The owner of Alaskan Security stepped back, making room for him to pass. "Come in."

The space Pierce and his family shared was nice as hell. Filled with a kind of luxury he'd never chased. It was a place he'd been plenty of times, but the way it felt inside had changed since Mona moved in. It was always a comfortable place to be, but it felt more like an extension of Pierce's office before. Now there were little touches of Mona and their daughter around that made it feel like a home. Maybe not the same kind of home he grew up in, but a family space nonetheless.

Pierce motioned to a chair situated across from the sofa. "Sit down. Would you care for something to drink?"

Reed lifted one hand, waving off the offer as he sat. "I'm fine."

He shifted in his seat, suddenly feeling uncomfortable. Working at Alaskan Security had never been his favorite thing. It was simply a means to an end. Something he did to ensure his father could live the best life possible.

And while he still wasn't completely on board with everything Alaskan Security did, the perception he had of his own position there had changed a little. Things no longer seemed so black-and-white. So clear-cut. Being around Courtney showed him there were shades of gray he'd never accounted for. Never considered.

He waited as Pierce situated himself on the sofa, carefully laying his daughter belly-down on a blanket spread across the floor. The baby immediately popped her head up like a turtle and started grabbing at the assortment of objects stitched to the mat beneath her.

Kids were another thing he hadn't considered. They suddenly seemed to be everywhere, but not once had he wondered what it might be like to have one of his own. So focused on taking care of his father, he hadn't given a single thought to the possibility of becoming one.

Pierce got the baby settled then glanced his way. "Zeke said he ran into you as you came in. How much was he able to fill you in on?"

"Not much. Just that some things had happened while I was gone and that someone blew up one of our cabins." Reed continued watching the baby, transfixed by the intense way she worked the flaps and rings. "I told him once I was settled I would go to the location and see what I could find."

He was more familiar with the area than most. Many of his teammates had more experience in some of the more dangerous parts of their job, but he carried the most skill in tracking. He knew the area like the back of his hand courtesy of years spent hunting with his father. He knew the best routes to take on foot and the areas to avoid, making it possible for him to determine where others had likely gone.

Pierce nodded. "That is an excellent idea." He paused, eyes holding Reed's. "But I'm sure you would like to pay your parents a visit first."

Reed narrowed his gaze. "What do you mean by that?" He worked hard to keep his private life just that. Private. While he was happy to spend time with his teammates, none of them had ever met his family. Not just because he didn't want people looking at his father with pity, but also because he didn't want his parents to discover what he'd given up to help them. That he sacrificed his own ethics to ensure his father's well-being.

But, like so much else, he wasn't as convinced that was exactly the case. Not anymore.

"You know I do thorough background checks on everyone I employ, Reed. Did you honestly believe I wasn't aware of your father's situation?" Pierce leaned back, continuing to keep one eye on the little girl at his feet. "Why did you think you were the first one I approached about the trip to Florida? I knew you were the one who would benefit the most from the extra income."

Reed huffed out a disbelieving laugh, a little surprised at his own blind spot. "I assumed it was because I'm the only one who's unattached." He shook his head, dropping his eyes to his lap. "You know this is none of your business, right?"

"I do. That's why I haven't brought it up until now. But it seems relevant to this situation." Pierce paused, waiting until Reed looked his way. "You know I will help in any way I can. If your father's medical needs ever become too much, there's always space for your parents here."

Reed worked his jaw from side to side, trying to ease the tension beginning to collect there. Deep down, he'd always resented Pierce. Hated him for presenting an opportunity that forced him to make a decision he struggled with every day. But, like his aggravation with Courtney, maybe he was once again being unfair. Putting his own guilt where it didn't belong.

Because at the end of the day, he was the one who chose to come work for Alaskan Security. He was the one who walked away from the law enforcement career he'd always wanted. He was the one who decided caring for his father was worth any price.

Except he hadn't acted like that was true.

Reed tipped his head. "I'll keep that in mind." He tapped

one finger against the arm of the chair before adding on, "Thank you for the offer." It was a blanket statement, even if Pierce didn't know it.

"Of course." Pierce's eyes dipped to his daughter. "Family is the most important thing."

"It is." Even as he agreed, his stomach clenched.

Courtney didn't have a family. Never had. She'd always been alone, her only companions bought and paid for in some way or another.

"If you're sure I'm not needed immediately at the cabin site, I think I'll take tomorrow morning to check in on my parents." He wanted to see them. Make sure they had everything they needed. That his father was doing as well as he claimed on the phone.

But his visit had a bigger purpose. One that didn't feel as rushed as it should.

"Of course. I spoke with Zeke and he has a few leads, so hopefully he's able to determine what exactly happened." Pierce's posture stiffened the tiniest bit. "Quite a bit has happened while you've been gone."

Reed forced his attention to the reason for the visit. Staying focused was always critical, and suddenly felt even more important than it had before. "What's going on?"

Pierce took a deep breath before blowing it back out. "It would appear someone is fucking with us." His words were tight and clipped. "A number of our safehouses have been identified and accessed at some point or another, whether it's cameras being disabled or perimeters being breached. A few have had the power cut. At another, the gas line was disabled."

It was such an odd form of attack and served no purpose outside of making things difficult. "Was anyone in them?"

Pierce shook his head. "We aren't currently harboring

anyone, thankfully." He scrubbed one hand down his face, and for the first time, Reed noticed how tired Pierce looked. "And then there's the sudden reappearance of Eloise's vehicle and the Jeep Nate was driving the night they were stranded."

Reed's brows lifted. "Sudden reappearance? Where?"

"One was delivered practically to the front gate, parked just outside of any camera's reach, so there was no way to determine who left it." Pierce ran his tongue across his teeth before sucking it free. "The other was parked in the garage at Eloise's old apartment. It was found when the complex manager did their final walk-through after she officially moved out."

"It was *inside* the garage?" His brain started running through the list of things that would've had to be done to accomplish that. "Let me guess. Nothing was caught on camera."

Pierce pointed his direction. "Correct."

Reed was speechless. More than a little confused by the odd collection of occurrences.

But there was one significant thing that connected them. Something that could help narrow down the possible culprits. "Who would have the access required to know about camera range?" That seemed to be the biggest limiting factor. One that should help them home in on possible places to investigate.

Pierce's lips flattened to a thin line. "That was the initial direction Intel took as well. But honestly, anyone able to employ someone as skilled as Heidi or Harlow would be able to accomplish it."

They'd dealt with situations like this in the past. Gone up against organizations attempting to limit Alaskan Security's ability to interfere with their own, frequently illegal, plans.

But all the main players in that were dead, so this had to be someone new.

"What does Vincent think?" He'd been key in helping them the last time this happened, but their relationship with the head of GHOST was currently strained, each party believing they benefited the other more.

Pierce pursed his lips. "It would seem Vincent has decided to limit his assistance after I refused to concede during our last interaction." Pierce worked his jaw from side to side. "So we're on our own."

"That's fucking great." Reed raked one hand through his hair. "I guess now is as good a time as any to put our money where our mouth is and prove we don't need him as much as he thinks we do."

Vincent and Pierce had been struggling to come to an agreement on how to move their partnership forward for months. Each one unwilling to concede or admit the other might have more value. But for the first time, Pierce looked uncertain if what he claimed was true. "Let's hope that's what happens."

Mona came into the room, smiling bright at where her daughter played on the floor. "Everything okay in here?"

Pierce cocked a brow at her. "I run the largest security company in the world, Love. I'm quite sure I can handle entertaining our daughter while you take a shower."

Mona leaned over him, giving him a quick kiss. "Of course you can." She turned to Reed. "How's Courtney?"

The shift in the conversation made him relax a little. Helped ease the tension building across his shoulders. "She's sleeping. I think our trip took a lot out of her."

Mona's eyes widened. "I can imagine. I can't believe how quickly you two got here."

He'd set a punishing pace because he wanted Courtney somewhere she would be safe. Unfortunately it seemed like maybe he'd simply traded one danger for another, which brought his next, and unexpected, question. "When will there be another townhome available?"

Mona's brows lifted in surprise.

She wasn't the only one a little shocked by his question. He'd never had any interest in living at the complex. But staying in the rooming house when he worked, and crashing in his childhood bedroom when he was off, no longer seemed like a viable option.

Plus, it would be nice to know Courtney was safe *and* taken care of while he was gone.

"Now. They're finishing up another unit, and so far no one has claimed it." Pierce also seemed a little more relaxed at their change of conversation. "It's yours if you want it."

"I'll let you know." Reed gave them a quick nod as he stood from the chair. "I should get back. It'll probably take her a while to get acclimated and I don't want her to feel alone."

Mona stepped his way. "I don't think you have to worry about that." She held up one finger. "Hang on. I have some things for you to take with you." She disappeared into the kitchen and came back less than a minute later with a stack of containers. "I know you're currently in one of the first-floor rooms, so I didn't want to give you anything that had to be refrigerated." She passed off the containers. "It's mostly cookies, but I figured I couldn't go wrong with those."

Reed stared down at her offering. "Thank you."

"You don't have to thank me. Courtney's had a hell of a week. I know chocolate won't fix that, but hopefully it will make it a little bit better."

He doubted the chocolate was what would make it better,

but Mona's gift would certainly make a difference. "I'm sure it will help."

He started to step away, but Mona followed him, blocking his path. "Make sure you let Courtney know we're here to help with whatever she needs."

His eyes shifted to Pierce, who nodded. "She's welcome to stay here as long as she likes."

Mona gave him a bright smile before facing Reed. "And we will do whatever it takes to help her get settled here. Heidi is already..." Mona tipped her head from side to side, "setting her up with some things she might need. She'll probably have everything ready in the next day or two."

The ease at which Mona and Heidi—and probably the rest of Intel—were accepting Courtney made him feel like an ass over all the shit he'd given her. "I'm sure she'll really appreciate it."

He said his goodbyes before heading out into the hall and back down to the first floor. He let himself into the room and stopped short when he saw Courtney sitting in the middle of the bed, knees pulled up to her chest, eyes wide.

"Where did you go?" Her voice was small. Quiet.

He moved toward the bed. "I had to talk to Pierce, remember?"

Courtney seemed to relax a little. "I guess I forgot." Her voice steadied. "I woke up and you weren't here and I freaked out a little."

Reed sat down beside her, setting the containers of cookies onto the mattress before pulling her close. "Mona sent you some cookies."

Courtney curled up against him, holding tight to his shirt. "That was really nice of her." She was quiet for a minute. "I don't know why I got so scared. I just—"

He slid one hand down the length of her dark hair. "I didn't think about that when I left. I should've stayed." They hadn't been apart for over a week, and she'd nearly been killed before that. It would only make sense that she'd panic a little at being alone.

It made sense, but it presented a problem.

He couldn't stay with her around the clock. He'd been hired to do a job, and Alaskan Security needed him now— maybe even more than ever. He was going to have to find a solution.

Courtney eased up, working her way to a sitting position. "It's not your fault. I just need to suck it up." She rolled her head from side to side, stretching her neck. "It's not like anybody knows I'm here. I'm just overreacting. I know I'm safe now."

He hated that it might not be completely true. That she might still be in danger.

And that this time it would be his fault.

That wasn't acceptable. No way would he be the reason Fairbanks would end up being just like Miami for her. She was going to have to stay somewhere she would be watched. Somewhere he could always have eyes on her in some way. That meant she'd have to stay on campus.

There was one other option. And her reaction to it could go either way. She might immediately be on board.

Or she might end up deciding it was better to stay locked in the rooming house.

He reached up to smooth back her hair as she bit into a thick cookie. "What would you think about going to meet my parents tomorrow?"

CHAPTER TWENTY-FIVE

COURTNEY

"I FEEL A little throw-upy."

Reed looked her over from where he stood in the open passenger's door of the Jeep they'd taken from Alaskan Security's garage. "Do it out here then. If my mom thinks you're sick, she's gonna throw you in a bed and force-feed you miyeok-guk until you swear you're better."

He said it like it was a threat, but the possibility actually sounded nice. Sure, she'd had nannies who took care of her when she was sick as a child but, like everything else, it had been compensated attention. Another funded and fraudulent interaction in a long line of them.

But barfing on Reed's parents' driveway still didn't seem like a great way to start this whole thing off. So she took a deep breath in through her nose before blowing it out, shivering a little as the frigid air cooled her throat and lungs. "I think I'm okay."

Reed lifted his brows. "Are you sure?"

She started to nod, but the front door of the small house they were parked in front of flew open. A tiny woman with graying hair stood in the opening, hands on her hips. "Are you coming, or not?"

Courtney plastered on a smile. But not because she was bothered by Reed's mother's clipped tone. If anything, it made her relax a little. It was familiar. Reminded her of the man watching her with a sharp gaze.

Her concern was that, while she was already unexplainably attached to the woman who raised one of the best people she'd ever met, Reed's mother might not like her back. She might find her just as lacking as everyone else always had. And there was no way she could bribe her to think any differently. It was a vulnerable and unfamiliar position for her— relying on her attributes instead of her bank account to convince people to let her hang around. Especially considering her attributes had been severely lacking for most of her life.

Courtney gave his mother a little wave before standing, bumping Reed out of the way so she could close the door. She started to reach for him, but wasn't sure exactly what he planned to tell his parents about them, so she tried to play the move off by adjusting the scarf wrapped around her neck. It was awkward and only made her feel more out of sorts. This was uncharted territory for her and she didn't know which way was up.

Considering the way most of her relationships had gone up to this point, it wasn't surprising she'd never actually met anyone's parents before. She'd kill for just a little experience to work with, because this whole thing was intimidating as hell. All the ways things could go wrong twisted around in her stomach, threatening to send the coffee and Danish she'd had for breakfast splattering onto the snow.

His mother waved one hand, hurrying them along. "Come

on. Come on. The house will be just as cold as the outside by the time you two get in here."

When Courtney tried to pick up the pace, her boot hit a slippery spot and she started to skid. Reed immediately grabbed her, steadying her with a strong grip that stayed as they finished their trek to the small front porch.

His mother's eyes flicked to where he held her before coming back to move between them, her gaze shrewd and assessing.

Reed helped her through the door, using his grip to keep her on the small rug just inside. He motioned to a line of shoes against the wall as his mother closed the door behind them. "Your shoes go there." He was already working on taking his own boots off. "Then you put on your inside shoes."

Courtney blinked, her stomach dropping as she leaned into his ear. "I didn't bring inside shoes."

His mother was suddenly right in front of them, shoving a pair of slippers her way. "These are for you. You will wear them in the house."

Courtney took the embroidered house shoes, a little surprised at how perfect they were. The main portion was pale pink and a set of roses tucked into greenery bloomed across the toe of each. "Thank you. They're beautiful."

Reed's mother nodded. "Reed said you like pink."

Her throat went tight. Not only because Reed told his mother at least enough about things to share her favorite color, but also because his mother went out of her way to choose something she would like.

Courtney ran one finger along the soft side of the slipper, swallowing hard as emotion tried to clog her throat. "He's right. I love pink. It's my favorite color."

Instead of responding, his mother looked her over again

before turning away and walking through the small living room they were standing in. "Come. It's time to eat."

After quickly slipping on her new house shoes, Courtney followed behind, ready to do her best to make friends with the woman in front of her. She wanted to make a good impression. Wanted to be liked and accepted by her. And not just because she was Reed's mom.

The house smelled amazing, and her stomach, which was threatening to revolt just a few minutes ago, was interested in what she would find in the kitchen. The house was small, making the trip from the living room to the kitchen short, but it was so sweet. Pictures of little Reed hung on the walls, following his progression from birth through high school and even into the Academy. None of the furniture matched, but everything looked comfortable and cozy and inviting. The ceilings of the home were much lower than she was used to, but that only added to the feeling of being cocooned in warmth and comfort.

It was a home. A place where a real family lived. And she wanted to soak up as much of it as she could.

Reed followed close behind her, his hand coming to rest on her lower back. As they stepped into the small but well-laid-out kitchen, his mother's eyes once again went to the spot where he touched her before moving from Reed's face to hers. She narrowed her eyes, standing a little straighter as she swung one hand in a beckoning motion. "Come here, Courtney. You can help with lunch."

Courtney hurried to his mother's side, her eagerness for any attention Reed's mom was willing to give her overshadowing the intimidation she felt in the woman's presence. She'd never had this. Never had any sort of motherly figure encourage her in any way and, even as a grown woman, she was still hungry for that kind of relationship.

His mother motioned to the sink. "Wash your hands first."

Courtney went right to the faucet, scrubbing down before drying off and turning back to face the tiny Korean woman who clearly had a huge amount of personality. "What can I do?"

She could swear his mother appeared surprised, but the almost imperceptible lift of her brows was gone in a flash. "You need to cook the carrots for bibimbap." She pointed to a pile of shredded carrots sitting beside a large bowl-shaped pan on the stove. "Do you know how?"

Chewing her lip, Courtney deflated a little. She knew the basics of cooking, but nothing extremely involved. And, while cooking carrots seemed simple enough, the tools laid out were not what she was accustomed to. "I know how to cook a little, but I've never made bibimbap before."

Reed's mother's lips pressed into an appraising line as she leaned back to peer at her. "Have you eaten bibimbap before?"

Courtney shook her head, a little embarrassed that she had to admit how unfamiliar she was with Korean cuisine. "No. I have not."

Reed's mother gave her another long look before moving to the stove. "At least you say it right." She grabbed a bottle and held it up. "You cook the carrots in just plain oil. No sesame oil." She shoved the bottle Courtney's way before turning her eyes to the pan.

Courtney tipped a small amount into the pan. The oil immediately rippled and started to smoke.

Reed's mother snagged the oil and pointed to the carrots. "Now put those in."

Scooping up the pile, Courtney dropped them in with the

oil. They were barely out of her hands before Reed's mom shoved a flat utensil that was a cross between a spoon and a spatula into her grip. "Stir."

Courtney did as she was told, moving the carrots around the pan. Reed's mother started tossing in different seasonings, adding a splash of this and a sprinkle of that. In what felt like under thirty seconds, his mother was grabbing the handle and pulling it off the heat. "Done."

Courtney blinked. "That was fast."

Reed's mother dropped the carrots into a waiting dish. "They are small pieces. They don't take long to cook." She set the empty pan on a cool burner before picking up the bowl of carrots and turning away. "Now we can eat."

She marched to the already set table in the small dining room adjacent to the kitchen, lining the bowl of carrots next to an array of other bowls. All were filled with varying items, from some sort of sprouty looking things to a green, shredded, leafy pile that almost looked like spinach. A giant pot of rice sat in the middle of the table with four place settings circled around it.

Reed rested his hand on her back again, urging her into the space before pulling out a chair. "You sit here. I'm going to go get my dad."

Courtney nodded, her stomach twisting into a knot. She knew Reed's dad had a stroke and that it greatly impacted him, but she didn't know exactly what his condition was, or exactly how to handle the situation. So she focused on his mother. Offering a smile across the table. "Thank you so much for inviting me to lunch."

His mother adjusted the dishes, moving them around. "Reed said you lived in Miami. Are you from there?"

Courtney's chin tucked in surprise. Exactly how much had

Reed told his mother about her?

"I was born there. I lived there up until recently."

Reed's mother's expression remained impassive. "You came to Alaska instead of staying in Miami?"

Courtney huffed out a little laugh. "I know it's a big change, but there's nothing for me in Miami."

In most movies, people ended up homesick when they left everything they knew behind, but that was difficult for her to imagine. Probably because Miami never felt like home. Nowhere had. Not a home like this anyway. There was no one inviting her to lunch. No one asking her to help cook. No one buying her slippers in her favorite color.

Reed's mother shrugged. "Korea is very different from here too. Much more to do. Many more people." The hard line of her mouth softened the tiniest bit. "But Alaska is not so bad." She leaned closer. "Once you get used to it."

Her eyes suddenly snapped away, zeroing in on the doorway leading to what was likely the bedrooms. Her expression softened even more as their final lunchmate made his entrance. "You are late."

"You can't blame that on me." The man sitting in the wheelchair Reed pushed in front of him was clearly where Reed got his height and bulk. He had the same long limbs and dark eyes, but his slightly slurred words carried a hint of teasing Reed's rarely did.

Reed's mother crossed her arms, but there was no hiding the warmth now lingering in her gaze. "Don't make excuses. You know when it's time to eat."

Reed's father continued giving her his slightly lopsided grin. "I know when it's time to come out and meet my son's lovely girlfriend." He spoke slowly and the words seemed difficult to form, but his tone was gentle and welcoming and reeled Courtney right in.

It was easy to smile at him as she reached out. "I'm Courtney."

Reed's father brought his hand her way, but his fingers were oddly positioned, making it impossible to give him a proper handshake. So she simply held his palm in hers, stacking her free hand on top of it. "I was just telling your wife how thankful I am that you invited me into your home."

Reed's father continued smiling, the expression crinkling up the surprisingly smooth skin around his eyes. "Of course. Our home is your home." His gaze shifted to where Reed stood beside him. "It's not every day my son brings a woman to meet us."

Reed's mother huffed out a breath. "It's no days. At this rate I will never get a grandchild." She didn't say the words loudly, but there was no missing them.

And it made her feel like both Reed's parents were more than excited she was here, regardless of how differently they showed it.

"You will have plenty of time to talk after we eat." Reed's mother stood up, snagging the bowl in front of the place setting beside Courtney and piling in rice. She set it back down before grabbing Courtney's bowl and doing the same thing. She filled the final two bowls as Reed angled his father in his mother's direction. Once all the bowls had rice, she gestured at the array of toppings. "Now you put on what you want."

Courtney looked them over, feeling a little like this might be a test. "How do you like yours?"

Once again, his mother's eyes barely widened before

quickly returning to normal. "You should try everything. Decide what you like."

Reed took his place beside her and started identifying each item. Beside the carrots she was tasked with making, there were bean sprouts, mushrooms, and cucumbers. She was surprised to discover one of the items was actually spinach—helping her feel a little better about things—but the rest were things she'd never heard of before. All of them sounded delicious, though, including the caribou serving as the meat option. There was also zucchini and green onion, along with the kimchi Reed told her would have made their first dinner on the road infinitely better. She added a little bit of everything to the top of her rice, watching as Reed added a hefty spoonful of a bright red paste to his own before stirring it all together.

Courtney leaned into his side. "What is the red paste?"

Reed lifted up the container. "Gochujang. It's fermented chili paste."

She pressed her lips together. As pretty as his bowl now looked, she didn't want to set herself on fire their first visit. "I think I'll wait and try that next time."

Reed's dad grinned at her across the table. "I'm glad you're planning a next time."

Reed's mother hushed him as she held up a small scoop from his bowl, carefully feeding it to her husband. "Eat."

Courtney went to work stirring together her own bibimbap, sneaking peeks at Reed's parents as she worked everything around her bowl. She'd seen happy couples on television and occasionally in real life, but not in a way that she felt connected to.

And she most certainly felt connected to them. It was their first time meeting, but their dynamic seemed similar to the way she and Reed were with each other, just with a little bit of role reversing. His dad seemed full of smiles and jokes while his mom was the more serious one of the pair.

But that wasn't what was stealing her attention more often than not. It was their clear affection for each other—the love they both had for the other, and the love they both had for Reed—that had her focus centered primarily on them.

They were a family.

And he'd brought her here. Offered this moment even though he'd never brought a woman to meet his parents, knowing full well the weight the visit would hold. He did it because he knew she needed it. It was the same reason he told his mother she liked pink. Because he knew his mother would ensure she had pink slippers and that it would make her feel welcomed.

And while she would've expected a moment like this to be overwhelming, it wasn't. Not at all. If anything, it was a relief. Because it was something she'd been chasing her whole life.

And he'd given it to her.

CHAPTER TWENTY-SIX

REED

"I HEARD YOUR trip with Courtney didn't go exactly the way you thought it would." Nate wiggled his brows as they worked their way around the perimeter of what remained of cabin number six.

Reed considered holding back. Continuing to keep everyone at Alaskan Security at arm's length like he always had. But that no longer felt as necessary as it once did.

"You could probably say that." He wasn't used to opening up to people. Courtney was the first person he'd told about his father's condition in forever, but sharing it somehow lightened his load. Left him feeling less isolated and alone. She'd proven it was more than the right thing to do because, as he expected, Courtney and his father were two peas in a pod and connected immediately.

She'd eagerly jumped into helping in any way she could, even volunteering to help him into the bathroom after lunch to wash his face and comb his hair. He came out of the room looking a hell of a lot different than he did when he or his mother was in charge, and grinning ear to ear.

Exactly like the woman who'd combed his hair into a mohawk.

"I think I love her." He hadn't planned the words. Hadn't even actually put a name to the way he felt about Courtney. Partly out of denial and partly out of fear. He should have known from the beginning she was exactly what he would be drawn to, if for no other reason than he faced down an example of it every day.

But admitting the way he felt about Courtney meant he would have to make room in a life that was already crowded. It meant she would take away from the time he was able to help with his father.

At least he thought it would. Then he saw the way she immediately fit in and wondered if maybe once again he was all fucking wrong.

Nate's brows lifted at his declaration. "Really?"

Reed considered, but only for a second. "Really."

She was one of the few people who didn't find his temperament completely off putting. If anything, she seemed to enjoy it. But it wasn't just Courtney's acceptance of him that led to this point.

She was fearless. Strong. Resilient. Ready and willing to fight for herself and the people she cared about. Hell, she'd even fought for him back when he drove her crazy, dragging his unconscious ass to safety.

Nate's lips pressed into a thoughtful curve. "I get it."

It was Reed's turn to be surprised. "You do?"

Nate lifted one shoulder. "Absolutely. It's always the one who pushes you the most." His head tipped to one side. "It's almost like you can't fall in love in your comfort zone."

Reed huffed out a laugh. "You're getting a little deep on me."

Nate grinned. "It gets deep fast, brother. Watch out, because it's coming for you."

Finding his match had always been the last thing he expected to happen. Honestly, it was the last thing he'd *wanted* to happen. There was never time in his life for relationships. Between work and making sure his parents were cared for, there weren't any extra hours left in his day. There wasn't any more space left in his life.

Never would he have expected someone might find their way into the cracks, sliding perfectly into the tiny little spaces that were left.

"Enough about the fact that you're now just as bad as the rest of us." Nate stopped, scanning the area around them, his breath fogging in the cold air as he squinted over the snowy landscape. "What the fuck is going on?"

Reed shook his head. "Hell if I know." They'd spent hours combing every inch of the area, looking for any sign that might clue them into who was responsible for the bizarre collection of events stacking up. "Whoever did this was familiar with the area. They took the least noticeable path. One that would still keep them from being caught on camera." He made a slow circle until he found the spot he was looking for. He lifted a hand, pointing at the tiny dip in the terrain. "My guess is that's where they shot the first camera out from." It was concealed further by a shrubby line of evergreen bushes that were even more of a blockage now that they were covered in snow. "After that they moved systematically around the property, using each new blind spot to their advantage as they took out the remaining cameras." He had to give it to them. They'd done one hell of a job and had clearly done their homework.

Which is what made it even more confusing. The kind of

homework a job like this required would involve access to camera feeds and data that were heavily protected.

Nate shook his head. "If Pierce is right, and whoever's doing this has somebody just as skilled as Heidi, we're fucked."

Reed started to agree with him, but stopped. "Are we?"

Nate barked out a disbelieving laugh as he motioned toward the pile of debris that was all that remained of the cabin they once used to hide clients. "They're blowing our shit up. They shot at me and Eloise and stole our cars. Yeah. I'd say we're fucked."

It did seem that way, but once he started thinking about it, things didn't add up. "They blew up an empty cabin. They shot at you and Eloise but didn't hit either of you." He thought it through another second. "Did you look at the cars when they bought them back?"

Nate held his hand out to one side. "Of course I looked at the cars. Why?"

Reed worked his jaw from side to side as a theory started to develop. "How close did they come to hitting either of you?"

Nate's nostrils flared, like he knew exactly what Reed was insinuating. "*They shot at a car we were both sitting in.*" He ground the words out between clenched teeth.

Reed held up one hand, hoping to calm his friend down before Nate let his own feelings get in the way of his objectivity. It was one of the reasons he was so good at what he did. He didn't have feelings when it came to their job or the events surrounding it. It made it easy for him to see things with a clear eye. "Did they come close to hitting either of you?"

Nate pursed his lips, eyes sharp. "None of the bullets that hit the car came within two feet of us." He barely paused. "But

I don't know that they even knew we were in the car. We slipped out the opposite side, so I think they believed the cars were empty."

It was possible, but not probable. "Why would they shoot at empty vehicles?"

Nate opened his mouth but quickly clamped his lips together again. His glare held a few seconds longer before his eyes finally moved away as he blew out a breath. "Fine. If they weren't actually trying to shoot us, then what were they trying to accomplish?"

Reed considered for a minute, but nothing about this made sense. "I don't fucking know." He pointed at what was left of the cabin. "What were they trying to accomplish with that?"

Nate shrugged, throwing out his hands. "I don't fucking know." He propped both hands on his hips, looking around. "They've gotta have a reason though."

He wasn't wrong. Whoever was doing this definitely had to have a reason, but it wasn't turning out to be as obvious as he'd hoped. "Pierce is going to be pissed when I don't come back with answers."

He knew Pierce was hoping he'd see something everyone else missed. That his knowledge of the Alaskan landscape and Fairbanks in general would allow him to make some miraculous discovery they'd all overlooked. It hadn't. If anything, it only raised more questions.

"He's going to be fine." Nate scrubbed one hand over his face. "We are all gonna be fine. We just need to figure out what the fuck is going on."

Before, his realistic expectations and ability to look at things from a more objective point of view might have had him arguing with Nate. But right now, he wanted to feel the same way. Needed to believe all this would work out just like it had so many times before. Because, for the first time in a long while, he was happy with the life he was living. Almost grateful for the decisions he'd been forced to make. Because if he'd stayed in Fairbanks and joined the police force, he never would've made that trip to Florida.

Would've never found a woman who was a complete pain in his ass and the brightest fucking spot in his life.

He and Nate trekked back to the Jeep they'd parked in the least conspicuous spot available, piling in before letting Harlow know they were on their way back.

As soon as they got back to campus, he traded out the Jeep they were in for another one, leaving back through the gate to go collect the woman taking up more and more space in his mind.

When he got to his parents' house, Courtney was sprawled across the couch. His mom and dad were each in their respective recliners, and all three of them were snoring away, completely oblivious to the fact that he'd come in. If they didn't have a state-of-the-art security system, he might worry about how oblivious they all were, but he'd wanted his parents to remain as untouched as possible by the life he chose. That was why, no matter what happened, he would never be able to take Pierce up on his offer. They deserved to continue living the way they wanted instead of being locked away in the rooming house.

Now, looking at how comfortable Courtney was, her face relaxed with sleep, he began to wonder if there might be another option. One he should've considered way before now.

Suddenly, Courtney's eyes popped open and in under a second she was up off the couch, grabbing for whatever she could get her hands on. When her glassy eyes focused, zeroing in on him, her shoulders slumped and she huffed out a laugh. "You just scared the shit out of me, asshole." She gently set down the decorative sculpture gripped in her hand. "I was about to try to kill you."

The fact that she was immediately ready to fight made him smile and sad at the same time. She was so ready to defend everyone she cared about, but that was because she finally had people to care about. And she was obviously prepared to take out anyone who tried to take them from her.

"I'm glad it was only almost, because my mom would have killed you if you'd broken that sculpture. It's her favorite." He turned to where his parents sat side-by-side, both sleeping heavily, his mother's hand resting on his father's arm. "We should get them to bed."

Courtney smoothed down her wild hair before offering a nod. She went straight to his dad's chair, gently resting one hand on his shoulder. "Tom?" Her voice was soft and gentle. "Are you ready to go to bed?"

His dad stirred, rousing and giving Courtney a smile before glancing at Reed. "Are you two staying here tonight?"

Reed shook his head. "Not tonight. I have to work for the next few days."

Courtney carefully helped his father transfer from his recliner to the wheelchair that made it easier for him to get around and saved his energy for things he enjoyed more.

Like talking.

"What about Courtney?" His dad sat back as she lifted each foot into place, looking like she'd done it a million times. "You can't just leave her on her own while you're busy."

Courtney gave his dad a conspiratorial smile. One that flattened out the second her eyes met Reed's.

He shook his head. "I should've known the two of you would be thick as thieves right out of the gate."

He couldn't be mad at it. Especially not since he'd realized just how much he wanted to keep Courtney in his life. And the extent of what that could mean.

"Spit it out. What do you two want?" Reed eyed his father and Courtney, hands on his hips as he waited for one of them to spit out the request he knew was coming.

Courtney stood behind his father's chair, gripping the handles. "We were just thinking it would be nice if I hung out here while you worked since I don't have anything else to do." She pressed her lips together on a short pause. "It would be nice to have an extra set of hands. And your mom promised to teach me some of her recipes."

He wasn't surprised Courtney and his father formed an immediate bond, but he was a little shocked at how eager she seemed to hang out with his mother. His mother wasn't only short in stature, but also in temperament. She wasn't overly warm or friendly. She didn't mince words and she didn't tolerate bullshit.

Glancing down at where the woman who passed on more than just her cooking skills still slept in her chair, he blew out a breath. Maybe he shouldn't have been surprised that his mother and Courtney were getting along after all. "Fine. I'll make sure she's dropped off in the morning."

Even if he wasn't available to do it, he could absolutely make sure Courtney got a ride to his parents' house every day. But, while he was in town, he planned to be selfish and make sure she spent her nights with him.

Courtney beamed at him, her smile bright and soft. "Awesome."

He moved in, taking his dad's chair from her. "I'll help him. You wake my mom up."

She didn't hesitate at the task he'd given her, making him wonder just how well she was getting along with his mother. Courtney was gently shaking her by the shoulder as he wheeled his dad down the hall. He helped him brush his teeth and get changed into his pajamas before moving him to the bed his parents shared and tucking him in. "Good?"

His dad nodded. "Really good."

Reed started to walk away but his dad reached out, not managing to grab him, but able to tap his arm. He paused, waiting as his dad collected his thoughts and slowly turned them into words.

"I'm glad you found someone. You've been alone too long."

He was right, but not entirely. "I have been single, but I haven't been alone." He patted his dad's hand when it fell back to the bed. "I've had you and mom."

His dad's crooked smile slipped. "We won't be around forever. I know you planned your life around us, but you need to start thinking about the future." His eyes held Reed's. "*Your* future."

His chest got tight at the meaning behind his father's words. On one level he understood it, but planning his life without including his parents would never happen. Not because of responsibility or other guilt, but because they were important to him. He wanted them in his life. Always.

His eyes lifted as Courtney peeked into the room, giving him a tenuous smile.

"Go." His dad rocked his head to the door. "You have other things to do now."

His father didn't seem upset, but the comment didn't sit right. It made it seem like his parents and Courtney had to be two separate pieces of his life. And that's why he'd been single. That's why he hadn't dated since his father got sick. He was already living two separate lives with his job and his parents, he didn't have time for three.

And he didn't *want* three.

Courtney gave his dad a little wave and a soft smile. "Good night. I'll see you tomorrow."

Her obvious comfort being around his parents was a perfect example of why Courtney, in all her snarky, difficult glory, was so easy to love. She was the perfect fit. Nothing had to adjust to make room for her. Nothing had to change for her to have a place.

And she saw him for all that he was and all that he lacked and accepted him anyway. Pushed his buttons so he expanded his views. She made him better. Challenged him in a way no one ever had.

Which was unexpected as hell.

His mother suddenly strode into the room, a giant bag of containers in her hands. She pushed it off on Courtney before making a shooing motion at both of them. "Go. I need my sleep."

Instead of being put off by his mother's abrupt nature, Courtney smiled. "I'll see you in the morning."

"You can only see me in the morning if you leave." His mother softened her words with a hint of a smile. "Make sure my son eats breakfast before he works."

Courtney nodded. "I will."

It was an important moment, even if Courtney didn't know it.

Food was important to his mother. It was how she showed she cared since physical affection didn't come easily to her.

Reminding Courtney about breakfast was her way of passing on a reminder of affection.

Of love.

And while Courtney might not love him yet, he most certainly loved her. Luckily, he was patient, which meant he was equipped to handle a woman like her.

And equipped to wait for her to love him back.

CHAPTER TWENTY-SEVEN

COURTNEY

"SO YOU STAY with your parents when you're not working?" Courtney eyed Reed as they walked through the quiet halls of Alaskan Security.

She'd learned a lot about him while he was gone, doing whatever Pierce needed him to do. His parents barely waited until he pulled out of the driveway after lunch before whipping out the photo albums and home movies. They were more than ready to spill all his secrets.

And they were definitely more than ready to see Reed in a relationship, which is what they seemed to think they were in.

She wasn't so sure.

Sure, they'd spent quite a bit of time together recently and seemed to get along and be compatible. Sure, they had some pretty intense chemistry. And sure, he didn't seem interested in putting her in her own room at night. But none of those things equaled a relationship. At least not as far as she knew. But she hadn't had much experience with relationships since most of her interactions with people were bought and paid for in one way or another, so trusting her own judgment about their circumstances wasn't something she was comfortable doing.

"I help my parents as often as I can." Reed swiped his badge across the sensor on the door to his room, opening it up and waiting as she walked in. "My mom doesn't like strangers in the house, so the second she could somewhat handle my dad on her own, she cut off all the help I'd hired."

That wasn't surprising. Even though she'd only known Reed's mother for a handful of hours, she knew Reed, and they seemed to be cut from the same cloth. "Your mother takes her responsibilities very seriously."

Reed tipped his head in a little nod as he stepped into the room, letting the door close behind him. "She does."

Courtney shrugged out of her coat, tossing it over the chair in the corner before moving his way. "And it seems like she's a caretaker. Not the kind of person who tells you they love you, but shows you instead." She went to work unzipping Reed from his coat. "Kinda like someone else I know."

She couldn't bring her eyes to his, because she wasn't so sure what she would see there. Would Reed be irritated that she not only saw him for what he was, but also blatantly called him out on it? Probably. But that was something he would have to get used to if he wanted to keep sharing space the way they were.

"Look at me, Princess." His voice was deep and dark. "Now."

She took a deep breath before lifting her eyes to meet his. "There. Happy?" She swallowed hard as his gaze held hers, simmering with the intensity and focus she liked so much. Especially since it was so frequently focused on her. Like she was worth giving attention to. Like he actually cared about what she was thinking and feeling.

Like she mattered.

Reed's full lips quirked up at the corner. "Mostly." He pressed one finger under her chin, tipping it higher as he stepped closer. "I'll be happier when you tell me what's wrong."

She shook her head, blinking at a sudden influx of emotion. "Nothing. I'm fine." Her eyes went back to his coat as she focused on dragging the zipper down before sliding her hands under the sides to push it off his broad shoulders. "Your parents are nice. I liked spending time with them."

"I'm glad." Reed snagged his coat as it slipped free of his arms, tossing it on top of hers before pressing his finger back under her chin, lifting her eyes to his. "But don't change the subject."

Courtney huffed out a breath, trying to rein in the tightness in her throat. "You're so fucking bossy."

His lips lifted a little more, eyes crinkling with an edge of humor. "So you've said." The fingers of his free hand slid down a piece of her hair before giving it a tug. "Now tell me what's wrong."

She rolled her eyes to the ceiling, needing to look at something besides his face. Needing a little bit of space from the realization she was desperately hoping this would be more than what it probably was. His parents made it clear Reed never dated, so there was a chance he wasn't looking for something permanent. "I'm just tired."

Reed was already shaking his head. "That's not what's wrong." He gripped her chin, bringing it down so her eyes had no choice but to align with his. "The only time you aren't dishing out a ton of shit is when something's wrong, so spit it out."

She wanted to. Tried to come up with something snarky to

say to appease him so she could step back from the fear and rejection waiting to pull her into their grasp once again. But there was nothing ready to come out, so she leaned into her other defense mechanism. "I'm more of a swallower." Courtney moved closer, pressing her tits to Reed's chest as one hand skated down his front to rub over his cock. "Speaking of, I still owe you that blow job I promised you."

Reed chuckled, shaking his head as he snagged her wrist and pulled it away, lifting her hand to his lips. He brushed them over the inside of her palm, eyes holding hers as he did. "You are a sneaky little shit, aren't you?" He pushed against her, the weight of his body backing her across the room. "But you're forgetting I'm not so easily distracted, Princess."

She sucked in a breath as her back hit the wall, pinning her between drywall and unrelenting man. "That's a shame. Because I would really love to have your cock in my mouth right now."

She wasn't lying. Sure, she was attempting to use sex to redirect Reed's focus, but she also really wanted to finish what she'd started in the shower at the campground. Almost as much as she wanted to move past this conversation and all the painful feelings it was bringing up.

Reed's eyes narrowed on her, his head barely tipping to one side as he studied her face. "Are you really still trying to distract me?"

Shit.

This man was too damn perceptive for her own good.

She shoved at his chest but he didn't budge. "I don't know why you're being like this." He was irritating her. Making her sit in this uncomfortable place she didn't want to be. A spot where Reed wasn't the only thing she would lose when this all went tits up. And she wanted to make him just as irritated and uncomfortable. "I would have been on my knees already with most men."

The flash in his eyes told her she might have taken things a step too far.

His hand came to bracket her neck, pinning her in place as his nose ran alongside hers. "I think you're trying to push me."

She swallowed hard as her heart rate picked up. Not out of fear, Reed would never hurt her. It was excitement, and a little arousal, that had her struggling to pull in a full breath. "That doesn't sound like me at all."

Reed's mouth pulled into a slow smile. "Don't act like I don't know you." He leaned close, the hand at her throat tilting her head to one side as his lips skated along her jawline. "Because I do know you, Princess. Maybe better than you know yourself." He nipped at her skin, soothing away the sting with a swipe of his tongue. "That's why I know you're upset."

Her head dropped back against the wall as his teasing teeth and tongue continued moving over her skin. One wide palm edged into the front of her pants to tease along the seam of her pussy with a barely there touch that quickly settled against her clit. It wasn't nearly enough pressure, and she tried to rock against him, looking for more.

But the asshole immediately pulled away with a wicked chuckle. "I don't think so, Princess. You don't get what you want, until I get what I want."

She gritted her teeth, trying desperately to fake indifference. "Fine." She wiggled her way loose from the pinning press of his body and started to walk away. "Be that way then."

"Oh, no." Reed snagged her hand, catching her before she

made it two full steps. "You're not getting out of this." His grip was firm but careful as he tugged her back, bringing her body to his. "You spent years making sure you were impossible to ignore. Don't pretend like you don't still want all my attention."

That was the problem. Even if she did want it, she couldn't have it. Shouldn't have it. Reed had much more important things to focus on, which was why he'd always been single. His job was demanding. His parents, sweet as they were, were also a demand.

And she was willing to admit that she might be a smidge demanding too.

Reed pushed against her, his wide chest warm and solid and inescapable. She tried to take a step back, but he immediately followed. "Don't try to get away from me." One hand came to grip her hip as the other laced into her hair, fisting tight. "Because I will find you."

She snorted, pretending like she wasn't even more turned on than when he had his hand in her pants. "We're in the same room. You *better* be able to find me or I'm gonna judge Pierce for hiring you."

Reed's lips worked up at one corner. "There's my girl. Where have you been all night?"

Courtney took a shaky breath, pretending she didn't know exactly what he meant. "I was with your parents. You're the one who took me there, and my feelings are gonna be a little hurt if you forgot where you put me."

Reed leaned in like he was going to kiss her, but instead his mouth slid against the line of her jaw, skating toward her ear. "Is that what you really think? That I would forget you?"

She swallowed hard around the lust and fear wrestling

through her insides. "You just have a lot on your plate, so I could see how it would happen."

Reed made a low humming sound like he discovered something. "That's what's wrong."

She had her mouth open, ready to spit out something snarky, when he gripped her thighs, hefting her up against him with ease. She yelped, immediately grabbing onto his neck as her legs hooked around his waist. "What are you doing?"

Reed hauled her onto the bed, keeping her suspended with one arm at her waist as he crawled up the mattress to deposit her in the center. "It seems like we've had a miscommunication." He released her and pushed up on his knees, smoldering gaze holding hers as he yanked at the laces of her boot, loosening it before sliding it free and tossing it over the edge of the king-sized bed. "But I'm not surprised." Her sock went next before he moved to the other boot, removing it like the first then stripping away the thick stock beneath it. "Have you ever been in a real relationship, Princess?"

She pursed her lips, irritated and sad and confused all at the same time. "You know I haven't. No one wanted—" her voice broke a little, giving her time to rethink the rest of her words. "No one wanted me."

She could blame her lack of connection on who she was and where the connection to her father left her. But at the end of the day, if someone had wanted her enough, they wouldn't have cared who she was related to, right?

That meant she simply wasn't enough. Not for her mother. Not for her father. Not for her friends.

And definitely not for a man.

"Then we're probably going to have this conversation a few times, so you should get used to hearing it." His hands came to the waistband of her joggers, fingers hooking in before peeling everything she wore from the waist down away. "People in relationships talk. When something's wrong you put it out there, okay?"

Her legs dropped to the mattress as he freed them from her pants and panties, tossing them over the edge. Her lower half was completely bare, but that wasn't why she suddenly felt very naked. Exposed.

"Why would we need to have this conversation more than once?" She was too afraid to hope she understood what he was saying. Over the years, she'd worn blinders more times than she could count. Let herself believe the people around her were there because they wanted to be, not because of what she offered. While she knew Reed wasn't here because she had anything to offer him, that didn't mean he was here to stay.

"Because sometimes it takes a while to see things for what they really are when you've spent years seeing them different-ly." He snagged her hands, pulling her up to a sitting position before peeling away her shirt. "And I think you're about to start seeing a lot of new things, Princess."

She sat still as his hands gently peeled away the rest of her clothing. It was a moment that was markedly different from any other time she'd ended up naked around him. It wasn't driven by frustration or aggravation. It wasn't bred from their intense and obvious attraction for each other. This was some-thing different. Something more.

And it was overwhelming.

Once he had her stripped down, his hand came to her hair, gently sliding through the long strands as his eyes roamed her body. She'd never been shy about nudity because it was simply more purchasing power in her arsenal. Something to barter with so she could have a taste of what she desperately wanted. Even if it was never real.

But there was more than physical appreciation in Reed's dark gaze as it swept her skin. More than need. More than desire.

The tips of his fingers slid from her hair to her shoulders, tracing a path down her arms before clasping her hands. He pushed against her, pressing her back against the mattress as he lifted her hands above her head, pinning her in place with his hold and his weight. "You should probably know a few things about me, Princess." His lips barely brushed hers as he spoke, the warmth of his breath fanning across her skin. "I wasn't single because I didn't want someone." His hands slid from hers as he pushed back to his knees, gripping the hem of his Henley and yanking it over his head to reveal the broad and bare expanse of his chest. "I was single because I don't like to waste my time." His fingers moved to the waistband of his pants, unfastening the fly before shoving them past his hips and kicking them away. "Because I don't have time to waste." He dropped back down over her, the heat of his naked body pressing into her skin. "I didn't think there was room for someone else in my life." He ran his nose along her neck, breathing deep. "But then I met you."

She sucked in a breath, both because of his words and the hard length of his cock as it rested against her belly.

Reed's callused hands skimmed their way back up her arms, long fingers twining with hers as he once again pinned her in place. "And you just wouldn't fucking quit." He nipped at her ear to punctuate the statement. "You dug at me and dug at me and dug at me until you were so far under my skin there was no way to get you back out."

She scoffed, insulted by the way he was describing her

behavior. "If anyone got under anyone's skin it was you getting under mine."

Reed chuckled, the sound low and deep where his lips brushed her hair. "I'm definitely planning on being inside you, Princess, but it won't be under your skin."

Courtney's head dropped back as he adjusted his hips to line his cock up with her pussy and rocked forward, dragging his length along her slit. "You are talking so much for a man who should be fucking me."

It was a gentle nudge. One she hoped would work. Because this conversation was a lot. More than she could handle.

And it only got worse when his head lifted, bringing his eyes to hers. "Don't get impatient. I'm going to fuck you." He leaned down to nip her lips, sucking the bottom one before pulling away. "Probably twice. But not before you let me finish explaining why I fucking love you."

CHAPTER TWENTY-EIGHT

REED

COURTNEY BLINKED UP at him, her mouth hanging slightly open. "I don't think I heard you correctly."

He wasn't surprised by her reaction. As much as Courtney needed to hear this, it would be a tough sell.

"You definitely heard me right, Princess." He leaned in to brush his lips against hers again, unable to stop himself from creating another point of contact between them. "I said I love you."

Her eyes stayed open as he continued teasing her mouth with his, drinking in the moment. A moment he hadn't expected to want so much.

Everyone else on Rogue had paired off, and he was happy for them, but he never once considered it happening for him. Not that he didn't want it, there just wasn't fucking time to even consider the possibility.

Maybe that's why it was so easy to recognize it once he finally opened his eyes. He hadn't been chasing or avoiding it, so he had no reason to resist identifying the way he felt about

Courtney. Plus, he had one hell of a great example when it came to knowing what love actually looked like.

Love was taking care of each other through the worst the world had to offer. Supporting each other. Protecting each other. Did it mean you were always sweet and sappy and mushy? Maybe for some people, but not for him. He needed fire. Someone who pushed him back. Someone who held their own and claimed what was theirs.

Someone like the woman still staring at him like he'd lost his mind.

Courtney shook her head. "You can't love me. You hated me not so long ago."

He smiled at that. "There's a thin line between love and hate, Princess. And you walk that line like a tightrope."

She rolled her eyes. "You're such an ass."

He relaxed a little more as she came back to herself. She'd been too quiet today. Too reserved. Almost withdrawn. It was fear, he knew that. And he was happy to do whatever it took to help her get back to her normal, pain in the ass self. "I am, but I'm your ass." He grabbed one leg, lifting it up and out, gaining more room to tease them both as he dragged his cock through the already wet folds of her pussy. "And you love me just as much as I love you."

She scoffed, but didn't deny it, which was good enough for him. He'd lived with his mother long enough to know that some people struggled to say the words, but Courtney had shown him more than a few times how she felt.

His eyes dropped to where he continued sliding along her slit. ""And while we're making confessions, I gotta tell you I really want to fuck you with nothing between us."

Courtney gasped as the head of his dick teased along the side of her clit. "That sounds messy."

There was a hint of snark in her voice, but the way her eyes glazed over at the suggestion made him think she wasn't entirely opposed to the idea.

Reed leaned down, lining his eyes up with hers, noses barely touching. "Are you saying you don't want me to fill you up, Princess?"

Her nostrils flared and her lips parted on a sharp inhale. "Why do you want to do that?"

He thought it was pretty obvious, but it was a reminder Courtney had no clue how to genuinely be with someone she trusted. That meant she wouldn't be able to identify it when it happened. "Because you're mine and I want to feel how wet you get for me."

The air rushed from her lungs as her tongue darted out to swipe along her lower lip. "I've never done it without a condom before."

Her admission made him groan with the realization that he would be the first to sink into her skin on skin. "Neither have I, but there's a first time for everything." He ran his thumbs over the palms of her hands as he continued rocking against her. "Eli makes sure everyone here is perfectly healthy every few months since we occasionally have to deal with each other's blood."

He dipped his head, catching the tip of one full nipple in his mouth as he let her think that over. He would never pressure her on this, but was more than willing to make it clear there were no barriers on his end.

"I'm not really interested in thinking about you getting hurt right now." Courtney whimpered, arching into him. "And I don't know who Eli is."

He pulled free of her nipple with a pop. "He's the staff doctor."

Courtney wiggled under him, unable to stay still. "That would make sense." Her hips rocked into his on his next glide. "I had them check me for everything right before I had my IUD put in a year ago, and you're the only person I've slept with since then, so..."

She stopped short of the permission he needed.

"So, what, Princess?" He nipped her lips again. "If you don't want to get messy, I can wait. I'm a big boy."

She sucked in a breath as he slid against her clit again. "Let's do it."

So close. Almost what he needed. "Let's do what?"

Courtney hooked one leg behind his knee, shifting her hips as he started to slide forward so the head of his cock notching into place. Her eyes held his, gaze unwavering. "Fill me up."

Hearing her say those words snapped the control he loved so much, sending him surging into her, a feral growl ripping free as her soaked pussy clenched tight around him.

He expected it to feel different, but this was—

This was—

Going to be a fucking problem.

He held himself still, buried to the hilt as his forehead dropped to hers and he closed his eyes, pulling in air.

Courtney squirmed under him, making desperate little sounds that pulled his balls even tighter.

He released one hand and gripped her hip, pinning her in place. "I'm gonna need you to be very still for a second."

She scoffed, hooking her other leg at his waist, to lock him in. "You better get your shit together, big boy, or we are never doing it this way again." She fought against his hold, each move making her clench around him, pushing him closer to an edge he was doing his best to avoid.

"If you don't stop moving, this is going to be over before it starts." Stamina had never been an issue for him. But, then again, he'd never been balls deep and skin to skin with a woman who drove him absolutely fucking crazy before. And apparently that was a deadly combination.

"Fine." Courtney's free hand slid between her legs, brushing the spot where their bodies joined as she started to work her clit. "If you won't get me off, then I will."

Gritting his teeth, he reminded himself this was the exact reason he loved her, but damned if it was putting him through hell right now. He sucked in a breath, digging deep for every bit of self-control he still possessed as he grabbed her hand and pulled it from between their bodies to pin it against the bed. "Fine. If that's what you want, then you better fucking hold on."

This wasn't going to be the sweet, slow interaction he'd expected. But when had anything between them been slow or sweet? They'd always been combustive. Gasoline and a spark.

And right now he couldn't fight that.

Courtney's fingers tightened around his, holding on exactly like he told her to as he pulled back, bringing himself almost free before driving back into her warm, wet, willing body.

He was lost, unable to rein himself in the way he always could. And for the first time in his life, he just let it happen. She made him wild. Broke him free of all the rules and expectations he did his best to fit into.

Releasing the hand above her head, he slid his palm to the back of her neck and held tight, keeping her in place as his hips pistoned into her, their bodies making a wet slapping sound every time they came together.

"Fucking fuck." Courtney tucked her chin, looking down

between their bodies, watching stroke after relentless stroke. "Reed, I need—" She stopped short of telling him what she needed. No one had ever given a shit what she needed.

But he did. Luckily he knew her as well as he claimed and didn't have to hear her request. Eventually he would make her give it to him—just so she knew she could ask for whatever she wanted—but not tonight. Tonight, hearing her demand pleasure would be more than he could handle.

So he shifted, dropping down to brace on his forearm, resting his stomach against hers, changing to long drags that ground his pelvis against her clit.

She clenched around him again, the sensation significantly more noticeable without a condom between them. Her legs jerked where they clamped around his waist, twitching as her nails dug into his shoulders. She was so wet, the sound they were making was obscene and ramped up the speed of the climax barreling at him.

"Come on, Princess." He ground the words out against her ear as he fought to keep going. "Give me what I want."

The words were barely out of his mouth when her body locked tight, squeezing hard and sending him right along with her. He ground against her as his cock jerked, swelling as he finally let go, coming inside her as she came around him.

He struggled to catch his breath as Courtney went limp under him, legs dropping to the mattress as one hand fell across her forehead. As his chest continued to heave in search of more oxygen, he brushed the hair back from her face.

Courtney squinted one eye open at him, looking over his face. "You sound a little out of breath." Her free hand came up to pinch his nipple, sending a zing of pleasure straight to his still half hard cock. "You should work out more."

She was giving him shit and he was more than happy to

offer it right back. "I plan on it." He gently eased away from her body, sucking in a breath as he slipped free of her warmth before making his way to the bathroom to retrieve a washcloth. He came back and sat down beside her, using the warm rag to wipe her clean. "Give me ten minutes and then we can go again."

Her eyes flew open. "What?"

He shot her a smirk. "You said I needed to work out more."

"SOMETHING'S GOING ON." Pierce stalked past him down the hall, feet moving fast as he made his way into Intel's office with Nate hot on his heels.

Reed raked one hand through his still-damp hair as he chased after them. "I just fucking got here and the shit's already hitting the fan?"

Nate barely slowed down. "Not our fault you're late."

Reed snorted. "I'm not late. I'm just not half an hour early."

Nate shot him a smirk. "For you that's late."

As much as he'd resented his job at Alaskan Security he'd always taken it seriously. It was how he helped care for his father and kept his parents comfortable in their house even when the medical bills never stopped coming.

"I had to drop Courtney off at my parents' place." Normally he wouldn't have explained himself. He'd spent his entire time at Alaskan Security making sure his work life and personal life were separate, but Courtney had changed more than just his morning routine.

She'd changed the way he looked at things. Made him realize she wasn't the only one he'd judged harshly. The only one he'd tried to put in a box to protect himself from shame. Shame he now knew was unwarranted.

Nate gave him a slow nod. "I get it." He offered a lopsided grin in spite of the situation. "My mornings have changed too."

Reed opened his mouth to ask Nate more about his new normal but was cut off by a screeching squeal of outrage coming from Intel's office.

They picked up the pace and cleared the door just as Heidi stood up, her wide eyes fixed on the screen of her computer. "You've got to be kidding me." Her face went pale as her focus snapped to where he stood,.

A chill settled in his veins. "What's wrong?"

Her eyes moved to Pierce before coming back his way. She held up one hand. "Don't get mad."

"That's not a good way to start a conversation." He scanned the room to find nearly every set of eyes on him. "What's going on?"

Heidi took a breath so deep it lifted her shoulders. "We might have put a few cameras around your parents' house." The words rushed out, but she didn't give him time to respond before continuing, words coming fast and rambling. "I know you were trying to sort of keep things separate so I didn't tell you, but you know there's no real way to keep shit separate with what we do and I was worried about them so I wanted to keep an eye on them." She pursed her lips on a cringe before repeating her earlier request. "Don't be mad."

Surprisingly, he wasn't. "Why does this matter now?"

She chewed her lower lip, looking panicked. "It matters because the cameras just started going out."

"Shit." He turned, racing from the room without waiting to hear any more information. It didn't matter. The last two times cameras went out, buildings blew up. And right now the building in question contained everything that mattered to him in the world.

Nate kept up with him, boots hitting the industrial carpet as they ran toward the garage. There was no time to waste putting together a team. No time to come up with a plan. No time to do more than grab their weapons, jump into a Jeep and peel out of the garage, knowing backup would be close behind them.

He called Heidi on the drive, getting as much information as he could on the way over. The minutes it took to get to his parents' neighborhood passed like hours, even though Nate was breaking all the traffic laws he'd expected to be enforcing at this point in his life.

When they finally reached the edge of the small cluster of houses where he grew up, Reed scanned the area for any sign of who or what might have taken out the cameras. But whoever installed them did a hell of a job making them hard to find, even with Heidi's description of the locations, so he was left using the skills he'd learned from his father to track the men responsible for taking them out instead.

And it was definitely someone with skill.

He pointed at an empty lot butting up against the end of the street. "Park there."

The Jeep was still rolling when he jumped out, taking slow steps through the snow as he followed the most recent path of tire tracks. He stopped where they suddenly distorted before changing trajectory, taking a slow spin, eyes moving over everything high enough to serve as a camera mount.

His boots skidded to a stop, eyes dropping to the base of an electric pole. There, scattered across the snow, were bits and pieces of what remained of one of Heidi's cameras.

He jerked his chin at the location as Nate reached his side.

"They parked here and took that one out in a single shot." Reed refocused on the tracks, following their path back to the road. "We need to canvass the neighborhood and we need to do it now."

"We should wait for backup." Nate's suggestion was reasonable and one he would have made not so long ago.

But he finally understood there were times you followed the rules and times you did whatever it took to make shit happen. Right now he was going to do whatever it took to make sure his parents and Courtney were safe. He'd break any law without blinking if it meant they would be okay.

Because there wasn't just a fine line between love and hate, there was also a fine line between right and wrong. And today he was going to walk it like a tightrope.

"You can wait if you want." Reed adjusted his grip on the rifle in his hands. "But I'm going in."

Nate held his gaze. "We don't have our earpieces. We'll be going old school." He gripped his own weapon. "But I'm game if you are."

He gave Nate a jerky nod, realizing how little separation actually existed in his life and how grateful he was for it. "I'll take this side."

Nate nodded back and took off, steps quiet as he moved to the other edge of the neighborhood, quickly blending into the snowy backdrop as he disappeared from sight.

Reed did the same, silently moving along the backside of the small homes. He knew this area like the back of his hand. He'd spent his whole childhood racing through the wooded space surrounding it, so it was easy to move quickly.

He was closing in on his parents' home when a single branch snapped behind him. He spun, rifle raised and ready to take out whoever decided to fuck with what was his.

A feral cat stared at him, furry body completely still. Reed let out a breath as relief flooded his system.

But before he could go back to his task he was hit hard from behind.

And then the world went black.

CHAPTER TWENTY-NINE

COURTNEY

"THESE ARE SO good." Courtney took another bite of the small, rectangular, slightly sweet confection Reed's mom gave her for second breakfast. "Tell me again what these are called."

"Injeolmi." His mother finished her own off. "They are one of Reed's favorites."

Courtney swallowed down her mouthful of the slightly chewy, completely delicious treat. "I can see why."

His mother stood up from the table where they were sharing coffee and a snack. "It's good to try new things." She went to the kitchen and topped off her mug from the giant pot sitting on the warmer. "Maybe you can show me some of the food your family eats."

The warmth that set up shop in her stomach the second she walked in and discovered Reed's parents seemed excited over her arrival, flatlined. "Oh." Courtney swallowed again, this time struggling around a tightness in her throat. "I don't really have anything like that."

Reed's mother's dark brows lifted. "You don't know your family's recipes?"

Courtney shook her head, forcing on a smile. "It's not that I don't know them. There aren't any."

Reed's mother studied her for a second. "Why not?"

She took a steadying breath, her smile faltering a little. "Because I don't really have a family."

His mother's lips pressed together as her eyes narrowed. "No family?"

Courtney shook her head. "No family."

It was humiliating to admit the people who were supposed to be there for her couldn't be bothered to deal with her on any level, let alone one that would involve discussing traditions and passing down recipes. It brought her back to that insecure place she'd lived in for so long.

A place she was just beginning to think might one day be as far behind her as Miami was.

"Well." His mother turned to the fridge. "I will teach you ours then." She pulled out a produce bag filled with something leafy. "Today we will make Kkaennip Jangajji."

She spent the next thirty minutes side by side with Reed's mother, plucking the slightly fuzzy leaves from their stems and cleaning them well before mixing up a brine of soy sauce, garlic, chili flakes, and a little sugar. That was poured over the leaves and thinly sliced chilis before being put in the fridge to marinate.

"Are those a condiment?" Courtney worked at wiping down the counter the way she'd seen Reed's mother do no fewer than ten times. She was definitely where he got his more regimented nature, and Courtney wanted her to know she understood and was happy to follow the house rules. She'd never had rules and it was oddly nice to finally be with someone who had expectations of her. Someone who thought she was worth the investment of time and energy.

"You eat them with rice or with bibimbap or with fish." She tipped her head, thinking it over. "You can eat them with everything."

Courtney considered the explanation. "Like kimchi?"

His mother smiled. "Like kimchi." She wiped her hands on a towel. "We will make kimchi later this week. You will need to learn to make that too. Reed eats so much."

Courtney smiled a little easier, that warmth from before blooming at the mention of him. He loved her. As someone who'd never been loved before, it was a pretty heady feeling. One she was still letting sink in.

If it had been any other man who said it, she wouldn't have believed him. Especially since he was practically balls deep when the admission came.

But this was Reed. Honest, assholeish, Reed.

Definitely not the kind of man to say something he didn't one-hundred percent mean, regardless of the location of his balls.

And he'd known she loved him back. Claimed her feelings for himself without hesitation. Also a very Reed thing to do.

Which was part of why she did, in fact, love the shit out of him.

"Then I definitely want to learn how to make kimchi." She gave his mother a smile. "And anything else you want to teach me how to make."

Reed's mother stood a little taller, like she was pleased. "Maybe one day you will get to cook for us too."

Courtney couldn't contain her smile at the possibility. "Maybe."

She'd been so alone for so long and the thought of having a whole family of people around her was unbelievably exciting.

Even after just a couple of days, she felt like a part of their group.

And she'd seen firsthand how much work it took for Reed's mother to take care of his father on her own. She was small but mighty, and able to help his father transfer from his chair to the wheelchair they used, but it clearly took all her strength. They needed an extra set of hands, but his mother was adamant she didn't want a stranger in her house. So maybe she could help out on a regular basis. Spend her days here while Reed worked.

His mother checked the time on the microwave. "The mail should be here. I need to go get it. It has medications we need."

Courtney immediately went for the door. "I'll get it. You stay in here where it's warm." She hurried toward the door, not waiting for agreement. Reed's parents were doing so much for her, the least she could do was get their mail.

After switching pink slippers for boots, she layered on her coat, tugged on a hat, and trudged out into the snow, sucking in a sharp breath as the cold air slapped her in the face.

"Fuck a duck, it's cold." She hugged her arms against her chest as she shuffled down the sidewalk to the driveway. The mailbox wasn't far, but by the time she reached it, her teeth were chattering and the shivers were setting in. Thank goodness she hadn't let Reed's mom come out here. The weather was freaking brutal.

And probably normal.

Prying open the mailbox, she grinned in spite of the freezing cold. It was impossible to be too upset if this was the worst part of her new life.

She'd just pulled out the pile of junk mail and the shipping envelope containing the medication Reed's dad needed, when a van coasted down the road. She hurried to grab the rest so she could get out of the way and avoid getting splashed with the mucky ice layered over the road. But the van stopped just as she snapped the hinged door back into place.

Courtney turned, half expecting to see Reed when the side door opened. But the man who stared out at her wasn't Reed. Or anyone else she knew.

She took a step back, wiggling her boot to check the traction as the huge, menacing looking guy climbed out. Before she had the chance to spin away, he was on her, grabbing her arms and attempting to drag her into the vehicle.

She'd worked so hard in Miami to make sure she was prepared for a situation just like this. But she'd been stupid enough to let her guard down here, thinking she'd finally found love and happiness and no one would ever come all this way to try to finish her off.

But it looked like she was wrong.

She dropped the mail—unable to hang onto it and defend herself at the same time—before gripping her hands together and using all the force she could muster to bring one elbow back into his ribs. The guy grunted, doubling over as he struggled to catch his breath. Courtney took full advantage of his momentary stun and again started to turn toward the house.

Then stopped.

That would lead them right to Reed's parents. And there was no way she'd put them in danger.

So she darted around the mailbox and took off down the road, screaming at the top of her lungs, hoping if she made enough noise a neighbor would call the cops and she might stand a chance.

But the guy who grabbed her wasn't the only one in the van. Two more men wearing white tactical gear ran after her, their long legs making it easy for them to close the distance between them. The first one to reach her tackled her from behind, taking her to the ground. He managed not to slam her full-force into the packed snow, but it still knocked the wind out of her and sent her face-first into a clump of filthy snow.

The other guy reached them half a second later. "Don't hurt her. We'll never hear the end of it."

The guy pinning her in place grunted as she bent one knee, sending her foot swinging in an arch that brought the heel of her boot right into the crack of his ass. "I'm trying. But in case you haven't noticed, she's a fucking handful." He managed to grab her hand right as she tried to claw at his eyes, gripping her wrist and wrenching her arm behind her back as his knees clenched together at each side of her thighs, making it impossible to move her lower half. "I could use a fucking hand."

Courtney narrowed her eyes at the guy who came closer, reaching for her like he hadn't learned anything from his buddy's struggles. The minute his ungloved hand was within reach, she twisted, craning her neck as far as it would go before sinking her teeth into the meaty muscle at the base of his thumb.

The other guy howled as he struggled to free his hand from her mouth, but she held on as tight as she could. The longer she managed to lay out here in the middle of the road, the better her chances were of being saved.

And someone would definitely try to save her. After a lifetime of being alone with no one having her back, knowing Reed would come for her only made her fight harder.

So, while she had number two by the hand, she lifted her upper body away from the snow. Bending back at the waist, and ignoring the protest of her abs, she clenched her free hand into a fist and sent it flying at his face. The impact with his nose was satisfying as hell. As was the almost immediate trickle of blood down his face. She finally unclenched her jaw, smirking as he fell backward.

The guy on top of her immediately snatched her fisted hand and jerked it around to meet the one he still held at the small of her back. "I know this probably isn't the right time, but if things don't work out with you and Reed, I'd love to take you out sometime."

She went still at the mention of Reed's name. They said it like they knew him. And it sent the chill biting her exposed skin straight to her gut.

This was bad. Worse than some thugs coming from Miami to finish her off.

Her wide eyes moved over the two men, taking in their white tactical gear and the arsenal of weapons at their waists and thighs. They were definitely not the same caliber as the men who blew up her house.

She yelped as the man holding her hauled her to her feet. He wasn't overly rough, but it was clear she was in deep shit. Shit that wasn't even hers.

He pulled a zip line from his waistband, looking at it a second before dropping it to the ground and grabbing his cuffs. "These will be more comfortable." He locked them into place around her wrists, finally glancing at his buddy on the ground. "Get up. We gotta go."

The guy spit in the snow as he stood, his saliva tinted pink. "I think she broke my nose." He swiped at the blood freezing on his face, smearing it up one cheek with the sleeve of his coat.

The prick holding her looked his friend over, grinning. "Oh, she definitely broke it. You're going to have to get it set when we get back to headquarters."

Courtney shifted her eyes, looking the guy at her side up and down, taking in everything about him as a possibility began to form. Everything about him seemed familiar. Not necessarily his face, but what he wore. The way he carried himself. The weapons and gear covering so much of his solid body. The earpiece nearly hidden behind the stretch of his white hat.

They looked almost identical to the guys at Alaskan Security.

But that wouldn't make any sense. Why would anyone from Alaskan Security do this?

The guy holding her pulled her toward the van, dragging her along as her mind raced.

Maybe Alaskan Security really was tired of her bullshit. Maybe they weren't as excited about having her living on-site as they acted.

Maybe they were going to try to send her back.

She needed someone to help her. Someone who carried a lot of weight. Someone these guys were likely to listen to. "I want to talk to Heidi." The guy dragging her along tried to urge her into the van, but she stiffened her legs, refusing to go easily. "I said I want to talk to Heidi."

He let out a heavy sigh. "I have a feeling you will have the opportunity to talk to Heidi soon."

His admission sent her stomach sinking. They didn't want her here but were too chicken shit to say it to her face. To Reed's face. They must not know how well-versed she was in the art of being rejected.

All the fight went out of her, and she was scooped up and dropped into a seat. Buckled in as they took off down the road.

Might as well get this over with. Might as well figure out where she could go from here. Her options were pretty slim.

Reed needed his job at Alaskan Security to take care of his parents. Needed the income it provided. And since she was no longer alive as far as anyone knew, she couldn't access any of her money to help him. That meant he would have to decide between her and his parents. And there was only one choice to be made.

She slumped down, sick to her stomach at the thought of losing Reed. Losing his parents. Losing what she'd wanted so much for so long.

But it was the only real option.

She blinked hard, trying to find the backbone that had carried her so far in life. "Just drop me off somewhere. I'll disappear. You don't have to go through all this."

Her Romeo wannabe shook his head. "No can do, gorgeous. We've got orders."

She rolled her eyes but couldn't decide if it was because he was still trying to butter her up or because he was acting like this couldn't all be over simply. "I'm sure Pierce won't mind if you just drop me off. It's fine. I get it."

Romeo exchanged looks with the one sporting a crooked nose before focusing on her. "It's not about easy. We have to follow orders."

She dropped her head against the metal side of the van, staring up at the roof. "Fine. Whatever."

It didn't really matter. Nothing really did. Not anymore.

She sat silently as they drove, ignoring the men across from her. When they slowed down, she glanced out the windshield, expecting to be pulling up to a gate. But the building in front of them was not Alaskan Security. It looked more like a warehouse. Rectangular and boring with a nondescript exterior that didn't remotely hint at what was inside. She sat a little straighter. "Where are we?"

The guy who tackled her unbuckled her belt and hauled her up. "You probably shouldn't worry too much about that." He led her out of the van and into the building, which was just as boring and nondescript inside as it was outside. The hallway was all beige. Floor. Ceiling. Walls. Doors.

He led her to one of those doors, pulling her through before dropping her into a chair set up in the middle of the room. "You okay? Can I get you anything to drink or eat?"

What the fuck was happening? "You can tell me what's going on."

He looked her over a second before slowly shaking his head. "That's above my pay grade." He backed toward the door. "Sit tight." He closed her in, leaving her alone, but it didn't sound like he locked the door behind him.

That was probably a mistake. One she would do her best to make sure he regretted.

Courtney looked around the bare space. The only thing inside of it was the folding chair she was seated on, leaving her little in the way of weapons. Getting out of the handcuffs was easy, but then what?

She needed a plan.

Before she could even begin to dislocate her thumb, the door opened again. But instead of one of the guys from before, someone completely new walked in. He was wearing the same tactical gear as everyone else, but his was all black, setting off the silver of his hair and cropped beard. He watched her with a sharp gaze. One that sent a shiver down her spine.

The guys before had been capable of terrible things, but she didn't get the feeling they were unwarrantedly dangerous.

This guy made her want to take a step back. His expression was unforgiving. His stance rigid and stern.

She swallowed hard, digging deep for what she knew she needed. Because this was definitely not Alaskan Security. And the man in front of her was definitely not Pierce. "Who are you?"

The man stared at her for so long she didn't expect him to answer. Finally he took a step closer. "That's information you don't need."

"Then why the fuck am I here? Did you just drag me here to sit in a chair and tell me none of this is relevant to me?" She lifted her brows. "Because it's seeming pretty fucking relevant right now, asshole."

She could swear the man's head tipped back the tiniest bit. Like he was shocked at her outburst. "Maybe you're just not asking the right questions, Courtney."

She rolled her eyes to the ceiling, getting more irritated by the second. "*Ohhhh*. You know my name. I'm *so* scared." She dropped her gaze back to him, bolstered by the knowledge she wasn't being kicked out of Alaska by Alaskan Security. They weren't abandoning her. Reed didn't have to decide between her and his parents. "I guess since you won't give me yours that's the name I'm going to go with." She leaned forward, narrowing her eyes. "*Asshole*."

The man blinked, again looking slightly surprised. "You aren't a part of this."

Courtney snorted. "Sure could've fooled me," she smirked, "*asshole*."

The man worked his jaw from side to side, the steel in his gaze hardening a little more and making her think she was getting to him. "Fine. One question."

Knowing his name wouldn't help her, so she skipped right

over that one. Plus she liked calling him asshole because it clearly stuck in his craw. So she settled on the answer that might actually give her something to work with. "Where am I?"

He slowly inhaled, nostrils flaring like he still didn't want to give the answer he promised. Finally he crossed his arms, staring her down. "You're at the headquarters of GHOST."

CHAPTER THIRTY

REED

"*WAKEY, WAKEY.*"

Reed fought the haze clouding his vision and his mind, rolling his head upright as he reached to rub the sting biting at his bicep.

At least he tried to.

His hands were locked tight together, the telltale cut of zip ties digging into his skin as he fought the bindings.

"Relax, man. We're not gonna hurt you."

Reed jerked his head upright as the last of the fuzziness cleared, narrowing his eyes at the men in front of him. "Who the fuck are you and where the fuck am I?"

"I'm gonna tell you the same thing I told your girl. That information is above my pay grade." The guy directly in front of him backed away, recapping the needle that must have just been in his arm, dosing his system with something that counteracted whatever they knocked him out with.

He must have still been a little bleary from it though, because it took a couple seconds for the prick's words to register.

Your girl.

Reed twisted, fighting against the plastic pinning his hands at his back and his feet to the legs of the chair he was sitting in. "If you've hurt a single hair on her fucking head I will disembowel you and feed your guts to the bears."

The second the two men took a step back, dragging Reed's attention his way. He blinked hard, making sure his eyes weren't playing tricks on him and the drug lingering in his system wasn't distorting reality. But the man's face was still as big of a mess as he first thought it was. "What the fuck happened to you?"

The guy in front of him grinned. "Funny story. Your girl was a hell of a lot harder to get a hold of than you were." He tipped his head. "Of course we didn't drug her, but still." He shook his head, smiling too wide at the memory of Courtney. "That's a wild one." His gaze settled on Reed. "You two serious?"

What the fuck was going on? This guy was acting like they were friends. Chatting him up, his tone casual, like he didn't think Reed would kill him just as easily for asking Courtney on a date as he would if she had so much as a bruise on her body. "What part about *I'll kill you for fucking with her* don't you understand?"

The guy held up both hands, having the sense to look apologetic. "Fine. I get it. I just had to ask."

Reed shifted in his seat again, jerking at the restraints, even more desperate to get free now that he knew they had Courtney too.

And now that it was clear at least one of them was interested in her.

"You're just gonna fucking hurt yourself, man. Calm down."

Death wish turned to the door. "Pierce should be here soon and then you can get back to your life."

Reed's head tipped back in surprise. *Pierce* would be here soon?

He went still, finally forcing himself to settle down and think. Thinking was what he normally did first. It was what he was best at. He always kept his cool. Almost always, apparently. It seems like maybe he lost his shit when Courtney was involved. And he wasn't even a little sorry about it.

The guy shot him another grin. "I figured that'd get your attention." He opened the door, letting his friend out first before following him out, giving Reed one last look. "I'll see you around." He closed the door, leaving him alone in the bare space.

None of this made any sense. What good would taking him and Courtney do? He blew out a breath, head dropping back as he tried to connect dots that formed nothing but a nonsensical clusterfuck.

If this was all connected, then these were the guys who shot up Nate and Eloise's cars. Towed them away only to deposit them back on Alaskan Security's doorstep. They would also be the ones who took the shot that killed Bryson's dad before he had the chance to hurt Eloise. They'd blown up a cabin and knocked out all the cameras in his parents' neighborhood, luring both him and Nate out without backup.

Which meant they probably had Nate too.

And now they claimed Pierce was on his way. There's no way they managed to nab the head of Alaskan Security. That meant he was coming of his own volition.

None of it made any sense. Who would fuck with them just to fuck with them and then—

Shit.

The answer hit him just as the door opened. He glared at the man who walked in. "Vincent." Reed shook his head. "You're lucky I'm fucking tied up right now."

The head of GHOST appeared unbothered by the barely veiled threat. "Or what?" He stared him down. "You'd kick my ass?" He shook his head. "I don't think so."

Reed's lip curled. "We're way past ass kicking."

Vincent laughed, but the sound was rusty and rough, like he hadn't made it in years. "Are we? Because it seems like I've proven Alaskan Security needs me more than I need them."

Reed rocked his jaw from side to side, fighting the rage that made him want to pull against the zip ties again. "That's all this was? You shot at civilians and blew up a cabin just to prove that Alaskan Security needs GHOST?" He snorted. "You're an even bigger asshole than I thought."

Vincent stiffened, stepping closer. "Don't blame me. It's not my fault GHOST can accomplish what your team can't."

Reed lifted his brows. "Are you sure about that? Because I'm pretty confident Heidi could take down GHOST in about two seconds." He smirked. "Actually, I'm pretty sure some random chick from Nashville could have taken GHOST down a few months ago if she'd wanted to, so I wouldn't get too fucking high and mighty. If a soccer mom can rock your world, then you probably need to do some work yourself."

Vincent clearly had an ego and Reed wanted to knock the feet out from under it. Hit him where it hurt.

At least until he could actually hit him where it hurt.

Vincent's nostrils flared. "How did you know about that?"

Reed shrugged, giving him a smirk. "That's above my pay grade."

He knew full well how they discovered GHOST's system had been breached. Pierce didn't just investigate the people who worked for him, he investigated everyone they interacted with, sending Heidi down any and every rabbit hole until they were able to discover all there was to know. And, unlike Vincent, Pierce shared his knowledge. Making sure his team was fully educated about everyone and everything they faced.

The realization threatened to make Reed shift in his seat. Courtney wasn't the only one he'd looked down his nose at over the years. Knowing he'd lumped Pierce and many of the men around him into a similar judgment zone made him feel like the ass Courtney had called him so many times.

But then he looked at Vincent, and felt a little better. Because he would never be as big of an asshole as that guy.

Vincent's hands fisted at his side, his posture stick straight and rigid as his jaw clenched. "I guess that's a conversation I'll have to have with your boss then."

Reed snorted. "Oh, I can guarantee you're going to have a conversation with my boss." He shook his head. "But I don't think it's gonna go the way you think it will." He almost laughed. Vincent had done all this simply as a show of strength. A way to corner Pierce into not just believing, but admitting Alaskan Security was beneath him. That he was the one with the power. The skills. The control.

But he knew Pierce. And while the owner of Alaskan was many things, stupid was not one of them.

But Vincent didn't seem to know that, because the hard line of his mouth softened into what might be the world's most awkward looking smile. "I guess we'll see, won't we?"

The knob of the door behind him jiggled and Vincent's smile grew. "Sounds like he might be here now." He turned just as the door swung open, flying so hard on its hinges that the knob punched its way through the drywall and stuck, wedging it in place. Reed barely had time to react as a slight figure rushed in, going straight for Vincent. There was a dull metal thunk as the folded frame of a metal chair connected with his body, hitting his head and shoulder with enough force to send him staggering to one side.

Courtney's eyes were wild as she pulled the chair back again, a set of handcuffs dangling from one wrist as she wound up to take another swing. "Stay the fuck away from him. He's mine."

Before she could take her second shot, men poured into the room.

This time, familiar men.

Pierce went straight for Courtney, grabbing her around the waist and hauling her, chair and all, away from Vincent.

She fought his hold, legs kicking as she screamed at the top of her lungs, obviously unaware she was now surrounded by friendly forces. "Put me down. I'll fucking kill all of you if you hurt him."

"A little help." Pierce barely managed to dodge Courtney's head as she swung it back, trying to butt his face with the back of her skull. "Someone get the fucking chair away from her."

Courtney suddenly went still, eyes widening as her head jerked around, trying to get a look at the man holding her. "Pierce?"

Wade rushed over, snatching away the folding chair as Zeke moved in to cut Reed's binds. The second he was free, he was up, kicking the chair to one side before grabbing Courtney and pulling her away from Pierce. She latched both arms around his neck, lacing her legs at his waist, gripping him tight in any way she could. "Are you okay? I was afraid they were hurting you."

He pushed her hair back from her face, looking over every

bit of exposed skin. "I'm fine. What about you?" The tension in his shoulders eased a little now that he had her. "Are you hurt?"

Courtney shook her head, but then squinted. "Well, *they* didn't hurt me." She loosened one of the arms squeezing his neck, bringing her left hand in front of his face. The base of her thumb was already starting to swell. "I did hurt myself a little getting out of the cuffs though."

Reed turned to where Vincent was starting to get up, one hand going to the side of his head. He stalked toward the head of GHOST, ready to add a kick to the ribs to the list of Vincent's pain points, but Pierce stepped between them. "No more." He rocked his head from side to side, neck cracking with the motion. "I think I deserve to be the one to handle this."

Reed tucked his chin, a little surprised. "You can't be the one to kick his ass, Pierce."

Pierce smirked. "Oh, I'm not going to touch him." His voice carried a hint of the ruthlessness few people got to see. "I'm going to do something that will hurt much worse." He turned to where Vincent was pushing to his feet, a trickle of blood sliding from a split at his temple. Pierce cocked one brow, looking him over. "Our business is done." He turned to Reed before scanning the rest of the men in the group. "Everyone out. I'm terminating our connection with GHOST. Effective immediately."

The team of men who'd accompanied Pierce quickly filed from the room, Reed bringing up the rear since he was still carrying Courtney. He had one foot in the hallway when Vincent laughed.

"You'll come back."

Pierce paused, turning to face the man who'd essentially

just thrown his version of a temper tantrum in an effort to prove he was right. Pierce looked him over as he tucked one hand into his pocket. "I wouldn't hold your breath, Vincent." Then he turned, ushering Reed down the hall in front of him as the team exited the building to a waiting van.

Nate was already outside, concern pinching his brow. "You worried the shit out of me, man." He slapped Reed on the shoulder. "When I figured out you were gone, I freaked the fuck out." His eyes shifted to where Courtney still clung to him. He blew out a long breath. "What the fuck is wrong with Vincent?"

Reed opened his mouth to answer, but Courtney beat him to the punch. She grinned wide. "Currently? Probably a pretty wicked headache." She looked ridiculously proud of herself.

Reed swatted her on the ass as he strode toward the van. "You shouldn't have done that." Courtney had no clue what Vincent was capable of. And while Reed was willing to bet Vincent wouldn't have hurt her, she didn't know that when she took a swing at him with a chair. "I need you to at least try to stop being a pain in the ass all of the time. You're going to get yourself hurt."

The possibility that she could have ended up injured, or worse, had him gripping her tighter as he hefted her into the van. Plunking her down onto one of the seats running up the side, he dropped next to her and hauled her tight to his side. "

Courtney raised her brows, chin lifted defiantly. "You wanted me to just sit there and wait, not knowing what was going on?" She shook her head. "No way. Especially not once I found out they had you too."

Reed gripped her chin as he leaned in close, lining his eyes with hers, his voice dipping low. "Are you just trying to get a spanking?"

He could admit that watching Courtney's ass pink up under his palms had been more than a little arousing and, after the shit she'd pulled today with Vincent, she was more than deserving of a paddle or two.

Courtney smirked. "I mean, I'm always trying for that, but I'm being serious too. If I think you're going to get hurt, I will beat the shit out of anybody with a folding chair."

She wasn't exaggerating. There wasn't a doubt in his mind Courtney would fight anyone for him. She'd proven her willingness to step up to the plate for him over and over again. And, while her defiant, stubborn, and snarky attitude once grated his nerves, now it was one more reason he loved the fuck out of her.

But it also meant she was going to be hard as hell to keep safe, so he was going to have to do something drastic.

"In that case, I'm going to have to move us into the housing complex." He'd been struggling with how to suggest this, but honestly, she didn't give him any other choice. Not now that he knew how quickly she would go rogue. "It's gated and there's a guard there twenty-four hours a day." He slid his thumb from her chin up the line of her jaw. "So at least if shit goes down you'll have backup."

Courtney's lower lip pinched between her teeth as her cautious gaze moved over his face. "But what about your parents?"

Reed took a deep breath, his own uncertainty matching hers. "I think they need to move there too."

He wanted so desperately to believe he could keep his parents separate from his connection to Alaskan Security, but it wasn't true. All the security systems and cameras in the world couldn't stop someone from getting to them if they were determined.

Clearly.

Courtney pressed her lips together, rocking a little closer. "With us? In the same place?" There was a hint of hopefulness in her tone. Like she wasn't only unopposed to the idea, but maybe even excited by it.

"Would that bother you? To have my parents living with us?"

She shook her head before he finished his question. "No. I think it's a good idea. Your mom needs help, but she doesn't want someone she doesn't know in her house, so I think it would be great." The concern came back, pinching her brow. "As long as it's the kind of place your dad could get around in."

That would be the trickiest part. The townhomes were beautiful. High-end with lots of space and light. But they were on three floors.

Reed turned his attention across the van to where Pierce sat looking deep in thought. "Pierce."

The owner of Alaskan Security's gaze came his way.

"Do you think we can put an elevator in one of those townhomes?"

Pierce's eyes moved from him to Courtney and back again, the tightness in his expression softening the tiniest bit. "I'm sure we could find a way."

CHAPTER THIRTY-ONE

COURTNEY

"DID I DO it right?" Heidi held out her cutting board of shredded carrot for Reed's mom to inspect.

"Close enough." Reed's mom gave her a pat on the back. "Much better than last time."

Heidi beamed, clearly understanding just how precious that complement was. "Does that mean next time I can chop the green stuff?"

Reed's mother looked her over. "Maybe."

Courtney muffled a laugh as she turned back to her own task. Reed moved his parents into the rooming house immediately after she'd been abducted from the end of their driveway. He'd avoided confessing the true nature of his career to his parents for years, but there was no longer any avoiding it. There was also no longer any way for them to safely stay in their home.

Part of her expected them to put up a little bit of an argument. She'd never had a place that felt like home, outside of their little RV, so she imagined a person who did have one would be extremely attached to it. But Reed's parents immediately agreed. Maybe it was because his mother knew she was in over her head caring for his father alone while Reed was out of town.

Or maybe it was because they were so happy their son was finally being completely truthful with them that they were willing to do whatever it took to keep it that way.

At any rate, she was loving their new living arrangement. Especially on nights like this.

"How's it going over there?" Helen, the woman who had cared for Pierce's niece for a number of years, sat with Naomi's son Emmett and a few of the other small people who helped make up her patchwork of a family.

And she wouldn't have it any other way. For the first time she felt accepted. Included. Wanted.

Loved.

And that was by more than just Reed. Everyone here brought her into their fold immediately, easily moving past her previous bad behavior. Ready and willing to see her in a new light. It was more than she would have ever hoped for.

At the beginning, she'd been thrilled just to have Reed in her corner. Someone who understood and appreciated her. Someone ready to protect her. Then she met his parents and her hope grew to wishing they might all one day be some sort of a family.

And now here she was, surrounded by the biggest, most extended sort of family she could imagine.

Bess, the earliest female arrival to Alaskan Security, leaned into Courtney's side, catching her attention. "Does this look right?" She was doing her best to squeeze the liquid from the chwinamul she and Reed's mother soaked overnight then boiled so it would be ready to be sautéed and seasoned.

Courtney gave her a reassuring smile. "It looks great." She

scanned the large island where the women who were starting to feel almost like sisters each worked at their assigned task, helping prepare Reed's mother's famous bibimbap in copious amounts.

"This all smells so good." Heidi continued working her way through the pile of carrots she'd been allotted. "I've been thinking about eating this all day."

Harlow snorted across the island where she was squeezing water from the gosari Courtney helped Reed's mother prep earlier in the day. "You've been thinking about this because you didn't want to think about the fact that Pierce cut off your best friend Vincent."

Heidi shot Harlow a scowl. "Vincent isn't my best friend. I just think maybe Pierce was a little dramatic about the whole thing."

Harlow's mouth dropped open. *"Pierce* was dramatic?" She motioned toward Eloise. "Vincent shot at Eloise and Nate and stole their cars." The tip of her finger swung Courtney's way. "And he kidnapped Courtney and Reed."

Heidi stopped what she was doing with a huff. "He also," her eyes widened, purposefully swinging to where Bryson sat playing video games with Emmett, "handled that situation that needed handling." Her wide gaze came back to Harlow, even more intensely focused. Like she thought Harlow wouldn't know she was talking about how Vincent also shot the man who was trying to drag Eloise to his car. The same man who had been abusing his own sweet son for years.

Harlow squinted her eyes, jutting her chin forward. "So what? We're supposed to forgive the fact that he fucked with us just to prove he could because he did something Reed would have done anyway?"

Courtney looked from woman to woman. She'd heard the

story about what happened to Eloise and how Reed had been right behind Nate when everything went down. And when the random shot hit its target with expert precision.

It was a crazy story. One she might not have believed not so long ago. But crazy stories seemed to be the norm around here. Hopefully that slowed down a little, because she was ready to live at least a somewhat boring and normal life.

Heidi went back to her carrots, still scowling. "Yes, Vincent is an asshole, but I think he just doesn't know what else to be."

Harlow snorted out a laugh. "I hope you're not about to say you think Vincent is just misunderstood."

Heidi lifted her brows. "Oh no. Vincent is definitely a prick, and at this point I don't see that changing." She again went back to her carrots, but only because Reed's mom shot her a look. "But I do think it's even worse now because he's unhappy."

Harlow took a deep breath, blowing it back out as her eyes rolled to the ceiling. "So you're trying to argue that the only reason Vincent lashed out at us is because he's unhappy?"

Heidi's face scrunched up as she considered. "That's not the only reason, but it definitely didn't help."

Mona, who'd been quiet up to this point, finally piped up. "It doesn't really matter why Vincent did what he did. All that matters is Vincent showed a complete disregard for the safety of the people who work here." Her eyes moved to Courtney. "And those close to us." She bounced her baby girl on one hip, watching everyone else work. "He crossed a line and changed everything. What we do isn't a game, and he treated it like one."

Heidi's shoulders slumped a little. "I know. I shouldn't feel bad for him, but he's like that mean-as-shit dog at the

Humane Society. You want to save them even though he would absolutely bite the hand that feeds him."

Harlow's lips pressed into a considering line as her head tipped. "That's actually a really good comparison."

Heidi smiled, perking up the tiniest bit. "Thanks."

That was what Courtney loved most about this group. They all had opinions. Every woman in this room had strong feelings and alliances. They were quick to protect the men they loved, but also quick to see someone else's point of view. To admit they were wrong and move on with no hard feelings and no judgment.

They almost made her grateful for everything it took to get to this point. Almost. She still wasn't particularly thrilled over nearly being blown up and having the head of a covert, government-adjacent group kidnap her.

Heidi sighed again. "I guess it'll be interesting to see what Vincent does now. I don't really imagine he's the kind of man who would go into hiding and lick his wounds."

Harlow shrugged. "Not really our problem, is it?"

"No." Heidi chewed her lower lip, unsuccessfully smothering out the hint of a smile. "But I'm definitely going to keep my eye on him. Just to see what he does."

Courtney shot Heidi a grin. "Nosy."

"Absolutely I am." She leaned Courtney's way. "Don't tell me you aren't just a little interested to see what kind of a fit he throws next." Heidi's expression turned serious. "Because he is definitely going to throw a fit and, honestly, I need to make sure he doesn't try to drag us into the middle of it again."

Courtney refocused on her task, just to make sure she didn't get the same dirty look Heidi got. "I don't care what he does, as long as he doesn't fuck with Reed."

Eva grinned across the counter from her spot next to Harlow. "You might want to keep a metal folding chair handy just in case."

Everyone around her laughed, enjoying the fact that she'd hit the head of GHOST up the side of his head with a folding chair almost as much as she did.

Harlow wiped at the corner of one eye with the sleeve of her sweater. "Man, what I wouldn't give to have been there to see that."

Heidi suddenly straightened. "Do you want to see it? It's pretty fucking hilarious."

Harlow's eyes widened. "Are you serious? You have it?"

Heidi smirked. "Of course I have it."

Harlow's jaw dropped. "How? I thought Vincent upped the security at GHOST to make sure you couldn't get in anymore."

"Pshh." Heidi rolled her eyes with a laugh. "Did you really think that was going to work?" Her mouth quirked as she eyed Harlow. "I'm a little surprised you didn't try to get it yourself."

Harlow groaned. "I've been busy. Pierce has got me hacking into shit all over the country, trying to figure out where the best place would be to put our next location."

Naomi raised one hand. "I vote for Florida."

Courtney wrinkled her nose. "I vote for anywhere *but* Florida."

Naomi cringed. "Fair point. Sort of forgot Florida sucked for you." She thought for a second. "What about Texas?"

Bess snuck a few slivers of shredded carrot from Heidi's pile, tossing them into her mouth. "Do we really care where the new location is? It's not like any of us are going there."

Naomi shot her a grin. "But we could visit."

Heidi finished up her task, scooting her carrots into a neat pile. "In that case, I vote for Hawaii."

"Me too." Mona blew out a long breath. "But I'm pretty sure Hawaii's not on the table. Pierce is looking for something a little more centrally located."

"What about Nashville?" Savannah, one of the quieter members of the girl gang surrounding her, made the suggestion so softly Courtney almost missed it.

But her sister, Sadie, made sure she wasn't ignored. "That's a really good idea." Sadie focused her dark gaze on Mona. "What about Nashville?"

Mona turned her attention to Savannah. "Have you been there?"

Savannah chewed her lower lip, looking hesitant as she shook her head. "But I see a lot about it on Instagram. It looks really nice. And the location might be what you're looking for."

"I think Nashville is a good idea too." Courtney piped up, adding more support. She'd heard bits and pieces of what Savannah had been through and wanted to make sure the other woman knew there were people who had her back.

And she would definitely slam someone with a folding chair for sweet, shy Savannah.

"Me three." Harlow focused on Savannah, her normally clipped tone softening. "Maybe you could help me scope the place out. See if we think it would be a good fit."

Savannah's eyes widened and she seemed to shrink back. "I don't think I would be very useful."

Harlow opened her mouth, probably to argue that Savannah was capable of being more than useful, but Sadie barely shook her head and Harlow's lips clamped shut.

Whatever terrible thing had happened was clearly still affecting Savannah. Making her withdrawn and hesitant. Or, maybe that's just who she was, which was more than fine.

Courtney finished up her task, wiped her hands, and went to sit at the table where Savannah and Sadie carried on a soft conversation, taking the chair on Savannah's other side. She gave her a careful smile, trying her best not to come on too strong. Especially since coming on strong was her nature. But she wanted Savannah to know she would be there for her. That they could be the two who didn't have their hands in Alaskan Security's mess together.

She motioned at Savannah's dress. It was feminine and pretty and a stark contrast to Courtney's new uniform of leggings and one of Reed's sweatshirts. "I really like your dress."

Savannah glanced her way before dropping her eyes back to where she wrung her hands in her lap. "Thank you."

Courtney stretched her legs out, leaning back in the seat, trying to look relaxed. "I've been thinking of updating my wardrobe. I probably need to have something to wear besides leggings and hoodies." She peeked Savannah's way, hoping the other woman might bite. "Maybe you could go shopping with me and help me pick some things out."

Savannah's eyes lifted to hers as she rubbed her lips together. For a second Courtney thought she was going to turn her down, but finally Savannah barely nodded. "I could do that."

Courtney smiled, feeling like she'd accomplished something enormous. "Awesome. I'll get with you after dinner and we can come up with a time."

Savannah gave another tiny nod. "Okay."

A chorus of deep voices suddenly amplified the already loud conversation filling the kitchen and common area as Rogue spilled out of the walkway, looking lethally attractive in their matching white tactical gear. The men went straight for the women and kids throughout the space, grabbing giggling toddlers and swinging them into the air before hauling wives close.

Courtney was on her feet before Reed made it halfway across the space, racing toward him before launching herself at him. He caught her easily, strong arms banding around her waist as their bodies collided. It was the way she greeted him every time he came home.

And this was definitely home.

His lips met hers in a quick kiss. "How was your day?"

She beamed up at him, even more happy now that he was at her side. "Awesome. I helped your mom all morning and then all the girls came to finish getting dinner ready."

"I think they're going to miss having her here to feed everyone." Reed caught her lips in another kiss. "But they're going to have to get over it. Because I'm ready to be moved into our new home."

Our new home. It was something she'd never get tired of hearing him say.

And it was a gift she would never take for granted. Alaska was supposed to be her new beginning and had more than fulfilled her expectations.

Her hopes.

Courtney leaned into him, looping one arm around his neck and pulling him close. "Me too."

EPILOGUE

REED

"NO PEEKING." REED cupped both hands over Courtney's eyes as he led her across the back lot at Alaskan Security's headquarters.

"How in the hell am I going to peek? I can't see through your freaking hands." Her steps were slow and careful, almost like she expected him to lead her right into a wall.

Or maybe an abandoned footbridge.

"I'm just making sure you're behaving. You have a history of not being a good listener." Reed stopped, parking Courtney in front of the early wedding gift he had for her. "Ready?"

She snorted. "I guess that depends on what I'm about to see."

"I think you'll like it." He eased his hands away, sliding them down to rest on her hips as Courtney blinked, squinting as she adjusted to the brightness of the late spring sun. He could tell the second she found focus. There was a brightening of her expression and her jaw dropped.

"Holy shit." One hand clamped over her mouth as she

stared, dark eyes swinging to him before going back. "She's *beautiful*."

Reed wrapped both arms around her middle, pulling her body against his. "You like?"

Courtney blinked a few times. "I love."

Bernadette had come a long way since they brought her back in January. Every bit of her mechanics had been gone over. Anything even close to being worn out was replaced before the engine was tuned and the tires were realigned. Now she purred like a damn kitten.

But that probably wasn't what Courtney was focused on.

His fiancée continued blinking, trying to control the shimmer of tears edging her eyes. "She looks the same, but completely different."

It was the thing he'd been most adamant about. While he definitely wanted Bernadette updated, she needed to still look like herself. Courtney was extremely attached to the RV, and he didn't want her to feel like it was gone forever, replaced with a stranger.

That meant the outside of her was almost identical. Anything on the body that needed to be replaced had to be as exact as possible. He'd hunted down the correct siding panels and lights. The new windows were as similar to the old ones as he could get his hands on. Even the paint job followed the style of the original, though the colors were quite different.

Courtney swiveled around, her eyes meeting his. "And she's pink."

He tipped his head because that wasn't entirely true. "She has pink *accents*."

The old paint job was originally white with brown and tan stripes running up the center. Bernadette's primary color was still white, but her stripes were now two different shades of pink.

Courtney turned back to refocus on the camper. "I can't believe you had them make her pink."

"Really?" He leaned in to nuzzle behind her ear. "Because you made it pretty clear Bernadette's favorite color is pink."

Courtney leaned back against him, hooking one hand around his neck. "I fucking love you."

He smiled against her skin. "I know." Releasing her, he gave her ass a playful swat. "Go look inside."

Without hesitation, Courtney took off, practically running toward the door of their newly redone home away from home. She stroked one hand down the side of the camper as she gripped the handle, giving Bernadette a pet before climbing inside. He was close enough behind her to hear the gasp of surprise when she saw the newly improved interior.

Courtney stood in the tiny walkway, her hands pressed against her cheeks, the diamond on her finger glinting in the sunlight streaming through the new, perfectly clean windows. "Holy shit, Reed. I can't believe this."

Everything inside had been redone. The RV restoration company stripped Bernadette to the studs before putting her back together again. Any water damage had been remediated and the parts replaced. Fresh, top of the line insulation now meant Bernadette could be used even as the temperature dropped. The cabinets in the tiny kitchen were all new, painted cream with gold fixtures. The couch had to be reupholstered since finding one that would fit was impossible, but the cushioning had all been replaced before it was covered in a pale pink velvet that perfectly matched the lighter of the stripes on the outside. The walls were the same soft cream as the cabinets, with the exception of the wall behind the sofa which sported feminine floral wallpaper. The new dinette sported beige cushions and the same marble-looking laminate as the counter. The floor was done in an easy to care for laminate that ran from the living room area back to the bedroom.

Courtney's eyes swung around the space as she slowly spun in a circle, taking it all in. "I can't believe this."

Her reaction was everything he wanted. Bringing Bernadette to her full potential had been expensive as hell, but seeing Courtney's face now was worth every penny.

And pennies had been easier to come by lately.

Pierce insisted on giving him the money he'd originally offered to go to Florida, saying it was only fair considering Reed had done exactly what he was supposed to do. His parents sold their house, which was paid off, and insisted on putting the money from it into the purchase of the townhome they all now shared.

And, while those things helped in many ways, they hadn't been the primary reason he had more money to work with. Pierce had also insisted on putting his parents on the company insurance, which reduced their out-of-pocket expenses enormously. So by the time the camper was done, he'd saved up enough to cover the price tag.

Which was good because now he had a summer wedding to pay for.

Courtney moved through the RV, touching nearly every surface as she checked out the tiny bathroom and the closet across from it. She turned and sat on the edge of their new queen-sized bed, bouncing a little on the mattress. "Oh my gosh. This is so much better."

She ran one hand over the bedding she picked out at Target what felt like forever ago. "You saved it."

"Of course I did. It's what you picked out." He stood in

front of her, reaching out to slide one hand across her cheek. "You like it?"

Courtney nodded. "I love it." She reached out to fist her hands in the front of his T-shirt, pulling him closer. "Almost as much as I love you."

Reed leaned down, bracing his hands against the mattress at either side of her hips. "You *better* love me since I'm going to be driving a pink RV named Bernadette down the road."

"First, you named her." Courtney's smile shifted to a teasing line. "Second, you don't have to be the one driving her. You could always let me drive."

He leaned in, brushing his lips against hers. "Not happening until you finish your lessons with Rico."

He'd taught Courtney everything he could, but, as pretty and funny and devoted as she was, the woman was a terror on the road. So he'd convinced Rico to help him out, hoping Rogue's primary driver could improve her skill set further.

Courtney rolled her eyes toward the ceiling with a groan. "Rico's never going to tell you I can drive this thing." She met his gaze. "He acts like I'm the worst driver he's ever seen. And I know that's not true because I've ridden with Lennie before, and she is just as bad as I am."

Reed chuckled. He'd heard Rico tell stories about the time Lennie drove him, Elise, and Abe around Cincinnati, and his recollection wasn't flattering toward his wife. "I'm pretty sure he wouldn't let Lennie drive this RV either, if that makes you feel any better."

Courtney frowned at him. "You know it doesn't."

Reed leaned in to press a kiss to the tip of her nose. "Then I guess you'll have to figure out how to get over it. Because there's no way you're getting behind the wheel of this thing until you can prove you're capable of handling her in any situation."

He wasn't just keeping Courtney out of the driver's seat because he'd invested so much money in the RV. He was doing it for her own good. If Bernadette ended up with so much as a scratch and Courtney felt like it was her fault, she would be devastated. So he was going to do as much as he could to prevent that possibility.

Courtney pushed her lower lip out in a pout. "Fine." She scooted closer to the edge of the bed, hooking her fingers into the belt loops of his pants. "Can we take her out now?"

He figured she would be itching to go on a trip but didn't anticipate she'd want to immediately take the new and improved Bernadette out for a maiden voyage. "We don't have any food. Or clothes."

Courtney shrugged, seeming unbothered. "We can grab food as we go and I'll just wear the same clothes tomorrow." She wiggled around. "Please, Sexy Pants."

He would give this woman anything he could, but unfortunately taking her out to camp now, even if it was just for one night, wasn't an option. "We don't have anyone to check in on my parents."

Courtney's chin tucked, head dropping to one side. "You know damn well we could hit up anyone on the street and they would happily go help."

"I know they would happily help, but imagine how my mother would react to an unexpected visitor."

Courtney stared at him a second before her shoulders slouched and she huffed out a breath. "Fine."

She'd been spending all her time while he was at work with his parents, so she knew damn well how much his mother would hate being surprised like that. His mom liked having the opportunity to make sure the house was immaculate. That her visitor had slippers waiting for them and a meal ready so she could guilt them into eating.

Courtney perked up a little bit, sitting taller. "What about tomorrow?"

Reed gave her a quick kiss on the lips before straightening. "We'll see."

Courtney jumped up from the bed with a scoff. "*We'll see* is what you say when you don't want to just tell me no."

"*We'll see* is what I say when we will see." He tried to give her a stern look. "Now, stop being a pain in the ass, tell me you love Bernadette, and get your sweet ass outside so we can go home."

Courtney's pout came back full force as she leaned close to him, running her hands up his chest. "But I don't want to leave Bernadette yet. I missed her."

He braced his hands on her hips. "I know you missed her and I will do my best to make arrangements so we can take her out tomorrow."

Courtney pushed her lip out a little more. "What if I want you to do better than your best?"

"Then I would say you're working hard at being a pain in my ass, Princess." He'd been pleasantly surprised to discover Courtney remained just as difficult as ever, even as she settled in and got used to being loved and taken care of and appreciated. It was fucking fantastic. Her attitude still made his dick hard almost instantly. And she regularly pushed his buttons until he gave her what she wanted, which was normally a few slaps on the ass before being fucked into the mattress.

Courtney's lower lip slipped between her teeth. "What if I offer to sweeten the deal a little?" One hand slid down his chest, over his abs to rub against the already hard line of his dick. "I'll suck your cock right now if you promise to take me camping tomorrow night."

He couldn't have dreamed up a woman like Courtney in a million years. One who was as willing to go to her knees as she was to sit by a campfire in the middle of nowhere.

"You shouldn't tell lies, Princess." He slid one hand into the dark hair at her nape, twisting tight as he ghosted his lips along the line of her jaw. "We both know you'll suck my dick whether I take you camping or not."

She gasped when he nipped the skin just below her ear. "True, but I'll do an extra good job if you promise to take me camping."

"Extra good?" He skimmed his lips down her neck. "How extra good?"

Courtney's hands went to his belt because she already knew she had him. "So good you'll want to take me camping every night."

He groaned as her hand slipped into his open pants, gripping his cock and pulling it free. "You make a good argument for camping."

He used his hold on her hair to tip her head back so their eyes could meet. "But first, you'll have to prove you can uphold your end of the bargain."

Courtney's lips parted, her pupils dilating. "I thought you'd never ask."

He pushed her against the tiny bit of wall between their bedroom and the bathroom door. "Get on your knees."

She slid to the floor, back to the wall as he leaned over her, arm braced above his head, chin tucked so he could watch as he fed his dick between her lips. Courtney swallowed him down eagerly as he slowly worked himself into the warm well of her mouth inch by inch, pulling back before pressing deeper, letting her get him wet and slick before sliding his palm to the back of her neck, holding tight as he slowly began fucking her face.

They'd done this just about every way possible, but this was the first time she was boxed in like this, so he was careful not to give her too much. He kept his movements shallow, but soon Courtney's hands came to his hips, gripping the open fabric of his pants to tug him deeper. She took more and more of him until he bumped the back of her throat.

Reed groaned. "Fuck, Princess. You could suck the soul right out of me, couldn't you?"

Her cheeks hollowed, the suction of her mouth pulling him deeper as her eyes lifted to his, holding as he shuttled between her lips in increasingly erratic thrusts.

"That's it. Good girl." His voice was rough, breathing ragged as he dragged one thumb across her lower lip, feeling where it stretched around him. "Look at how much of me you can take."

When she used her hold to pull him even deeper he lost it, balls pulling tight as the tension fisting the base of his spine shattered. He held her in place as he came, cock twitching against her tongue as he filled her smart mouth.

Courtney sucked in a breath when he pulled back, her wicked lips pulling into a smug smile as she wiped at the line of saliva glistening down her chin. "How'd I do?"

He hauled her up from the floor to pin her against the wall with his body. "You know damn well how you did, smartass." He skimmed one hand down her side, reaching back to cup her ass before giving it a light slap. "It seems like we're going to be doing a hell of a lot of camping."

❄

Made in the USA
Monee, IL
29 January 2024

52592744R00218